THE GROWING AX

ROB NEUTEBOOM

The Growing Ax

Print ISBN: 978-1-66786-237-8
eBook ISBN: 978-1-66786-238-5

For Idgy and Suzy Q

CHAPTERS

~

Mjölnir owes its very existence to Sif's golden hair.

Loki, trickster of the gods, stumbled upon Sif slumbering in her chamber. Drunk and feeling particularly mischievous, he removed all of her beautiful hair at the roots that it may never grow again. Of course, when Sif arose and ran her hand over her shorn scalp, she wailed. Thor rushed into their bedchamber and found his wife bald and grieving, for her hair had been her greatest and most treasured feature. The mirror had been shattered, and her white hand bore traces of red blood. No inquiry was needed to ferret out the person responsible for his wife's grief. Thor summoned Loki. As Loki entered the room, Thor greeted him by gripping his throat and lifting him above his head. Despite Loki's protests and denials, Thor knew the truth. He threatened to break every bone in the trickster's body. The prank quickly lost its humor. Loki pled for mercy. Thor demanded his wife's hair be returned and restored to its original condition. But Loki could not return something so thoroughly extricated. Sif would never grow hair again. That was supposed to be the funniest part of Loki's prank. Thor's temper, which far exceeded all others, burned in his faculties. He gripped Loki's throat harder. With his free hand, Thor snapped the pinky bone on Loki's left hand cleanly in half.

Loki shouted one anguished word, "Dwarves!"

Thor paused. He held Loki's left ring finger between his thumb and index finger, preparing for the next break. He aimed to take his time to draw out the pain and make Loki's suffering last, a bone for every one of Sif's tears. "What did you say?"

"Dwarves," Loki repeated. "They can make anything. Hair shouldn't be a problem."

"And they would be willing to make this for Sif?" Thor set Loki down.

"Yes. But if you break my bones, I won't be able to visit them to plead our case."

And so, it was arranged that Loki would speak to the dwarf craftsmen in Nidavellir. Of course, Loki could do nothing without some measure of guile, so he stirred up trouble between the dwarf artisans to leverage their talent to his advantage. He pitted the Brothers Ivaldi against Sindri and Brokkr in a contest to determine whose work was more exquisite. The products of their labor would become gifts to the gods. Odin and Freya would judge their work. To secure his own safety, Loki beguiled the Sons of Ivaldi into fashioning golden hair with incomparable beauty to pacify Thor and restore Sif's dignity.

On the day of the judgment, the Brothers Ivaldi and Sindri and Brokkr each presented three gifts to the gods. Among these gifts, of course, was hair to replace that which Loki had stolen from Sif. It worked a charm. The hair attached itself to Sif's head and shone even more radiantly golden than before. Sif was pleased. She swished her hair about and ran her fingers through the strands. She stared at its shimmering luminosity in the large mirror hanging on the chamber wall. Hair fit for a princess. The dwarf craftsmen gifted many magical and beautifully wrought trinkets to Freya and Odin. Each pleased the gods greatly: a golden armband that multiplied wealth, a ship that could be folded like a scarf, a flying boar wrought of gold to pull Freya's chariot.

But the greatest among these gifts was a stubby-handled hammer Sindri and Brokkr introduced as Mjölnir. Among its mystical features, the hammer was unbreakable, would never miss its target, and would return to the wielder's hand when summoned. Thor, to whom it was gifted, marveled at its functionality, its invulnerability. He had broken or lost many weapons in his battles with the frost giants. To have a hammer with such power and endurance—Thor could only imagine the possibilities. He soon forgot all about Sif's hair. He ran his fingers along the hammer's smooth face. He saw his smile reflect clearly in the hammer's polished metal, which was of a workmanship he couldn't begin to understand. The hammer enthralled him.

The other gods agreed that this hammer was the best gift of any they had received. Not only was the workmanship excessively fine, but it had the strength to protect all of Asgard against the giants. One could overlook its short, stout handle. Besides, the weapon was light enough for Thor to manage with one of his mighty hands. Brokkr went on to explain that the hammer could grow or shrink according to Thor's desire. It could become the size of a massive boulder to increase its impact or the size of a miniscule gnat to secret into safeguarded spaces.

In his hand, the hammer pulsed with a heartbeat. Thor noticed for the first time an inscription on the hammer's gleaming cheek. It declared matter-of-factly that Mjölnir chooses his champion. A weapon that chooses? Didn't that imply thought, and wasn't thinking the domain of living creatures? Why had the dwarves inscribed the hammer with such a strange proclamation? Perhaps Loki had put them up to it. Another of his tricks? Thor finally asked what the inscription meant.

Brokkr explained: "The objects we craft in the smithies of our realm do not remain inanimate. The bellows breathe life into them. How else would a hammer be capable of the virtues we described to you?"

"You're telling me this hammer is alive?" Thor turned it over in his hands, held it to his ear, but the hammer did not breathe. Yet somehow it did speak. Not in words, but in something else, in a feeling, as the quiet hum in the mind.

Brokkr nodded. "Yes."

"How is that possible?" Thor challenged.

Brokkr didn't answer Thor's question directly. Instead, he shared a story.

"There was once a man whose wife was barren. Because she could not have a child, her life felt empty, and her grief could not be consoled. The man loved his wife. It caused him much pain to see his wife so sad. By trade, the man was a potter. Although his skills were average at best, he set to casting the perfect child out of clay to bake in his kiln. He spent many evenings sculpting and spinning, only to throw away his work in the wee hours of the morning, disgusted and exhausted. At long last, his fingers found the right form, and the shape of a child emerged in the clay. He hoped to present this gift to his wife, a symbol of his love for her. That night, he placed the child-shaped pot into the kiln to bake. When the mud dried and the form was fixed, he pulled it from the fire. He left it on his workbench to cool. Just before going to bed, he placed a single kiss on the clay child's forehead. In the morning, the potter could not find the clay child on his workbench. He searched the floor, fearing the thing had toppled in the night and shattered. In a corner of his shop, a child, as real as any he had ever seen before, slept soundly on a pile of old sacks. When the small boy awoke and stood, he was unmistakably the same child he had sculpted out of clay. You see, love had brought the child to life. When you ask me if it is possible for an object to have life, I answer you this: through its creator's love."

Thor grinned. "A fine fable."

"As it is," Brokkr responded.

"I see. Tell me, how does one care for a living weapon? Water and feed it?" Thor joked.

"Think of it as a companion rather than a servant to your whims. If you care for Mjölnir with honor and integrity, he will bring you glory unimaginable. If you neglect him, he will betray you. In this hammer resides the future of your kingdom, of your world."

Thor pondered this prediction for some time. Finally, he nodded. A green spark coursed across the hammer as he lifted it. As light as it was to pick up, Thor could feel another sort of weight bearing down on him. One day, he knew, Mjölnir would determine the fate of the realms. One day, in some way Thor could not yet grasp, this hammer would save his people, and it would happen through love, not hate.

THE GROWING AX

CHAPTER 1

THE SUMMONING

ASK BANYUN SETTLED INTO HIS faded white rocker on the front porch and thought about his father, who had mysteriously disappeared two summers ago. He often reminisced about how the two would sit silently and observe nature perform its predictable patterns. His father would point when a squirrel skittered across the lawn with an apple gripped between its teeth, dragonflies flitted amidst the milkweed just below the deck, or deer peered curiously from the tree line south of the house. Ask loved those times.

On this summer night, he attempted to recreate that feeling, but the years of his father's absence dulled that sense of comfort, reducing it to some fleeting and elusive wish that would vanish if he thought too hard about it or wanted it too badly. In the end, he was left only with this night, those memories, and a fading hope his father would return. As the sun continued its nightly descent toward the western horizon, Ask watched green shoots stretch in the failing sun, yearning to become corn by fall, and listened to cicadas chittering on thick oaks. The trees' shadows spread across the lawn like giants' hands with fingers extended, plucking away at the tendrils of light still lingering. In the pasture, just beyond the shadow's reach, a single goat gnawed at tufts of grass, as evening rendered the air soft and languorous.

Like every night since his father disappeared, Ask studied the end of the long dirt road, where he hoped, ached, to find his father coming back to him. Each night, Ask would squint until the sun cast its final shadows before succumbing fully to night, and until he submitted to one more disappointment. This night was no different. He fought the urge to run down the road to close a distance he couldn't measure, between the ambiguous separation created by his father's disappearance and Ask's hope that his father would return. Perhaps this small exercise of faith would be enough to bring his father home. But he did not go down the road, because he was afraid all he would find was yet another disappointment and lose what little hope he had left of ever seeing his father again.

His mother joined him on the porch, a few wisps of blonde hair escaping from two long braids that always reminded Ask of German operas interpreting Norse mythological characters. Wagner's "Ride of the Valkyries" in *Der Ring das Nibelung*, which his mother listened to often, came to mind. "Beautiful evening," she said—the tiniest hint of an accent, but neither German nor Scandinavian. No one in the world sounded quite like his mother.

"Yeah," Ask said. "Beautiful." They both stared into impending night.

To lighten the mood, perhaps sensing her son's disillusionment that their family would one day be whole again, Ask's mother resumed the game they played most nights before calling it a day. She pointed to a cluster of stars, just beginning to punctuate the darkening night sky. "What's that?" she asked.

Ask tilted his head, squinted, and smiled. "That's Draco. Obviously."

"Obviously. And that?" She pointed to another cluster of stars.

"Lyra," Ask said.

She nodded. "And that one?"

Ask looked, shot his mother a confused glance, and then said, "You're messing with me. That's the moon."

She laughed—a sound Ask loved more than any other sound in the world—and this tore at his heart as well. How could his father leave her, even if he was tired of raising a son?

There were dark days, Ask recalled, when it was clear that his father would not be returning. Even Ask's backpack seemed to drag him down as he lugged it from home to the school bus to home again, a perpetual task that felt pointless in light of what he'd lost. One day, about two weeks after his father was gone, Ask came home after school to what appeared to be an empty house. He searched for his mother in the living room, the kitchen, even in the cellar. Next, he checked the garden, but he could not find her. Back inside, he ascended the stairs. At his mother's bedroom door, he paused. Inside, he thought he heard two voices having a heated conversation, one melancholic that kept sighing between indiscernible words, and the other stern, even reprimanding, in tone. He was still standing close to the door when his mother opened it. Her eyes were red, as if she'd been crying. Ask looked around her into the room, but his mother had evidently been alone. Not even a cell phone in hand or in sight. She didn't explain anything, and Ask didn't pry, not knowing even what to ask her. Plus, he was distracted by the tears his mother tried to dry quickly with a sleeve and her disheveled, exhausted appearance.

He didn't know why her laughter this evening would prompt such a painful memory.

The game ended, all the star clusters appropriately labeled. Ask's mother announced, "Alright, let's get inside."

The mosquitoes were beginning their nightly foraging, and Ask was always ripe for their harvest. He stole one more glance of the sky as he pulled the screen door shut and reached for Heim, the family's white shepherd named for the Norse god Heimdall, the great guardian of the Asgardian bridge connecting all the known Norse realms. Ask always thought the name unsuited for a dog who would welcome anyone and everyone into the house with wagging tail, as long as they might feed and pet him. All the same, Dad said the Norse were their ancestors, were in their blood. For this reason, his father made a point of naming everything in the world around him consistent with that tradition.

Even Ask's name was Norse, mythological. He was, his father had explained, the first and, as it turned out, his parents' only child. The first of what, Ask never thought to inquire. His full name was Askr, but his parents had called him Ask for as long as he could remember. They did so as if he were an enigma for which they had no solution, as if they hoped one day Ask himself would provide the answer.

Once inside, Ask encountered another puzzle. Here, in the small farmhouse in North Dakota, his father's presence still lingered in the thick winter coat hanging on a peg near the backdoor; his watch, which he had left for some reason, still ticked on an end table; a telescope, through which Ask and his parents explored the cosmos, stared blankly at the sky from a family room window; and a cowboy hat his father wore working the fields lay upside down on top of a built-in bookcase, which his father, incidentally, had also built. Yes, although his father was gone, he remained as these objects scattered throughout the house.

Ask found himself looking out the picture window across an expansive lawn cast in varying shades of shadow. Though dark, he could still make out the darker outline of a shed a quarter of a mile west of the house. It was his father's work shed. He recalled filling the shed with seed in autumn and then loading the truck with that same seed in spring for planting the crops that were now managed by a neighboring farmer who lived on the other side of their twenty-acre lot.

Lately, he often found himself staring at the shed for long minutes before retiring for the night. At times, he swore that shed was calling to him. But sheds don't call people. He chalked it up to further manifestations of missing his father. But tonight, a voice called to him, indiscernible but powerful.

"Ask," it said, but not in a language he knew. Again, his name, but not quite his name, "Ask." This time he felt the words. That was it. The sound was like the thump of a heartbeat. His name coursed through his veins. He involuntarily checked for a pulse in his wrist. He then raised his right arm and, if by some instinct, reached for the shed, touching the windowpane.

"You okay?" a voice shattered the impression, bringing Ask out of something akin to a trance. He looked quizzically at his hand on the glass and wondered how it had gotten there.

“I’m fine,” he said, lowering the hand. He wasn’t sure he believed what he said. “I’m just tired.” He rubbed his eyes, forced a yawn. “I suppose I’d better get to bed.”

His mother hugged him. “You and I are going to be alright, you know, as long as we have each other.” This expression, which she repeated from time to time, Ask knew, was meant to reassure herself as much as him that they were still a family, even without his father.

He gave her a hug, whistled for Heim, shuffled up narrow stairs to his bedroom, closed the door, and sat staring at his hand. Was something trying to communicate with him? If so, what did it want?

“Weird,” he whispered to Heim, and then he lay back on his bed. Soon, he fell into a deep and dreamless sleep.

CHAPTER 2

LISTENING TO FISH

SINCE IT WAS SUMMER VACATION, the days stretched long before Ask and the work, though plentiful and constant, left hours of leisure time in between his chores. Ask fed the goat, the animal with a filthy beard his father ironically called Babe, set to a few farming chores in the immense garden his mother insisted they maintain—"Better to have it and not need it, than to need it and not have it," as she always said—and then kicked a soccer ball against the garage wall until Deonte, his best friend, showed up with poles for their usual midday fishing foray at the nearby Sheyenne River.

As they meandered the short mile to the river, Ask kept stealing glances over his shoulder of the shed that continued to call, or rather to summon him, with its peculiar impressions. Deonte first squinted at Ask, then turned toward the shed, and finally whispered in feigned surreptitiousness, "Are we being followed?"

Ask forced a smile. "No." He hesitated as the impulse to tell Deonte the weird sensation of being summoned by the shed tugged at his conscious mind. He knew, however, that even best friends can think you're either on drugs or imagining things if you tell them inanimate objects are "speaking" to you.

"Why do you keep looking behind us? It makes me, well, a little nervous, to be honest," Deonte said.

"It's nothing, really," Ask said, convincingly enough that he didn't entirely doubt his own words.

"Then stop it." Deonte readjusted the tackle box, his pole, and the bucket, which they would fill with water to keep their catch fresh until it could be cleaned, and then marched more deliberately toward the river.

The friends set their lines about fifty paces from a bridge. The highway noise would be minimal this time of day. They chose this spot because the bank was low and wide and provided an oddly shaped tree with a large branch that protruded sideways, which made for a comfortable bench for Ask to sit on while he fished. Deonte, on the other hand, had a more active approach to fishing. He liked to wade into the water a few feet, so he could be, as he once explained to Ask, "in the middle of the action." To accommodate Deonte's approach, this spot also offered a shallow inlet to the river for safe wading. Ask watched his friend roll-up the legs of his jeans to his knees.

"I wonder why he did it," Ask pondered aloud.

"You know we can't answer that question," Deonte said. Deonte, like Ask, was also being raised by a single mother. They'd had this discussion enough that Deonte didn't need Ask to clarify.

"Yeah," said Ask. "I know."

Deonte's father had also vanished one day, never returning from the BNSF Railway Company in Fargo, where he worked at the railyard repairing faulty connectors between the cars. "Making sure the cars stay together on the tracks," Deonte had explained it to Ask once. "You got to be strong to do that work." Deonte was proud of his father, that was evident. Ask recalled Deonte accompanying his father on a weeklong trip one summer to fix a line that was separating and splitting from its railroad ties. When he returned, he regaled Ask with stories of strength and stamina, of camping on the prairie, after long days of cutting, welding, and grinding, lifting steel, and driving in spikes, until the line was repaired. He met some colorful characters, he said, too, like Chip, whose long explanations taught Deonte expletives he'd never even heard before. He liked how everyone laughed, even when the work was hard, especially when the work was hard. He told Ask that he liked how his father never complained, even soothed the others with a smile and a hand to ease their burden. "It's like he always has their back," Deonte told Ask. "They can always trust him. I could tell." Then one night, his father just didn't return from his shift.

Deonte showed up at Ask's house a few days after his father left. "It's like I expect him to walk through that door any minute," Deonte said, staring out Ask's bedroom window, the character in his POV video game stalled against a wall, legs moving without anywhere to go, the controller not even in Deonte's hand.

Deonte's father was there one day and then gone the next. Ask put his arm around his friend's shoulder to comfort him, not realizing at the time that the same fate would befall him just a couple of years later. It would then be Deonte's turn to both comfort and mentor Ask into a life that would feel incomplete.

Ask had asked Deonte then, too, "Why did he leave?"

"I ask myself that question a lot," Deonte said. "It doesn't help." He continued, "Look, it won't get easier, but the pain does eventually dull. Things start to feel, well, normal, as normal as they can anyway."

Ask nodded in acknowledgment of Deonte's experience and in acceptance of their shared trial. From that moment on, Ask and Deonte could talk about their dads, openly and honestly, without alarming their mothers.

To Ask's question now, Deonte said, as he had said many times before, "I don't know." Deonte seemed quite a bit more reserved than usual. "Is that why you kept looking back? You thought you saw your dad?"

Ask, taken aback, said, "No," and then amended his answer to, "I-I don't think so." This revised response surprised Ask, but he knew it was true.

Deonte paused mid-roll, leaving his left cuff loosely hanging halfway up his calf. "You mean, you might have thought you saw him?" Studying the river's edge, he added, "Where? Where do you think you saw him? By the shed?"

Ask suddenly started, wide-eyed. *Yes*, he thought. *By the shed. Well, more like from inside the shed, but how was that possible?* He tried to describe this to himself as much as to Deonte. "It's not that I saw him," he clarified. "It's more like I heard him."

"What? Like, call your name or something?"

Ask considered the insistent thrumming of the previous night emanating from the shed. A voice had called his name, sort of, but it didn't form any words. More accurately, it had seeped into his body, pulsed within him like blood, animated his cells, gave rise to a yearning to recover some part of himself that was missing. That was it—the impulse to be whole, to be complete, and his father was somehow part of that. "Not like that, exactly," Ask finally answered. "I just sort of felt the way I did when he was around."

"Ah, déjà vu. I would sometimes come home and think Dad was back. But Mom told me I just sort of remembered another time and the feeling was a memory or the feeling of a memory or something." Deonte knelt to finish preparing his pants for the river. He took a few steps into the water.

Ask shrugged. He wanted to keep talking about the source of this feeling, the shed, the other night, the immense desire he had even now to go to the shed and decipher the message muddling his mind and throbbing in his heart. Ask had an itch that needed to be scratched, but he couldn't reach the right places to alleviate the discomfort.

"Could it be his voice you're hearing? Could it be your dad's watching over you, somehow? Like a guardian angel?" Deonte asked. Deonte attended a Catholic church in West Fargo. Years ago, he told Ask, who didn't attend a church, about a sermon in which the pastor spoke of guardian angels. Since that sermon, Deonte would reference angels whenever something happened no one could explain, like the time he was climbing a tree and slipped from a high branch. For reasons he still couldn't explain, a thin branch, lower on the tree but well above the ground, managed to stop his fall by catching a belt loop. "Tell me," Deonte said to Ask, "that's not the work of a guardian angel."

Deonte even found his own guardian angel by researching his ancestors after his mother shared the results of her AncestoryDNA test with him. He showed Ask the breakdown of the data on his computer at school a couple of months ago. Deonte had been studying his genealogy ever since. He told Ask about one great grandfather who owned a general store. With nothing but a pitchfork, Deonte's great grandfather chased off three would-be thieves. He often told Ask this relative was his guardian angel. "I don't know—maybe your dad is protecting you," Deonte said.

Ask tensed at the thought of his father being an angel, which would mean his father was not only gone but dead gone. Ask had accepted that his father was no longer around, but he had not considered death. An ache crawled up his chest and lodged itself sharply in his throat. What if his father was dead? Even though such an explanation might make the pain of separation more tolerable in some respects—knowing that his father simply did not leave but was forced to leave by virtue of his mortality—it also meant he would not see him again, at least not in this lifetime.

"I'm sorry, man. I didn't mean to imply. . . Look, I was just trying to work it out." Deonte put a hand on Ask's shoulder.

"It's okay. Honestly, I don't know what any of this means right now. I'm probably just wanting to believe I hear him. You know what, let's just forget it and fish." Ask forced a smile.

Deonte stared at him for a moment, as if to say, "Are you sure?"

"We're burning daylight," Ask added, something his dad used to tell him when he dragged his feet on a project.

Deonte nodded and grinned. "Alright." Casting his line, he said, "Yeah. I'm going after the biggest fish in this river. The kingfish."

Transformed into a fish by magic to escape capture and death, thought Ask. He remembered a time he was fishing with his father. He was very young, perhaps five or six. His father told him to be gentle with his catch, to listen to its secrets. "You never know, son, when a fish is not just a fish."

His father recast his line. After a few moments, his father told him, "A long time ago, son, there was a great war between gods and giants. The heavens ran red with their blood as the mightiest heroes battled." Raising a fisted hand above his head for emphasis, his father continued, "Thor, wielding Mjölnir, crushed his enemies before defeating Jörmungandr, Loki's son, only to succumb to the great serpent's venom. All were lost, except a few, who fled to the mortal world. One beautiful goddess," his father explained, "transformed herself into a fish to hide from a relentless enemy that strives even today to finish what it began millennia ago."

Ask watched his father place each catch to his ear and listen. Because his father laughed, Ask thought he was teasing him. But, as his father listened to one fish, his face grew serious, and he placed the fish back into the river. He didn't say a thing.

Why did Ask think of that now? And why was the call to run home to the shed more intense than ever?

CHAPTER 3

CONFRONTATION

ASK PACED THE LIVING ROOM while his mother prepared the walleye he caught for dinner with the bread she made that morning and potatoes and green beans she had picked from the garden. Two things weighed heavily on his mind. The first, of course, was the perpetual and intensifying desire to go to the shed. He wasn't sure why he resisted. Some part of him dug his heels in deep against it, not wanting to be summoned, afraid, perhaps, of what he would find. The second was Deonte's suggestion about his father being a guardian angel. What if this were true? What if a ghost was tugging at Ask's head and heart to entice him to enter a place he considered more and more dangerous? Although he couldn't explain it, he somehow knew there would be no going back once he unlocked the shed door.

"Why don't you sit down or go for a walk outside?" His mother was standing in the doorway to the kitchen. "Dinner won't be ready for another half hour."

Ask suddenly felt overwhelmed, anxious, and frustrated. Everything seemed out of his control. He stopped pacing and looked at his mother. Why hadn't she told him anything more about his father leaving? He stared at her, an intense anger simmering in his veins, rising in the blood pulsing at his temples.

He swiped fingers through his blond hair. Was she keeping secrets from him? Did she know something she wasn't willing to share?

"What is it?" Her face furrowed with worry as she approached, a hand reaching for him.

He pulled away. "Where's Dad?"

The worry on her face gave way to weariness. She dropped her hand. "We've talked about this," she said. "For now, he's gone."

"Gone, as in he's coming back, or gone, as in he's dead?" Ask said.

She fell heavily onto the plush sofa, displacing a couple of crimson pillows, and studied the distant fields through the living room window, deep in thought. "I don't know how to answer that question," she finally said. "It's complicated."

"It seems pretty simple to me. Either he is alive and returning or dead and gone." Ask had never confronted this issue so directly. He was always afraid of where it might lead, the hope he might end up abandoning by knowing. Even so, he seemed to gain a stubborn confidence with each question he asked, each word he uttered. "Tell me," he pleaded.

She was quiet a long time, so long, in fact, that the timer beeped, and she had to rush to the kitchen to rescue the cooked fish from the oven, where it continued to sizzle in butter and herbs, a scent that would typically entice Ask into the kitchen to hover over his mother's shoulder with the impatience of a hungry hyena ready to pounce. Not tonight. Ask waited in the living room. He didn't feel like following her. The strength of his confidence seemed rooted to where he stood, and he didn't want to chance losing it by moving. He would stand his ground on this issue until he knew the truth.

She returned and surprised him by saying, "Your answers are in the shed."

His heart pounded in his chest. He felt lost for a moment, as if this truth was both exactly what he expected to hear and entirely the last thing that made any sense. "What... What did you say?"

"Your answers are in the shed." She nodded toward the red and white structure, slightly smaller than a barn but larger than their garage, a few feet from where Babe chewed tufts of grass and bleated. "But don't go in there. Not now. Maybe not for a while."

This recommendation relieved him—he feared as much as he yearned to go and see and know. He whispered, "But if the answer is there, why shouldn't I go right now?" Despite this threat of action, Ask remained standing in place. Then he added, "Why didn't you tell me last year, last month, last week?" He realized that, even when he spoke these words, he was in no hurry to open those shed doors.

"You have to know, Ask, that once you find your answers, nothing will be the same."

Ask puzzled over this cryptic remark. "Because I'll know?" He suddenly feared finding his father's body decaying in one of the shed walls. He kept hearing Deonte say that ghosts protected the living. "Is. . . Is he there?" He found the courage to ask.

She sighed. "Not like you're thinking. Nothing corporeal."

So, he was a ghost? "What does that mean? Nothing corporeal?"

"Like I said, it's complicated. I don't fully understand it myself." She peered up at the ceiling and exhaled loudly, shook her head, as if remembering something. For a moment, she appeared to be arguing with herself, silently but furiously, as if she were two minds sharing one body. She closed her eyes, rubbed her temples, and said, "Just do me this favor and wait a little while before you open that shed."

He found himself nodding. Something still bothered him, though, nagging at the corners of his logical mind. He didn't know if he should tell her. His mother's reaction worried him. He was afraid to push her too far. But then, he figured she probably already knew. "The shed has been calling me?" he said. Is that the reason she mentioned it?

She grew suddenly concerned, more serious. "It what?"

"You told me about the shed when I asked about Dad. I figured maybe it was calling to you, too. It's been, well, tugging at me. . . whispering to me."

He thought that may have been the "voice" with which she was arguing.

She was standing by him now, eyes wide and wilder than Ask had seen them before, as if a force darker than his mother's calm attempted to surface from deep within her. "What is it saying to you?"

He hesitated and took a step back. "I don't know." He added, "I can't understand it."

With a strength and certainty Ask hadn't seen in his mother for some time, she said, "You will. When you do, you must resist it."

The shade from a large cottonwood cast a shadow over the shed. To be true to his mother's wishes, he buried deep inside himself the desire to discover the mystery in that darkening structure that appeared more and more ominous yet more and more enticing as each minute passed.

CHAPTER 4

THE GROWING AX

THE WEEKS THAT PASSED PROVED an excruciating exercise in self-control for Ask. Often, the impulse would strike him, and he would be compelled toward the shed. He would come to himself with his hand on the door, his heart thumping in his chest. While he dreaded the chores on the farmstead—mowing the several acres each week, collecting and burning branches severed by the unrelenting North Dakota winds, gathering beans, peas, carrots, cucumbers, and zucchini from his mother's garden—he threw himself into these tasks with focused fervor in an attempt to quell the incessant temptation to give in to the pulsing urge always calling him.

One day, when he found himself standing only a couple of feet from the shed door, having left the half-empty basket for harvesting beans and peas at the garden entrance, Ask wondered why he so persistently resisted going inside. It was such a little thing, after all. He crept closer until the door handle was within grasp. Instead of reaching for the handle, he suddenly stepped back, away from the shed. His mother had warned him about an irreversible change. Plus, he had promised to wait. Of course, neither he nor his mother established what waiting entailed, nor how long or for what specific reason. But he could swear that, at times, when the summoning was strongest, like now, a stronger impulse of resistance settled into his mind, as if another power, a balancing power, was producing a sort of equilibrium. This impulse to resist reminded him of quiet moments on the porch. It reminded him of his mother.

As Ask returned to his work, Deonte arrived and waved from the end of the dirt driveway, his mother having dropped him off. As Deonte's mother drove away, Ask nodded toward the departing SUV. "How is everything? I haven't seen your mom much lately."

Deonte shrugged. "Me neither. She's been pulling extra shifts at the hospital."

Ask remembered Deonte's parents visited often before the disappearances of their fathers. During these visits, Deonte's mother chatted with Ask's mother about anything from politics to physician practices to education, while Deonte's father wandered around looking for something to do, something to fix. Ask's father usually guided his friend to a broken machine or a section of fence in disrepair, and the two would set to working on it. Deonte's father always seemed to relax when he was puzzling over an engine that wouldn't turn. Wrench in hand, his smile was genuine, and he could talk comfortably, about the task, about the day, about life. Ask remembered him saying once, "The best thing anyone can do is to fix something broken." Ask thought about that often, but neither he nor Deonte could figure out how to fix the things that simply disappear.

Despite their early introduction, Ask and Deonte didn't become fast friends. Their friendship was first one of convenience. They argued as toddlers tend to do over toy trucks, sippy cups, and attention. Later, they noticed their differences—Deonte's athleticism and Ask's diminutive frame, his preference for stories and books. These differences first created a separation, like how Deonte would play basketball, baseball, or foursquare during recess, and Ask would chase dragonflies, not having been invited to join him.

It wasn't until fourth grade that they found friendship. Ask had been pushed in a mud puddle at recess behind a dogwood bush where adults couldn't see, by Tate Chism, the class bully. It was unfortunate that Ask had followed a frog into that concealed part of the schoolyard. Deonte happened to see the whole thing after catching a fly ball to deep left field.

"What's going on?" Deonte asked, nudging his way between Tate and Ask.

"None of your business," Tate said.

"Yeah? I'm making it my business. You can't just go pushing people in the mud. It's not nice."

"So?" Tate laughed. "Maybe you need a mud bath, too."

Deonte pressed up close to Tate. He was nearly a head taller. "Try it."

"Whatever," Tate said and ran off.

"Thanks," Ask said.

"Don't mention it. Come on. I have an extra shirt in my gym bag you can wear."

Ask followed Deonte. "Why'd you do it?"

"Do what?" Deonte asked.

"Stop him?" Ask struggled to keep up with Deonte's broad strides.

"Because I hate bullies, especially when they mess with my friends."

Just like that, Deonte's declaration solidified their friendship, a friendship born of two very different personalities, strengthened by those differences.

In response to Deonte's comment about his mother working extra shifts, Ask said, "That's too bad. Has it been that busy?"

"Naw. She just takes all the shifts she can, staffing shortage or not. Has since Dad disappeared," Deonte added.

Deonte followed Ask to the pasture, where Babe had somehow gotten his nubby horns caught in the fence wire. Over the weeks, Ask had developed an impatience for the animal. Babe always seemed to do what he wanted and what he wanted often put him in a tricky position. Ask may have tugged a little too hard to extricate the animal, as Babe's bleating seemed excessively accusatory.

Once Babe was free, Ask and Deonte made their way to a maple tree on the south side of the house, where swings had been attached to a thick horizontal branch. They sat on the swings, as they had for so many years as children, and pumped with their legs to see who could go higher. The combined weight of bodies much larger than they were as children caused the branch to moan as they gained altitude.

"School starts next week," Deonte lamented.

Ask nodded, looking west to the fields of ripening corn, green soybean plants, and golden wheat, ready for the first harvest. Summer break seemed like a dream. He'd filled his time with chores, fishing, and anything to occupy his mind. Truth be told, the unceasing call of the shed had taken a toll. He was exhausted. It kept him up at night and forced him to stay busy. He'd easily read two dozen books during too many nights of extreme insomnia. He wasn't ready to start school in this condition.

"What's going on, Ask?" Deonte stopped swinging. "It's like you've been gone or something all summer. You're here, but you're not. What's up?"

The weight of keeping a secret and resisting the pull to the shed compounded into a burden he could no longer bear alone. Still, he hesitated, started to explain but then stopped a few times. Finally, he said, "There's something in that shed I have to see, but," he hesitated, "I'm scared of what I'll find." Already, he felt a little lighter having shared just that much.

"Okay," Deonte said. Then he added, "Something in the... what?"

Once he shared a portion his secret, Ask knew he had to explain, fully. "A few weeks ago, if you remember, I felt this... well, urge to go to that shed, as if something was calling me. It's wild, I know, but every day since I've been doing everything I can to stay away from it. I'm positive that once I open that door, there will be no going back, whatever that means."

"Have you been watching those sci-fi movies late at night again? I told you that stuff messes with your mind," Deonte teased.

"I'm serious," Ask continued. "It's impossible to explain, but I know something is in that shed, and I'm supposed to find it."

"Why in the hell haven't you just done it, then?" Deonte asked, perplexed. "You always got to make things so hard on yourself. It's like that time you wanted to ask, oh, what's her name. . . Sheryl Ann. . . on a date in middle school. You remember that. You paced all over, said you needed to find the right time, the right place, and catch her in the right mood. And, so you waited, and then that jerk, Jepp—"

"He's not a jerk. He was our friend," Ask interjected.

"No, he's a jerk," Deonte said. "Friends don't turn on each other. They stay loyal."

"But it must be hard for him, you know? All the pressure to win, the expectations he has to live up to," Ask replied.

"No, those aren't the hard things, Ask. Going with the flow is easy. When he made the football team, he changed. You know that."

Ask nodded. "You're right, but I can't help but think he's had to make tough decisions, too."

Deonte rolled his eyes. "Whatever. . . So anyway, your buddy Jepp walks up two weeks after you started mulling over your big move, asks her out, and now they've been dating for like two years. Same thing all over again."

Ask couldn't help but smile at how Deonte simplified everything Ask made too complex. His friend liked things that were clear, direct, and actionable.

"I got a solution," Deonte continued. "We walk over now and get it done." He pointed to the shed. "No more moping around, turning this thing over again and again in your head. You'll see real quick there's nothing to be afraid of. I'll even show you it is *all* in your head. There ain't nothing in that shed except for some old tools, dusty burlap sacks, too many bugs, and maybe some tore up snow fencing." He hopped off his swing and started walking toward the shed. "Come on."

"Wait," Ask said. How could he explain to Deonte that his mother knew and that she admonished him to wait, that she told him everything would change? That *he* might not be ready.

"Oh no. You've waited plenty long. It's time to just do it." Deonte took broad steps toward the shed. He hit a growth spurt the past year and was now a full head taller than Ask. Most of his height seemed to be in his legs.

Ask jogged to catch up, Heim loping along at his side, and he arrived just as Deonte was pulling the shed door open. A flurry of flies and moths filled the opening as the door exposed the shed's interior. It was relatively dark inside, since the only light was sun filtering through gaps between old boards. Ask stayed behind Deonte, beyond the shed's threshold, peering inside after his friend. Deonte brushed cobwebs aside, clucked his tongue, and scanned the walls, floor, and rafters. "I see you've neglected this place. It's a mess." He added, "Looks like I remember it." He grinned.

Ask quickly scanned the inside once his eyes sufficiently adjusted to the muted light. Nothing was out of the ordinary. A twinge of disappointment settled in Ask's chest. He expected something extraordinary, supernatural, or even a little scary. He thought of the hours he spent fretting over what he now saw was nothing but cobwebs and some old odds and ends. The scene was entirely anticlimactic.

"See. Nothing to worry about," Deonte said. "Now, can we enjoy the last week of vacation before school starts?"

Yet, still, despite what was in front of him, Ask felt the yearning return, more intensified, more concentrated, here at the threshold of the rickety shed. It occurred to him that he was standing outside the shed; some persistent hesitation kept him from stepping inside. But he had to know, so he placed a foot on the bowing wood floor. Heim let out a single bark. Ask couldn't tell if the bark was meant as encouragement or a warning. Once inside, he noticed that the space was suddenly brighter than it had been, illuminated by a slight pulsing green light emanating from behind a stack of old grass seed his father had planned on spreading over a stretch of field Babe had chewed to nubs.

Deonte took a step back from the light. "Whoa. What's that? You have one of those bug zappers hidden back there?"

Ask, too, found himself seeking a reason for that light. "I don't think so."

The light pulsed like something living. It resembled the sensation he had felt and constrained the past several weeks. It was the beating of a heart, the breathing pattern of something living. Ask took another step and another, until he stood at the stack of grass seed bags.

He peered over his shoulder at Deonte, whose wide eyes seemed to say, "Don't." But Ask wasn't afraid anymore. The closer he moved to the light, the less unbearable the itch in his veins, and the more at peace he felt. The summoning of the previous weeks had been leading, Ask realized, to this moment. He knew, although he couldn't explain how, that he and the light were one. If he were ever to feel whole again, he needed to be that light. "I have to," he told Deonte.

On the other side of the stack of grass seed, leaning against the wall on the floor, he found a rusty old ax he remembered using on camping trips with his parents. It would have simply been ordinary, even a little underwhelming, if its steel head hadn't been pulsing green. Ask's initial thought was to look for some glow-in-the-dark paint splattered on the ax or something else that might explain the light. It didn't make sense, and so his mind worked to create a plausible, natural, normal explanation. The only rational action, he surmised, was to pick it up, to study it closer. Notwithstanding, some subconscious part of his mind knew that's exactly what he had to do. And so, Ask picked up the ax.

He felt a rushing in his head and a peculiar sensation in his nerves and muscles, as if he'd been stretched like playdough. For a moment, he lost track of himself and his surroundings. The green light appeared to be all around him. He was somehow caught up into it.

He regained his senses when he bumped his head. He turned around to ask Deonte what hit him. He found Deonte staring up at him, and he was looking down at Deonte. "What's going on?" He didn't sound like himself. His voice was deeper, bigger. He took an awkward step toward Deonte and bumped his head again. He gazed up and found that he was inches from the roof of the shed, which was at least twelve feet high.

Deonte screamed and ran out of the shed.

Heim observed Ask from just outside the open door, his head cocked to the side, but he didn't seem worried or surprised.

Ask wanted to follow Deonte, but he realized it would take some careful maneuvering to get out. Not only was he twelve feet tall, but he was also much wider than usual, with—he marveled—bulky, muscular arms. At the end of his right arm, gripped tightly by his massive right hand, the glowing green ax he had picked up no longer appeared to be old, rusty, or glowing, but a weapon with a bright silver head and bearded heel. As he observed it carefully, he found that the blade was extremely sharp and embossed with words he could not decipher, from a language with which he was unfamiliar. The old ax had also engorged to an enormous weapon, a battle-ax reminiscent of some centuries past.

Regardless of which way Ask turned, he couldn't quite shimmy through the shed door. He seemed to be getting larger. The ax—which was now about his normal height, five and a half feet—proved an awkward accessory when pressed against bulging shoulders. He had to readjust. He leaned the ax against the south wall and released his grip. As he did, he felt a dizzying sensation, as if he had been spun quickly several times and then dumped on uncertain feet. He placed his hand out to brace himself, only he was standing in front of the open shed door, so his hand settled on nothing but air. He tumbled out of the shed, reduced to his usual size and shape. A sudden and splitting headache came over him. He ran to the side of the shed and threw up.

Deonte had just about made it to the house. Ask could see that Deonte had stopped, noticed him, and was sprinting back. "What the hell was that?"

Ask couldn't talk. He was sitting in the grass, slowly coming out of the sweep of nausea and recovering from the excruciating yet now subsiding pressure in his head. Heim licked the side of his face, which didn't help him feel any less nauseous. The smell of Heim's breath was surprisingly rancid. What were they feeding that dog?

Deonte peeked in the shed. "You do that with mirrors or something? You messing with me?"

Ask shook his head. "No. What happened?"

"What? You mean you don't remember turning into a giant Viking? Seriously, how'd you do that?" Deonte looked at the ax leaning against the wall just inside the shed near the door. It was no longer pulsing green. It was just an old rusty ax. "You just picked this up?" he asked.

"Yeah. Then everything went a little blurry."

Deonte reached his hand out. He looked at Ask, who nodded. Deonte paused, pulled his hand back, and then reached once more, lifting the ax in his right hand. Nothing. He stepped into the shed and closed his eyes, lifting the ax above his head, as if the transformation might come from the sky. Again, nothing. He pointed the ax at Ask. "You picked this up and then you grew. You had a red beard, man. Like I said, you must've planned this. I don't know how you did it—"

Ask cut him off. He pulled himself to his feet. "No. That light called me. It told me to pick up the ax."

Deonte furrowed his brow. "That ax didn't say a thing." He paused, looked Ask over. Perhaps something in Ask's shaky stance, or the fact that his clothes were shredded to strips that barely covered him, softened Deonte's voice. "You okay?"

"I guess so." In the back of his mind, Ask pondered over what his mother told him. She said that he would find all the answers he needed once he went into the shed. But he didn't find any answers, only more questions. His father certainly wasn't there.

He thought he caught a glimpse of his mother, then, inside the house, peering through the window below the west gable. He feared she would be disappointed in him. *No,* a voice whispered in his mind. *That wasn't true. She wasn't disappointed.*

As he leaned over, hands on knees, trying to catch his breath and find his bearings on ground that seemed to wobble beneath him, made even more unstable by Heim performing figure eights between his legs, Ask closed his eyes. As he did, he saw himself suddenly standing in his house, staring through his mother's eyes. He thought what she thought and felt what she felt. She was afraid and tired beyond anything he could imagine, as if she had been traveling the world for ages, only to arrive at the same empty place where she began. And then he envisioned an image of his father presented to him through her memory. The brown-red hair, the sharp jawline, the broad shoulders, and those jade green eyes. He'd forgotten about those eyes, how they sparkled at times like a peridot refracting moonlight, like the glow on the head of a rusty old ax.

"Alright. Sure. Look, I'm going to take off. You should, I don't know, drink some water or something." Deonte played on the basketball and football high school teams. He was no stranger to overexertion. He'd had his fair share of summer two-a-day trainings and muscle cramps. Not surprising, then, his go-to advice for Ask whenever he was sick or injured echoed that of his coaches: walk it off or go get a drink of water.

After accompanying Ask to his house, Deonte said, "Well, I guess I better head home." He added as a joke, though it fell awkwardly flat, "Looks like you've got your hands full."

Ask nodded, grasping and pinning the remnants of his torn and disfigured clothes against his body in bunches. Fortunately, he'd worn shorts with an elastic band, so they remained intact; however, the elastic had been stretched beyond its capacity to rebound to its regular shape.

Deonte returned the nod and then quickly pivoted and ran down the road, cell phone against an ear, calling, Ask assumed, his mother to pick him up.

When he could no longer see Deonte, Ask turned to his immediate problem. He needed to sneak into the house as quietly as possible. To avoid his mother's questions, he made sure to climb the stairs slowly, careful to make as little sound as possible. He decided that he couldn't talk to her, not now anyway.

He gently closed the bathroom door behind him. He loosened his grip, and the tatters of torn cloth fell to the floor around him. He wiggled out of the pieces that still clung to his body. Because the August afternoon was humid and hot, and the effort of transformation produced a stream of continual sweat, he started water for a quick shower. Before pulling his tired body, worked unnaturally to exhaustion, into the cool drizzle, he glimpsed himself in the mirror. He noticed a few small bruises at his elbows and shoulders. *Must have been from the expanding and retracting*, he thought.

And then he caught sight of his eyes. Light blue irises had been replaced with bright green ones, the shade and brilliance of the light that had emanated from his father's ax.

CHAPTER 5

ORLA

THE FINAL DAYS OF SUMMER vacation accomplished, Ask found himself standing by the metal sculpture of a mustang raising up on hind legs, the school's mascot, guarding the south entrance to his high school's multipurpose sports field.

Deonte would likely be in the locker room cleaning up after early morning practice. They hadn't spoken much since the day it happened, the day he'd transformed into a giant. Because Ask remembered only a few sensations and a powerful headache, he referred to the incident as "it." Somehow, calling whatever happened "it" made it feel less scary. He was also able to push it to the back of his mind more easily. "It" was impossible to forget, however. Whenever he saw his friend after it happened, Deonte avoided eye contact and said he was busy. The alienation and excuses from his friend hurt more than anything else.

He shuffled toward the main entrance.

It was Thursday, and the humidity of late August hovered in the air as a hazy mist. Sheyenne High School, in West Fargo, was about fifteen miles from home. Ask had one more year of taking the bus and then his permit would become a full-fledged license, provided he passed the exam and his mother let him drive. She'd become overprotective when Ask's father disappeared and put in place rules and restrictions about where, when, and with whom he could travel. He hoped his license would loosen some of those restrictions. He didn't worry too much about the driving portion of the exam. Like most of his friends who grew up on farms, Ask had been driving a tractor since he could reach a gas pedal. The practical exam would be a snap. He just had to remember all those rules. Of course, everything he needed to know was in a booklet.

If there was one thing Ask could do and do well, it was read. His mother instilled in him at an early age a respect for story. He was raised on Aesop's fables, the lyrical cadence of epic battles detailed in Homer's *Iliad* and *Odyssey*, and grew up idolizing the heroes of Norse mythology. He recalled how his mother spoke as if she knew those gods and goddesses, describing for him little idiosyncrasies—Thor's propensity to clench his jaw whenever someone poked fun at him, how Bragi curled his beard around his index finger when he puzzled out a particularly complex problem, or how Vidar's lip curled slightly to the left when he was amused. These insights made these characters feel more like uncles than fictions.

Ask walked the long hallways lined with lockers. The first task of the day was to find the one to which he was assigned. He pulled out his locker combination and made his way to locker number 1165.

Two things happened rather quickly as he was loading books into the locker. First, Jepp walked by and slammed Ask's locker shut, just as he was about to place another handful of books on the lower shelf.

"Think fast," he joked.

Jepp, Deonte, and Ask were best friends in elementary and middle school. Unlike Ask, Jepp grew a foot between middle school and high school. He was also naturally athletic, which made him a prime subject for the football field, where he now enjoyed the position and social praise of star quarterback. The best, critics around the area claimed, in the school's fifteen-year history. He could run, and he could throw accurately.

The second thing that happened is that Deonte pushed Jepp against the locker and told him, "Don't be a tool." To which Jepp responded with a snigger, yanked his shirt free of Deonte's grasp, and nudged a couple of his friends on the football team. Then, Sheryl Ann settled in next to Jepp, who pulled one of his arms over her shoulder.

"Hi, Ask," she said. She looked at him square in the face for several seconds.

Was she staring at him? He felt both elated and a little unnerved.

"Your eyes are green," she finally concluded. "Did you get some of those colored contacts over the summer?" Before he could answer, she said, "I've always wanted purple eyes. Like those anime cartoon characters. My parents won't let me, though."

She knew the color of my eyes, Ask thought to himself excitedly.

Jepp was already pulling her away. "Watch yourself," he called to Deonte over his shoulder in reference to the shove. With Jepp, there would likely be retaliation.

"Jepp was just playing around," Ask told Deonte after they left. "It's alright."

Deonte rolled his eyes. He opened the locker and shoved a gym bag, a backpack, and a couple of books in a pile on the locker floor. "Look. He's not good, he's not nice, and he's not your friend anymore."

"Are *you* still my friend?" Ask blurted, not sure why he thought this was the best time for such a question.

Deonte threw him a look like "seriously?" and then left.

"You looking for a friend?"

A tall, slender, pale girl with dark black hair leaned against a nearby locker. She had a nose piercing and striking beauty. He'd never seen her before, not in previous grades and not around town. "I'm Orla." She smiled. "And you are?"

"Ask," he said.

"I already did," she said.

Despite himself, and because he had a tendency toward self-deprecating humor, he returned her smile. "That's my name, Ask. Do I know you?"

Orla's smile grew. "Not yet. I'm new. Just moved here from the north."

"North isn't a place. What, north like Canada?" Who was this girl?

"North," she repeated. The first bell rang. Classes would start in ten minutes. "How about we meet up at lunch?"

Ask nodded.

"By the way," she whispered, passing close to him, "I know those aren't contacts. Though I will say the color is *transformative*."

Ask's heart both leapt at the soft, cold puff of her breath on his ear and lurched at her assertion that she knew something about what happened to him last week. How could she? *He* didn't even know what happened.

CHAPTER 6

THE PROTECTOR

ALGEBRA AND PHYSICS—THE DRUDGERY OF formulas and integers—behind him for the day, Ask made his way to the cafeteria for lunch. Tray balanced in hand, he scanned the rows of tables for the enigmatic Orla, whom he hadn't seen at all after their encounter that morning. He would surreptitiously glance about during breaks, as classrooms released students into the halls. He wondered if she was in Wood Shop or French, subjects offered in another wing of the school. He imagined she might be in both. He imagined other things about her, too, like what it might be like to be close to her, but he tried not to dwell on those thoughts too long.

While he was searching for Orla, he saw Deonte at a corner table, his shoulders and legs pulling toward his core, declaring he didn't want company. For another time, he thought. Then, he spotted Orla leaning in the entryway of the west cafeteria entrance. From a distance, she was not at all awkward, like so many of the other kids around her. Her easy posture and the smirk of indifference on her face revealed a confidence Ask lacked and craved in his life. Oh, and she was gorgeous. He felt an urge akin to gravity pulling him close to her, another kind of summoning.

"You eat that?" she asked, nodding in the direction of the overcooked pasta slathered in a tomato-like red substance that sort of passed for sauce. The garlic bread was virtually a rock, edible only where the sauce had seeped into a corner. He looked at the food on his plate. He vaguely remembered getting in line for lunch, passing the gauntlet of food options, and holding out his tray to servers who filled it with the sad contents now cooling into something even more unappetizing. Only the apple wobbling near a small box of milk seemed a smart choice.

"Should have gone with the pizza," he retorted.

Orla rolled her eyes. "Dump that and come on."

Ask shrugged, pocketed the apple, and placed the otherwise untouched tray at the cleaning station. The worker at the station shot him a disapproving look.

He followed Orla outside, where the August sun was high and bright. Groups of teens were scattered on the lawn, texting and laughing. He envied them. Ask hadn't felt much like laughing since he picked up that rusty ax. While the intense summoning had dwindled to an occasional whisper, he now experienced flashes of what felt like memories, sensations, even traumas of a past he was too young to know. Sometimes when he closed his eyes, especially at night before falling asleep, he pictured himself in a forest, a massive hand gripping a tree trunk, the other the throat of the ax handle. Disembodied cries in the distance, a squiggle of smoke curling from the chimney of an old cabin, a pounding in his heart, an acute need to help.

"Been thinking a lot lately, haven't you?" Orla asked.

Ask furrowed his brows. "Who are you?"

She pulled him toward a large tree with expansive shade. "I hate the heat, but we need to talk as privately as possible. This humidity. It's hideous."

It dawned on Ask that he was holding hands with this girl he'd never met. She was dragging him behind the trunk of a large oak. Neither being pushed against the tree for a passionate kiss nor slammed against the tree for sheer spite would have surprised him at this point. Regardless, he relented to being pulled along. *I mean*, he rationalized with himself, *she's hot*, even if her hands were cold, freezing cold, in fact.

"I know what you're thinking," Orla continued. Ask blushed, perhaps imperceptibly, but he blushed. "That I'm pushy for someone you just met. Perhaps even a little bossy." She winked. "Maybe a little. Look, this may sound forward or ridiculous to you, but I'm here to protect you." He let go of her hand because his was burning from an intense chill, as if he'd been squeezing a chunk of dry ice.

"Protect me?" he asked. "Look, Jepp isn't always nice, but I can handle him. We used to be friends, you know. He's just confused."

Ask noted clear humor in Orla's glacial blue eyes. "Yeah. I'm not concerned about your friend. And, once you fully manifest, you won't be either."

"Once I what? Manifest?" The word felt right, fit into a vocabulary his body had been learning since being summoned to pick up the ax, but Ask rejected the feeling, afraid it might change him permanently. "You aren't making any sense," he stammered, his conscious mind attempting to deny the knowledge already embedded in and currently restructuring his cells.

He didn't tell her that he could lift an extraordinary amount of weight or that he cut himself a week ago, nearly down to the bone, and didn't shed a drop of blood before the wound closed itself up. Yes, there were manifestations—a glowing green ax, a surprising transformation, and now the sudden appearance of a stranger who seemed to know all about it.

"Just don't do it again. Not now. They felt it the first time, knew that the ancient weapon had chosen its new champion. They'll be listening closely for the full transformation. You won't be strong enough to face them, not yet." Orla's hand on his bare arm seared with cold. "Promise me you won't touch that weapon again. Resist for a few weeks until they think it was a false alarm."

"Who are you talking about? What transformation?" Ask inquired.

The bell sounded signaling the end of lunch period. Kids who had eaten lunch outside began to pass the tree, as they headed toward the door. Orla looked around, quietly pleading, "They're dangerous and will hurt you and the ones you love to get what they want. Please. Promise me."

Because he could no longer muster a façade of protest, he simply nodded. Orla nodded as well and rounded the tree. When Ask followed, he couldn't find her. It was as if she had vanished. His arm, where her hand had gripped, still bore the print of her palm and fingers, his flesh red and cratered with goosebumps.

CHAPTER 7

AN UNUSUAL GIFT

THE SAME DISTRACTION THAT HAD made it difficult for Ask to focus on his final classes of the day accompanied him home. He wandered the farmstead, mindlessly working on chores he had neglected in his haste to get to school on time that morning.

Two things Orla had said were particularly weighty on his mind. She had told him others, enemies, knew about his transformation, and they would harm him if he took up the ax again. These enemies, she had told him, wouldn't hesitate to hurt him, his family, or anyone else that got in their way. Of course, this was a terrifying prospect. Part of him wanted to go immediately to the shed to test Orla's prediction and, thereby, determine how much he could or should trust her. He hesitated because he wasn't sure he had enough courage to chance it.

This brought him to the second assertion Orla made. She said the weapon had chosen a champion. Clearly, she wasn't talking about him. Ask was no athlete and certainly no hero. He had tried out for sports teams a few times over the years, but he'd always been passed up for faster, stronger, more talented peers. He made decent grades, but that's because he worked hard at it, not because of some innate intelligence. Although he cataloged his shortcomings in this way, Ask wasn't trying to demean or insult himself. He was a realist. He was the very definition of the term "average." For this reason, any implication of specialness seemed absurd to him, destined for someone else.

Again, he thought about the ax leaning just inside the shed. He could test that theory as well. Would the ax make him a champion? The idea of greatness, of being better than he was, created a temptation nearly unbearable to resist. He then noticed that he had, during his musings, come quite close to the shed. He felt his blood quickening in his veins as he neared the door. But resist he did. For Ask was above average in one thing—he generally kept his word, nearly to a fault. He told both his mother and Orla he would not touch the ax for a while, and so he backtracked to the pasture, where Babe bleated persistently by the water trough. In his hurry to leave that morning, Ask had forgotten to fill it. He grabbed the hose and pulled the pump handle until water streamed into the plastic container. Babe dipped his mouth into the water and drank deeply. When he raised his head, Ask swore he heard the goat say, "It's about time," amidst the cadence of his bleating. Ask let out a single guffaw and shook his head. Now he was hearing animals talk. "Sorry," he answered as he walked away.

He turned toward the house and realized he had not kept his word in every instance in recent weeks. His mother had also asked him to wait before going to the shed before his first transformation. He rationalized that Deonte's insistence that he do it somehow minimized his involvement and lessened any blame that could be assigned to him. He was following his friend, after all, and didn't initiate the disobedience. Despite his effort to justify his actions, Ask knew that he had willingly defied her. For this reason, he made a point to avoid telling his mother what happened. She would, he feared, be disappointed in him after all.

He settled into his chair on the porch, the one next to his father's chair, now vacant for more than two years, and tried to hold on to parts of himself and his past he felt were somehow and suddenly slipping away from him. Gripped by a melancholy that signals change, Ask began to feel a sudden and intense sense of grief. Why had he taken for granted those lazy mornings by the river fishing with his father or the slow walks with Mom, Dad, and Heim, down the dirt road bathed in the soft indigos of evening? Instead, he was alone on the porch, missing a delinquent father and worrying his lonely mother. Deonte avoided him, and now this strange person cornered him at school to tell him his life may be in danger. What had he gotten himself into? He stared down the dirt road where he would find no answer.

When his mom joined him on the porch, he felt a tinge of guilt coated with anger. Yes, he had disobeyed her, but she had told him the shed held answers about his father. Not that day and no time thereafter had his experience in the shed brought him any closer to knowing anything about what happened to or where he could find his father. He wrestled within himself. Should he get up and go inside, ignore her standing near him, apologize for not keeping his word, or yell at her because she had lied? Such questions exhausted him, so he settled on staying silent.

In fact, neither spoke for some long moments. His mother started to speak and stopped again, as if she didn't know what to say to him or how to say it. Eventually, she said, "I put an awful temptation and burden on you, Ask. That wasn't fair of me. I was just concerned about what you might find, what might happen."

"Nothing happened." Why did he lie?

Her whole being seemed to exhale with relief.

"In fact, I didn't find anything." This statement tipped his emotional scales toward anger. "You told me I would know what happened to Dad."

"I wasn't sure." She seemed genuinely perplexed. "I thought for certain… Oh, well, it's not important. I guess I was wrong. I'm sorry."

"Wrong about what?" Keeping his transformation a secret from her, albeit a deception, was proving a useful way to figure out what his mother knew, and why she was reluctant to tell him.

"Your father," she said, hesitating. "Your father, he was—how do I say this?—endowed with a responsibility and given a gift to help carry it out. I thought, perhaps, you might be called to a similar responsibility. When you said something in the shed called to you, well, it had called to him, too."

That *was* his father's ax, Ask realized. Not just an object that belonged to him but a power he wielded. Had he also grown in stature as he took up the ax? What exactly did his responsibility entail? The woods, the cries for help in the cold night, the cabin tucked beneath snow-laden pines—were those his father's memories? He made eye contact with his mother for the first time since he went into the shed.

She gasped at his now green irises. "It is true, then. You said you found nothing in the shed," she said.

"An ax. It was glowing. Green. I picked it up. It wanted me to hold it." He didn't tell her that he transformed into a twelve-foot-tall Viking warrior. Still, the implications started to dawn on Ask—the transfer of the light from the ax to his body. The scattered thoughts like memories finding life in between consciousness and dreams. Could this be what Orla meant by manifestation?

Her relief gone, replaced by what Ask interpreted as a mix of despair and acceptance, his mother fell into his dad's chair. "How often have you picked up the ax?"

He shook his head. "Just the once." She eyed him suspiciously. He knew he shouldn't have lied. "Just once," he repeated.

"That's all it takes to begin the convergence, but perhaps not often enough to pinpoint the source," she said mostly to herself.

"What do you mean by convergence?" Ask said.

"Combining your energy with the ax's." Without elaborating, she continued, quite seriously, "This time, don't touch the ax again for a while. It's our best shot."

"That's what Orla said," Ask let slip.

His mom furrowed her brows, concern spreading over her face. "Who is Orla?"

He didn't tell her that he hadn't met her until today, nor did he mention that she warned him about enemies and offered to protect him. Instead, he simply said, "She knows."

LATER THAT EVENING, HIS MOTHER called to him from the living room, "Ask, will you come here a moment?"

He was factoring polynomials for Algebra class. The integration of numbers and letters—these two separate rhetorical spaces—mimicked, to some degree, his own growing sense of incongruity. He dropped his pencil on the desk in his room, next to an upended metal toy stock car, abandoned by a childhood he now felt years gone, and a picture of his family taken about five years ago. In the picture, Ask wore a red Minnesota Twins baseball cap because his father always wore one. He quickly looked away.

Downstairs, he found his mother standing in front of the couch, a large cardboard box balancing on the cushions. Next to the cardboard box was a mangled t-shirt Ask recognized as the one he had been wearing when he transformed.

"We both agreed you would not pick up the ax again for a while, right?" his mother said.

Ask nodded.

"However, it will and must happen again at some point. I'm not naïve to that fact." She held up his shirt. "We certainly can't have you tearing your clothes each time you do."

She riffled through the box, pulling from its contents a plain muslin cotton tunic. The tunic was white and without embroidery or embellishment and, when he held it in his hands, was surprisingly light. *How medieval,* he thought, holding it to up to study it in its full unfolded ordinariness. As Ask fumbled around with the tunic, his mother cryptically said, "This will help. Wear it under your shirt. It was your father's."

Quite perplexed, Ask said, "Ah, okay. Thanks." Was this gift her way of saying it was time to return to the ax? Didn't she just confirm his waiting awhile longer? Why gift it to him now? "What does it do exactly?"

"Let's just say it will make everything stretchier." She slid the lid back onto the box and then carried it upstairs to her bedroom. Ask stood in the living room holding the tunic as if he had just gotten stuck with the one white elephant gift no one at the party understood or wanted, the punchline of a peculiar inside joke. He held the tunic against his chest, sizing it up. Did this mean his father also transformed?

He found himself formulating an equation in his mind to make sense of the perplexing occurrences the past few weeks, this most recent especially baffling. So, he hypothesized, if A (Ask) + G (Growing Ax) = T (Transformation) does t (tunic) multiply G or divide from T? How did F (his Father) factor into all of this? He realized he couldn't simplify the equation in any way because none of the variables matched. If only he could get the ax alone on one side of the equation, maybe he could figure out what it all meant and why he was in the equation in the first place.

CHAPTER 8

FEVER

AT SCHOOL THE FOLLOWING DAY, Ask couldn't concentrate on his classes. His mind tried furiously to piece together the bits of mysteries, disparate and shrouded, that had surfaced in seemingly unrelated fashion over the past several weeks. His father's disappearance, the ax, the light, the summoning, the convergence, Orla's so-called manifestation—it was all too surreal to make sense within the boundaries of rational thought. Then, there were the snippets of dreams or memories that dragged him exhausted through the night, always to end at the cabin in the woods, the screaming, and, most recently, the sensation of floating, of becoming nothing and everything all at once.

He wandered from class to class and then to lunch and to class again. The piece that made the least bit of sense to him was his mother. How did she know about the shed? The ax? His eyes? She used the word "convergence" but didn't explain it. What did that mean? What else did she know? Even Orla, who had not returned to see him since the first day of school, made more sense than his mother. Perhaps that was because Orla could be explained away as an illusion. As the days passed and he didn't see her again, the more he was convinced she didn't exist. He hadn't dismissed the possibility that he might be insane. A diagnosis of insanity, in fact, was the only conclusion that aligned the pieces into a clear picture. Orla may well have been the "manifestation" of his mental illness.

As he pondered on the relative causes of his insanity—grief over not letting his father go, a bite from a hallucinogenic bug, genetics—he bumped into Deonte, literally. "Watch it!" Deonte turned around.

"Sorry, I, uh..." Ask stammered, unsure how to continue. Since the transformation, Deonte had more or less cut ties with him. They had been friends since grade school, had known each other even before that. Regardless, their friendship seemed to have suddenly ended the day in the shed when Deonte was teaching Ask to act instead of just think. Oh, and then there was the transformation thing, and the way Deonte had looked at him, and left as quickly as possible.

Deonte offered a similar look now. He then surprised Ask by saying, "It's okay," but quickly added, "Don't let it happen again."

Drawing courage from the source of their long friendship, Ask responded, "What did I do to make you so angry with me?" A crowd was starting to assemble as Ask raised his voice.

"It doesn't matter." Ask could see Deonte was retreating from the conflict, afraid of the judgmental eyes of bystanders who would later poke fun at him. Deonte had a reputation to protect. Arguments about friendship with someone not as popular as Deonte, like Ask, might not help that effort.

Intuiting this, Ask nodded his head toward the entrance and led Deonte down the hall and out of the school. He was again surprised when Deonte followed. "What's the deal?" he asked when they could no longer be observed, by the oak where Ask thought he had visited with Orla. "Look, I'm not sure what I did to you, but we were friends, and now it seems we're not. Why?"

Deonte hesitated, studied the football field, appeared to be weighing the cost of what he was about to say. "You know, I work hard to run faster, jump higher, get stronger, and you, well, you read books and watch the stars, and then one day all you do is pick up an ax, and you turn into a superhero. I mean, what the hell, man? And so, I wonder to myself why do some just get what others have to work so hard for but can never achieve?"

"Really? You're angry at me because I turned into a freak for like thirty seconds? Trust me, it was no gift. It was awkward and meaningless and hurt like hell," Ask said angrily.

Deonte shook his head. "Look, dude, whatever."

After an awkward pause, during which neither had answers to the questions posed or the accusations implied in their exchange, Deonte softened. "You weren't a freak. You looked like a comic book barbarian. You were like Dwayne Johnson standing on Arnold Schwarzenegger's shoulders." Deonte laughed.

Ask laughed too. To Deonte's original point, Ask said, "I get why you're upset, but I didn't ask for it." He continued, "You're the only one who saw what happened. I've been trying to work through it, figure it all out, but I can't, not alone."

Deonte nodded. "There you go thinking about it again. That's your problem—you think until you don't know what you're thinking anymore. Sometimes, you just got to take action. Pick up the ax again and see what happens." He paused. "You need a partner, like Black Panther."

"Unless you have 'vibranium' hiding in your closet, we might be out of luck," Ask retorted.

Deonte grinned. He added, "You'll make the biggest, baddest sidekick a hero could ask for."

Ask nodded. "Right?!"

"You think your dad has a glowy machete in that shed?" More seriously he said, "I'm sorry." To drive home how sorry he was, Deonte gave Ask a playful nudge to the arm. He was surprised that Ask not only didn't move, but Deonte's larger hand hurt a bit from the gesture. Ask's arm was like a rock. "What the...? You know about this?"

Ask had grown stronger since picking up the ax, but he didn't know that his muscles had undergone some kind of transformation as well. He shook his head.

"Let me try something." Deonte picked up a thick stick that had been lying next to the oak. He hauled back and swung the stick as hard as he could against Ask's arm. Ask winced as the stick came toward him. It shattered on impact. Ask didn't feel a thing. "Holy crap. What? You're like invincible now? Viking Hulk. I told you—superpowers."

"I don't know about that."

While his body had been apparently growing stronger, his immune system seemed to be weakening. He suddenly felt rundown, feverish, and even sick. In fact, although his body didn't hurt when Deonte hit him, Ask felt more worn out with each impact. Ask had never been this sick before, at least not like this, feverish and unable to concentrate. These sensations were new, and he didn't know what to do with them.

"Let's try this again." Deonte picked up a rock. Ask held out his hand in submission. "You okay?" Deonte asked. "You don't look so good."

"I..." It was as if the world spun a little on the wrong axis. "I just need to sit down." He flopped onto the grass and leaned back against the tree, taking deep breaths. After a moment, he stood up again, but he couldn't find steady footing.

"Man, I'm sorry about the stick. You didn't look hurt." Deonte tried to brace Ask's unexpectedly heavy frame.

"So much for superpowers," Ask mumbled.

The bell sounded, so the sidewalks began to fill with kids filing back into the building. Ask tried to propel himself forward by using the tree trunk for balance. "I can make it." He shuffled a few feet and then things normalized a bit.

"You going to be okay?" Deonte asked.

Ask nodded.

As they entered the school, Deonte said, "You need to pick up that ax again."

That was exactly what Ask was thinking. He wondered if the ax held some kind of healing power or if the light needed its source, like a cell phone needs its charger. "After school. My place," he told Deonte, who nodded and then took off in the opposite direction, where he would no doubt anxiously tap a foot through Ms. Crowley's North Dakota History class.

As Ask neared Mr. Wheeler's English class, a hand gripped his and pulled him into an alcove near a drinking fountain. Orla pinned him against a narrow bit of wall between the fountain and an adjacent corner. "I see we're running out of time," she said cryptically, staring deeply into his eyes. "Meet me after school." She was so close that her cool breath puffed against his lips. In the haze of fever still gripping his mind, Ask leaned forward to kiss her but missed the mark. Orla held his face between her hands. So close now that he could see the frost gathering around her pupils in glacial sweeps. "We are definitely running out of time. After school by the mustang." She disappeared down the hall. Giddy from such intimacy, from a fever growing in his veins, Ask nearly bounced into his classroom.

To say that Deonte was unimpressed by Orla would be an understatement. From his perspective, Ask guessed, she must have been nothing more than a gangly Goth consumed by too much dark drama. She kept looking too intently into Ask's eyes and turning his head this way and that. Was she trying to read his mind or hypnotize him?

As Deonte watched Orla fret over Ask with his arms folded across his chest, Ask was reminded of the first time Deonte met Jepp, both friends with a friend in common but not with each other. Deonte stayed quiet for the most part, while Jepp talked about a trail he and Ask had found the week before riding bikes near Kindred. Every so often, Deonte would counter with an experience only he and Ask shared. "Remember that catfish you pulled in last weekend? Must have weighed ten pounds. Your mom fried it up real good—that breading. Holy crap. Delicious." Jepp would redirect the conversation with some reference to the soccer team he and Ask both played on, how Ask had passed the ball to Jepp between two defenders and facilitated a goal. "We killed them! Five to one. We should go kick the ball around." It was competitive like that for a few weeks, but, eventually, Deonte and Jepp created enough shared memories that all three of them just sort of found themselves in a friendship.

What happened to that friendship still eluded Ask. One day, he and Jepp were eating lunch together, riding the bus home with Deonte, and meeting up later to hang out. Seemingly, the next, they were like moths circling different flames. First, it was football practice that separated them. Ask was shorter and smaller than Deonte and Jepp. So, he didn't make the team. He would head home after school and catch up with them the next day. Soon, Jepp was sitting with his teammates and then he was a letterman jacket Ask passed in the hall on Tuesdays and Thursdays. He remembered the day he realized they had somehow lost their friendship. He went to a home game one Friday in October. Jepp had thrown three touchdowns and run one in himself.

Ask rushed onto the field to congratulate him after the game. "That was awesome, Jepp," he said.

Michael Jostad, a defensive lineman, pushed him out of the way. He fell to the ground. "Get off the field, dork." Instead of defending Ask, Jepp turned his shoulder, smiled and nodded at Michael, and jogged off.

Deonte pulled Ask to his feet. "What happened? You okay?" Ask nodded, though he didn't feel okay. Deonte looked at Jepp leaving the field. "Forget him. He's not worth it. He's just another bully."

Jepp found ways to enact revenge on a past his new society deemed unacceptable by tripping Ask, making fun of him between classes, and saying, "Ask? What was the question?" Apparently, the cost of his popularity was to erase Ask's friendship. Ask represented a past that could not be part of Jepp's future.

Even now, almost two years later, Ask occasionally lamented losing Jepp as a friend. It was silly to admit, but he missed the memories they made together. Deonte was more adept at closing emotional doors. When he said, "Forget him," he meant it. Ask held out hope for Jepp, reserved access to friendship if he wanted it; his the kind of longsuffering hope that compels a boy to sit on a porch night after night waiting for his estranged father to come home.

Ask hoped now that Deonte and Orla could find better common ground. Deonte broke the ice by stating, in his most undiplomatic tone, "Who the hell is she?"

Orla gave Deonte an exaggerated once-over and smiled. "I'll wait while you say goodbye to your. . ." She paused, looked Deonte up and down once more, and then added, ". . . friend." She made the word "friend" sound unappealing, juvenile.

This was not a good start. If only he'd thought to prepare them both for the encounter, but the fever made coherent thinking a monumental task. Even now, as they waited for him to resolve this awkward stalemate, Ask couldn't concentrate. What were they doing again, standing outside the school? Shouldn't they go into their classrooms if they didn't want to be late? He felt a sudden urge to march quickly down to his English class and put his head down on his desk. He closed his eyes.

"You there," a distant voice was calling. "What are you doing?"

Was that a ferryman next to a longboat with a hand extended awaiting payment for passage? The water was clear all the way to the pebbled bottom. Some of the stones were so smooth and so clean they shone like jewels. Cliffs about the fjords swept up into pined peaks. "Once you go, you won't come back. They never do." A stranger at his shoulder told him.

"But I've paid the toll," Ask explained. While Ask had no idea what was happening, somehow, he knew exactly what to say, as if his mind read from a script buried below his consciousness. This place, too, felt familiar, even though he'd never been there before.

"Aye. Is it worth the price, so little in exchange for so much grief?"

He nodded. "I promised her."

"Well, a promise then. Yet even now you can change your mind. She'll understand. Some do."

Ask felt himself shake his head. "I keep my promises."

A swift slap to his face brought Orla and Deonte back into focus. "We are running out of time," Orla said.

"Why did you hit him?" Deonte asked.

Weakly, Ask said, "This is Orla." He felt himself slipping again, the school vanishing beneath a thick forest, verdant and untamed. Orla grabbed him, and again, he was staring deeply into her eyes, the forest now draped in a snowy cloak.

"Look. I need to get him home. There's something he has to do. Or. . ." She hesitated.

Ask whispered, "He knows."

She nodded abruptly. "He needs to finish what he started."

"The ax?" Deonte asked.

"The convergence," Orla corrected.

Orla and Deonte loaded Ask into a relatively compact car that smelled of artificial vanilla and had the AC cranked up rather high. On the trip to his house, Ask fell in and out of consciousness, vaguely remembering riding between Orla and Deonte and listening to them argue.

At some point, Deonte said, "Why are you stopping here? The shed's half a mile away."

Orla replied, "You'll have to carry him the rest of the way."

To this, Deonte responded, "Are you kidding? Do you know how heavy he is? Just pull up to the shed. It won't hurt the grass."

Then, silence.

Ask heard himself say, "Pull up to the shed, Orla. It's okay. You're welcome here." Why did he feel the need to invite her?

He then blacked out only to imagine himself sailing across an expanse of open water, the breeze chilling his cheeks to an uncomfortable numb. The cold from the AC finally slowed the fever a bit, and Ask was able to fully concentrate when he was finally standing, with Orla and Deonte's assistance, in front of his father's shed.

"You know what you have to do," Orla whispered, still distrustful of Deonte.

"I do," Ask said softly, "but I'm not sure how or why you do." He smiled. "One of you is going to have to bring it out here for me. If I pick it up in the shed, I'll be stuck. Viking in a bottle." A loopy giggle.

Ask turned first to Orla, who seemed, to this point, the person in charge. But for the first time since he met her, she didn't take the lead.

She deferred instead to Deonte, who rolled his eyes and pulled open the door, muttering, "Sure, Deonte will fetch that for you. Sure thing." A moment later, he presented the ax to Ask. "Will there be anything else?"

The giddiness coming upon him more strongly now, Ask said with great flair, "My horse, good squire." He pointed to Babe and howled with laughter.

As Deonte went to press the ax into Ask's hand, Orla said, "Wait! Not here. Let's go someplace a little more discrete." Deonte, Ask noticed, looked at the house and the picture window facing the shed. Orla, on the other hand, looked out over the fields west and north.

Each taking an arm, they pulled Ask into the trees south of the garden and Babe's pen. In a clearing surrounded by massive cottonwoods and a thick undergrowth of untamed prairie grasses and boxwood and dogwood bushes, they handed Ask the ax.

At once, the ground beneath him seemed unstable as the components of his body enlarged unevenly, one leg and then the next, an arm engorging before his neck thickened, a foot taking its sweet time to steady the increasing weight associated with a massive and momentarily lopsided frame. But, as he finalized the transformation, he could think more clearly than he had been able to for the past few weeks. The fever was completely gone, and, in its place, a strength coursed through his veins. He turned to Deonte and Orla and said, in a booming voice produced from a broad chest, "That's better."

"The convergence needs time to imprint on your cells, fully, so don't put down the ax, not yet. It didn't happen the first time you transformed because you changed back too quickly. Things stay precarious until the convergence is complete." Orla grinned, perhaps an attempt at support, Ask inferred. But it was an odd look for her and came off more like a grimace.

Deonte stared at Ask, and his eyes grew large. "Where in the hell did that armor come from?"

Ask peered down at his chest, his legs, and his feet. It was true. Somehow, he was wearing thick leather cuirass armor, loose-fitting but padded leggings, and massive black boots. *That's new*, he thought. "I have no idea."

"Seriously?" Deonte shouted, half in jealousy and half in admiration. "How cool is that?"

It dawned on Ask that he had worn the tunic his mother gave him under his clothes religiously since that odd exchange a few nights ago. Was the way the tunic grew to fit him what she meant by "stretchier"? What caused it to change? More to the point, how did she know it would help? What else did she know?

Orla stepped in front of Deonte. "Okay, real nice. The armor will help. Let's focus now."

"Okay, I'll say this again," Deonte cut in, "Who the *hell* are you?"

Orla didn't answer right away, as if she were calculating the right response. "Let's just say I'm a friend. A protector of sorts."

Deonte pointed at Ask, whose balance was becoming incrementally surer, better in fact than he'd ever known it in his entire life. "You saying he needs protection? Like that? With that big ol' ax?"

Again, careful, guarded, Orla responded, "There are other forces, dark forces just as powerful. The wielder of the ax isn't invulnerable. The ax has powerful magic, yes, but it isn't invincible." They both paused as Ask tried taking a step and tripped on his own foot. "Plus, it takes time and training to understand that power," she added, pointing to Ask steadying himself against a tree for proof.

"What I don't get," Ask whispered, trying to temper the projection of his massive voice, "is how you know anything about this."

Deonte nodded. "That's right. How do we know you aren't with those dark forces? You give off a sort of goth-y, vampire-y vibe to me. Why else would you be so cold?" Deonte got close to Orla, posturing. He quickly backed off. "Like, wow, literally, really cold."

"I'm not," Orla said, quickly, "one of them. They want to destroy things. I don't. I like the world the way it is." She didn't elaborate.

"And, what, you're some sort of super-thin superhero with the power of poor circulation?" Deonte added. Ask couldn't help but chuckle. At first, Orla glared at Ask, her glare like sharp points on two icicles, but then her eyes softened a bit, and she chuckled, too, genuinely.

Deonte returned her smile. "You know, ice queen, I think we can get along."

Ask reached down and picked them up in a giant embrace. In doing so, he dropped the ax. Suddenly, the three of them were lying on the ground in a clump where they'd fallen, as Ask returned to regular Ask-size, laughing.

Back on their feet, Orla pointed to the ax. "Not done yet. Pick it up."

"How much longer before this convergence thing is done?" Ask whined a little. The transformation this time was less intense.

"You'll know."

CHAPTER 9

A STORY OF GIANTS

THE THREE OF THEM MADE a routine of gathering in the wooded clearing near Ask's house most days after school. As it turned out, Orla was a skilled coach. She showed Ask how to swing the ax from several different positions, how to use his weight to advantage the strike, and how to defend himself with blocks and counterstrikes. She used a long pole made of a metal as strong as the ax that shimmered a greenish-purple when it reflected light and sparked madly when it came into contact with the ax.

Ask had once been in a school production of *Hamlet* as Laertes. To prepare for the final fight scene, he remembered Mr. Childers scripting every step, choreographing every swing of the plastic sword. He recalled thinking how practicing the scene was like a dance recital. He hated the deception of the whole thing—Hamlet and Laertes wouldn't practice how they were going to fight each other. They would take up their swords and swing, responding to each other in the moment, spontaneously. He felt that same way now. He told Orla as much after she corrected his stance and told him to swing the ax a particular way. "If I actually ever fight someone, they aren't going to follow the script. What's the point in doing the same thing over and over again?"

Orla leaned on her pole and nodded. "You're right. They won't. They'll be trained, though. Like this. They'll know all kinds of ways to attack you and defend themselves. I know it seems like you're just doing the same movements over and over again, but that's how you develop muscle memory, that's how you'll be able to fight effectively *when* the time comes."

Her emphasis on "when" struck Ask. He set the ax down, so he could speak to her eye-to-eye. "What aren't you telling me? We've been going hard at this for, like, three hours, as if you're preparing me for war." He glanced over his shoulder, scanned the tree line. "I don't see any immediate threat."

"The minute you picked up that ax, the threat awoke. Each time you transform, the threat increases. That threat has been looking for this ax for a long time and will stop at nothing to take its power. It will tear right through you if you aren't ready. That war I'm preparing you for started a very long time ago and will continue until that threat, or you, are dead."

"But what is the threat? What is he supposed to fight against?" Deonte had shuffled up close to Ask. Always protecting him.

Orla seemed reluctant to answer.

"What if *they*—whoever *they* are—find me tomorrow, and I don't know who they are, when the ax is in the shed and I'm at school? If they feel the energy, they must know where I live by now. They must be plotting something. How can I fight against an invisible foe?"

Orla nodded. "You're right. It's time you know." She motioned for Ask and Deonte to sit, and she relayed to them the following story:

"A war started millennia ago between giants and gods in another world." She looked at Ask. "You know this story."

He shook his head. "I don't."

"You do because your father told you. I'm certain of it. He told you the story of Ragnarök, didn't he? The final battle of the gods?"

"But that's just a fairytale." He reconsidered his statement. "I mean, it's a story, a myth."

"Yes, it is a story, a myth, and a history. This may startle you, but I was a child when the giants raided the halls of Valhalla, marching in legions behind

Loki. He would stop at nothing to have Thor's head. To secure his prize, he enlisted every enemy Thor had ever made to coordinate the attack, make it impossible even for Thor to survive."

Ask added, "As the story goes, he didn't. He died fighting Jörmungandr, the Midgard serpent, killed by the creature's poison as he severed its head."

"Yes. Many gods fell those long weeks as the battlefields filled with blood. The bloodlust couldn't, wouldn't, be satiated. Though the giants depleted their ranks, they were numerous like the stars. Some of us, too young for battle, kept hidden in the hollow of a large rock near the sea. We passed long hours scratching at sand with seashells and listening to the ocean rushing through conchs. I played a game with another girl. We used the small shells littering the floor of the dark cave to recreate what we remembered of our village: the merchant kiosks with their wares lined in rows or hanging from hooks; the market with fresh fish lined up in a beautifully appetizing display; the houses with their colorful and welcoming façades. We decorated our homes as elaborately as we could, every detail both a sweet memory and a painful reminder of what we lost, what we would never have again after our village was torched to cinders.

"At night, we sneaked out to forage for food, wading out into the sea to try our luck catching fish braving the shallow water, crabs skittering across the shoreline, or, most often, seaweed gathered from low tide. We ate the catch raw, regardless of what it was. The few elders with us warned against a fire, as it would signal our whereabouts and summon patrols. We knew they would kill us, even though we were children. Both sides, at this stage of the war, were bent on genocide. Each day, we feared no one would be left when the war ended. Our future felt as empty as those shell villages we had constructed in the sand.

"So, we sat starving in our cave, pretending not to be afraid. This girl, a few years younger and, well, more delicate than I, clung to me whenever we heard swords striking pikes in the distance. Surely, they would come for us and flay our small bodies and stuff our skin into the pouches they carried at their waists. These weren't unwarranted fears. The giants and the gods practiced terrible atrocities—tying the other down for wolves to devour, removing arms and legs and watching the victim bleed and starve to death, pulling on limbs until a body literally tore in half.

"The most violent, powerful, and bloodthirsty warrior of all was a giantess named Hyrrokkin. She rode atop a massive wolf and crushed gods with her bare hands. She agreed to enlist in Loki's war because she wanted to kill every god that ever existed. She hated them for exiling her to an enchanted dark forest, where the trees would fill in overnight any space she cleared for a home. She often lost her way, since the foliage in the forest always changed, wrapping itself in tangles over and around tree trunks, reaching even higher than she was, creating a suffocating canopy. One day an open path would be a wall of thickets and thorns the next. Her lot was a perpetual battle against a foe that would never die, an enemy she could never defeat. So, when Loki appeared and tricked the bramble and stunned the trees, she was able to escape to fulfill a vow she repeated in her anger-twisted heart: 'Asgard will be their eternal tomb.'

"Even after Loki was killed and the ranks of the surviving gods diminished, her lust for vengeance was not satisfied. She rallied the few remaining giants and pressed the surviving gods. Most finally succumbed to the unrelenting hunt, their heads severed from their bodies and mounted on pikes. Yet, despite her efforts, a few escaped. They transformed themselves—"

"Into fish," Ask said. He remembered his father holding the walleye to his ear and then releasing it, that grave look on his face.

Orla nodded, a bit taken aback. "Yes, some of them transformed into fish. And they came here through the crumbling bridges and portals by land, sea, and sky, which once connected our worlds. One of them, Hyrrokkin's greatest threat, seized Mjölnir, Thor's hammer, and brought it here. Hyrrokkin desired its magic and wanted to use its power to annihilate the gods once and for all. She sought Thor's corpse, expecting to find the hammer yet in his grasp. He had been laid in a stone sepulcher dug into the side of a mountain and sealed by magic with a massive stone. She pounded at the stone for hours, and then days, and then weeks, chipping away a few inches at a time. Finally, she broke through and dragged herself wearily into the tomb. Thor lay on a granite table, adorned in gold armor, a shield bearing the standard of the great hammer spread over his chest. Hyrrokkin pulled the shield from lifeless arms and hurled it against a wall, where it clanked loudly and then clattered, dented badly on one side, to the floor. She expected to find the hammer beneath the shield. When it wasn't there, she filled the tomb with an anguished yell, bursting with all her rage. Her wolf steed howled just outside the cavern. So, the story goes.

"It wasn't long before she knew one of the surviving gods had taken it. With Thor's death, the hammer would give strength to whoever wielded it. Forged in the smithies of the dwarves, the weapon commanded great power. Those who took it knew Hyrrokkin would be unstoppable if she got her hands on it. So, not only did they take the weapon away, but they also hid it with spells and incantations. They prayed to the forces that made the gods for protection and then disappeared among the people of Earth, abandoning their identities, their best bet to blend in and forget Asgard. But Hyrrokkin was a great sorceress as well as a giantess of immense strength and intellect. She made her way to Earth and fashioned her own façade. Somehow by dark magic, persistence, or both, she began finding the gods who had escaped. One by one, she killed them. Today, only a few remain. Some who heard rumors of Hyrrokkin's success in uncovering the secret identities of their friends sought to fight back. They performed an ancient ritual designed to bring the spirit creators into the realm of the living to protect them. When that didn't work, they tried a spell to combine their powers in Mjölnir, so it might slay Hyrrokkin. This second effort failed as well. And so, it is said, a goddess of great power split the hammer into two separate weapons, both mighty but neither as powerful as the hammer. One is a spear that hits its target with every thrust. The other, an ax that gives its champion strength greater than that of a giant."

Ask studied the small rusty ax laying on the grass next to him. "I see. This is the ax that was the hammer."

"Yes," Orla said. "A spell enchants the mind to see it, well, like that—old, dull, ordinary. It was also protected from location spells when it was dormant."

"But it's not dormant anymore."

"No. Not anymore. Now, Hyrrokkin will come for it."

"And the spear?" Ask said.

Orla frowned. "She has it. Its keeper was hunted down until she couldn't hide any longer. Her enchantments to disguise the spear failed, and she died, pierced by the thing she swore her life to protect."

A knife of panic stabbed Ask in the heart. A spear that never misses. "Is. . . Is the spear what killed my father?"

He was surprised when Orla said, "No. As far as I know, the spear didn't kill him."

"How did Hyrrokkin do it, then?" Anger swelled in his breast. "Did she pull him apart limb by limb?" His teeth were clenched. He would avenge his father.

"Ask, Hyrrokkin didn't kill your father. Many of the giants wanted to kill him, but none of them did," Orla said.

His anger deflated to a dull sense of disorientation. Finally, he'd found the answer to his father's disappearance, a noble one, one he could accept and avenge, only to have it yanked away before it could take root in some great sacrifice. "What do you mean? You said she hunted down and killed the keeper of the spear. He was the keeper of the ax. I thought. . ." He paused and then asked, "How did he die, then?"

"I don't know." Orla's expression softened. "Nobody knows what happened to your father."

A new anger sprouted in his heart. It wasn't fair that he might never know what happened to his father. He sat silent, nurturing his growing anger. Orla placed a hand on his shoulder, but he shrugged it off, hard. "How do you know all of this anyway?"

"It's what I saw and what I pieced together these many years from the stories of others when we've crossed paths."

They sat in silence for a while, birds serenading them from the trees, most prominent the call of the killdeer. Its peculiar singsong resembled a sort of mockery, a kind of cruel teasing.

Deonte, who had been quietly listening, chimed in. "So, what happened to you?"

"What?" Orla asked.

"You said you were hiding with old people and another girl. What happened?"

She hesitated before continuing. "One day, we were out late scavenging for food when a soldier happened upon us. He slit the throats of the elders with us. We ran. We hid in some trees on a hill above the sea until daylight and then carefully made our way deeper into the forest. The war had been raging for many years by then. The land showed it. No one to tend the fields, no one to live in the houses burned to ruins we encountered along the forest path, no destination for two children running from a threat that would never relent. The world was eerily quiet and overwhelmingly devoid of life.

"Weeks after we ran from our hiding place near the sea, we encountered a patrol of five warriors. They detained us for 'questioning.' The leader, a hard sort with a long scar on his face, slapped the girl who was with me, and she fell unconscious to the ground. Then, he slapped me, but I stayed on my feet and spat in the man's face. Spittle traced the scar across his left eye. They all laughed. So did the man who hit me. He told me I had 'a warrior's heart' and that I would 'fight with them now.' I had no choice but to go with them. I pleaded, so they brought the other girl as well. If I'd known why they brought her and what they would do to her, I would have asked them to kill her that day. Eventually, they did kill her. A morning some weeks later, one of the men caught her trying to escape. Koerl choked her until he crushed her neck, and she suffocated. It was not the worst thing they did to her. Her name was Solveig.

"I lived with them in fear for several decades. They fought me every day to harden me for the hunt. In time, their quarry diminished and then disappeared altogether. The gods had escaped to Earth. Hyrrokkin called the remaining patrols together, no more than twenty giants remained. Atop her beloved wolf steed, she led us through an intermittent portal to Earth and assigned us partners. Because we were so few, she dispatched us in pairs. As soon as I had the chance, I put a sword through my partner's heart and ran away. That was several hundred years ago."

"These remaining giants—they are the ones who will be coming?" Deonte asked.

"That's right. And when they do, they won't come to talk. Now you see, Ask, why it is so important we prepare you."

"For the spear that never misses?" he asked petulantly. How could he protect against such a weapon? He felt angry and afraid. "Seems a bit like a lost cause. We don't even know what happened to my father, and he knew what he was doing."

"I know it's overwhelming. The more you wield the ax, the more powerful you will become. It has a powerful energy that fuses with its keeper. Its strength will become your strength."

"And how do you know that?" Deonte fist-bumped Ask.

"Because I saw it with the spear. Hyrrokkin is so much more powerful with the spear, and she was extremely powerful without it. Of course, her convergence was unnatural. The spear did not willingly connect with her. She had to trick it, so the power is unreliable at times. The ax chose you, Ask. In time, you will have its full power at your command." She popped onto her feet. "Storytime is over, boys. Back to work."

Ask stood up. The ax laid several feet away. He reached out his hand, and, to his surprise, the ax came to him. He heard Deonte say from across the field, "No freaking way! You're a Viking Hulk with the 'force'? Sweet!"

CHAPTER 10

THE MAN WITH THE SCAR

OCTOBER BROUGHT THE FIRST FROST of the season. The green lawns of the high school glistened as the sun rose above dusty fields, where tractors in the distance harvested soybeans and corn. The angle of the light cast everything in a golden hue. Ask was distracted as he sat in class, elbow on his desk and chin balancing in his palm. He watched geese formations land on a nearby pond. Mr. Wheeler droned on about the use of metaphor in Orwell's *Animal Farm*. Ask caught bits and pieces of the lecture, something about governments, agendas, and how power corrupts. He thought about Hyrrokkin. Corruption and power, her hallmarks.

Despite Orla's warnings and their intense preparations—often extending for hours after school and well into night—Ask hadn't been attacked. In fact, as two weeks turned to three, he questioned the existence of this general giantess and her remaining army. Perhaps the magic Orla described had diluted over time. Maybe Hyrrokkin had just given up. A millennium is a long time to hold a grudge.

As class dragged on, Ask wished something would happen, just to break up the tedium. His attention lagged and drifted toward the window.

Outside, a man wearing a dark parka with a dog walked by on the sidewalk below. The dog was large, even from Ask's vantage. It could have been an

Irish wolfhound, a Scottish deerhound, or a long-haired Great Dane mix. The dog wasn't on a leash, but it stayed close to the man. There was something ominous and disconcerting about the man that caused Ask to shift in his chair. Just below the window through which Ask watched him, the man suddenly stopped and looked up. From that distance, and shaded by a tint on the glass, Ask knew the man wouldn't be able to make out anything in his classroom. Yet, somehow, the man made eye contact with Ask, or at least Ask felt as if the man made eye contact with him, and grinned. As if looking through binoculars, Ask clearly saw minute details on the man's face: hard lines around the mouth, the grin mirthless, more a threat than a friendly gesture, and a scar running at an angle from lip to temple, ending in a white star above his left eyebrow. He kept the man's gaze for several moments. Then, the man nodded, as if an acknowledgment, as if to say "I'll see you soon," and took quick, long steps to catch up to the dog sniffing grass down the way.

Ask caught Deonte in the hall between classes and told him what happened.

"I don't know," Deonte responded. "Sounds like your brain is playing tricks on you."

"Because you don't think it could happen?" In a whisper, Ask continued, "You know, some unbelievable crap has been going on lately."

"But some guy staring you down from outside, two hundred feet away? I mean, why? He wasn't even a giant, was he? Could it be you're imagining it because of what Orla told you?" Deonte asked.

For a moment, Ask second-guessed himself. Maybe he had invented the whole thing. It wasn't inconceivable that no sign of impending attack the past few weeks forced him to create one. But, the details, that scar. "Maybe," he compromised.

"Look, I gotta run. Game tonight, so I won't be able to hang after school," Deonte said.

"I could come to the game," Ask offered. Then he added, "I could bring Orla."

Deonte, who had taken a few steps down the hall, paused. "Do you think she'd go?" And then, "Whatever. See you later."

AFTER SCHOOL, WHEN ASK DESCRIBED what he saw from his classroom window to Orla, she had another take on the man. She paced in the clearing among the trees, while Ask practiced summoning the ax. He also discovered, as he transformed each afternoon, that he didn't need to hold the ax. Enough of its energy had been transferred to him that he could change as long as he was just a couple of steps away from the weapon. This made the process much less tenuous, even if it was not entirely reliable. The transformation itself, the actual enlarging of his body, no longer hurt or disoriented him. He and the ax were becoming one, as Orla had promised.

"You said he had a scar?" Orla asked.

"Yes," Ask repeated, "from his lip to right above his left eyebrow." He drew the ax in front of his face to demonstrate.

"And he looked right up at you through the window of your second-floor classroom?"

"Again, yes. I don't know how. He just. . . Look, Deonte thought I'd maybe imagined it. He said it sounded far-fetched."

"Your senses are, well, enhancing as you grow closer to the ax," Orla said. "It isn't unrealistic to think you could have seen the man's face up close, even from that distance. Plus, Hyrrokkin's warriors have powers, too. As I told you before, they can sense the convergence, feel the energy shifting from the ax to you. They are drawn to that energy."

"So, he could be one of her giants?" Maybe he wasn't losing it.

Orla didn't respond immediately. When she did, it surprised Ask. "I know a giant with that same scar. He condemned Solveig to death and conscripted me to fight for him. Remember the story I told you? His name is Koerl."

"The warrior who found you in the woods," Ask said.

She nodded. "He is one of Hyrrokkin's deadliest soldiers. His grin means he's marked a victim."

Ask stopped phasing from large to regular size to pursue a point that perplexed him. "But you're talking about a giant. The man I saw was average-human sized."

"Yes." Orla nodded. "Giants have a way of making themselves appear normal when they need to."

A sudden anger gripped Ask. "Let him come," he said. "I'll drive that gash deep into his skull."

"I like the enthusiasm." Orla smiled. "But I don't think you're quite ready for him."

Ask clenched his jaw, furrowed his brows, postured as if he would strike. "Let's get to work, then. I'll be ready."

Ask attacked Orla with fervor, his ax clanking loudly against Orla's pike, pushing her back; the first time he'd been able to gain an advantage in their sparring. Orla rebounded quickly, but she also readjusted her pike before striking back. He sensed the slightest tinge of worry in her cold blue eyes.

Ask's mother was waiting for him on the porch that evening. It was a clear night, so she had the telescope pointed at the darkening sky, but she wasn't using it. She sat in her chair instead, squinting into the distance. Ask had been avoiding her for some time, partly because he was ashamed to have gone back on his promise again regarding the ax and partly because he was angry at her for telling him he would know why his father disappeared by going in the shed. These emotions combined made any conversation with his mother uncomfortably volatile. He found it easier to sneak in after dark and slip up to his room to work on homework or ponder the day lying in bed. She had let him do it for the most part, bringing him a plate of dinner or calling up to see if he was okay.

But not tonight. As soon as he climbed the porch steps, she asked him, "Who is that girl?"

Ask dropped into the chair next to her. "I told you about her a few weeks ago. Her name's Orla."

"She goes to your school?"

Ask hesitated. Did she technically go to his school, or did she show up when the world seemed on the brink of some impending tragedy? He settled with, "Yeah, that's where I met her."

His mother nodded. Then she asked, "What do you know about her?"

Ask turned to face his mother. "She, uh. . . Well, she's an exchange student from up north." True enough, he rationalized. Isn't that what Orla had told him when they'd first met?

"Used to the cold, then?" his mother asked. "I haven't seen her wear a coat."

It did feel rather chilly this evening, Ask realized. "I guess so. She's a bit peculiar," he said. His mother's sudden interest and careful attention wasn't lost on him.

"Oh yeah? How so?" Now his mother met his eyes.

Ask looked down. "I don't know. She's had a rough life, I guess. Orphaned, on the run from bad people, kind of an outcast."

"Sounds lonely. Maybe you should ask her to stay for dinner one of these days."

Had Ask actually seen Orla eat? Her lanky limbs suggested a high metabolism or a low-calorie diet. He wasn't sure which. Though, she was strong, even when he was transformed. Someone significantly limiting their calories wouldn't be able to fight like that. "Yeah, sure," he said, curious not only to see if Orla would accept the invitation but to see if she ate human food. Hadn't Deonte once compared her to a vampire?

"Look, I know things have been a little strained between us lately," his mother said, changing the subject. "I haven't been fair to you. There is a lot going on right now, things you never expected and probably never believed could happen. I'm sure that's the reason you haven't told me about the clearing you use to practice transforming."

Startled by her directness, Ask knew he wouldn't be able to pull off a lie if he wanted to. Plus, he could feel how his mother felt, just like before. It was a sort of empathic, extrasensory connection made possible, Ask guessed, by the ax's energy. There was no anger, no feeling of betrayal, just that same tired acceptance he'd sensed in her before. He wondered if she had come to peace with or stopped struggling against something. Because this strange power didn't allow him to see her thoughts, he could only conjecture what sort of understanding had produced such a feeling.

"I'm sorry," Ask said. "I-I was losing my mind, and the only way to save it. . ."

"Was to pick up the ax and finish the convergence," she said, completing his sentence.

He nodded. "I didn't want to break my word, but I didn't have much of a choice."

"I know," she said. Then she added, "What I can't quite figure out is how your friend Orla fits into all of this. I can't say that I've ever seen her before."

Yeah, Ask wanted to retort, *she's like a thousand years old and from some other world. Why wouldn't you have met her before?* Besides, and perhaps more to the point, Ask worried that his mother might not like Orla. Orla wasn't exactly the Taylor's daughter, who was going through an emo phase, or Sheryl Ann, who beamed on the arm of the star quarterback. You didn't just run into Orla when you delivered potluck casserole to the church picnic or scanned the condiment aisle at the supermarket for relish or mustard. She wasn't working behind the counter at the fabric store or taking tickets at the Cineplex. No. She materialized from thin air, stepped between people in the hallway without them noticing, and kept a pike close at hand to finish off the man who killed her friend and kidnapped decades of her life. Why would his mother think she would have seen her before? He was almost certain no one had. She was a shadow in the interstices of the worlds of reality and fantasy.

"I'll invite her to dinner," he said.

"Be careful," she warned. "People aren't always who you think they are. Sometimes, they wear masks to get close. And then, it's too late to get away."

Ask knew she was warning him about Orla, but his mind went right to Koerl, the man with the scar. To defeat such a man, he would need allies, and having allies sometimes meant trusting people, even when you didn't fully know them or their motives. Perhaps he was a bit naïve, but Orla didn't feel like a threat, at least not as big of a threat as Hyrrokkin's best warrior.

CHAPTER 11

WATCHED FROM THE STANDS

ASK CONVINCED ORLA TO GO to one of Sheyenne High's home football games with him to show support for Deonte. Partly, he was making good on his promise—or threat to Deonte—that he would invite Orla. He also had an ulterior motive: in this venue, perhaps Orla would let her guard down and reveal more about herself. He recognized that he'd accepted her sudden and inexplicable appearance at his school weeks ago almost without question. For weeks, he'd been dodging her pike in training bouts and taking her advice. He truly had placed himself in a compromising situation. Maybe his mother was right to encourage caution. On the other hand, the game was another reason to spend time with her. He found that he really liked spending time with her.

Since it was a junior varsity game, kickoff was in the afternoon on a Thursday. JV games offered better opportunities for freshman players like Deonte to see some action. In fact, it wasn't long at all before Ask saw Deonte lining up on special teams for the first play of the game, decked out in his blue and orange uniform, the profile of a mustang glowering across his helmet. Always fast, Deonte was first down the field and in position to tackle the player who caught the ball. He wasn't able to connect directly for a tackle but slowed the returner enough for a swarm of teammates to finish the job, pinning the opposing team, the West Fargo Packers, at their own ten-yard line.

Ask stole a glance at Orla. She looked confused. "What was the point of that kick and attack? Why would you willingly hand over the ball? Isn't the object of the game to keep and protect it?"

"Haven't you seen a football game before?" he asked.

Orla shook her head.

"You mean to tell me you've been around for centuries, and you've never seen a single football game? I find that hard to believe."

Orla shrugged. "I'm a bit of a nomad. I didn't go to school in this or the previous century, until now that is, and I don't own a television. Plus, I've never been very interested in silly human games."

Ask shook his head. "Well, the kickoff is how they start the game. They flip a coin to see who kicks and who receives. Then, the kicking team gives the ball to the opposing team. Now, the object is to stop the team with the ball from advancing to the defending team's goal. The offense tries to push past the defense into the end zone to earn points. The team with the most points wins."

"Ah, it's a military game." She nodded approvingly. She straightened up and appeared to focus on the field more intently.

"Yeah, I guess you could say that," Ask said.

"It's similar to playing Siege the Castle or Victor's Trophy." She might have added, "you know," by her tone, though Ask clearly did not know. These titles sounded like they belonged to card games, RPGs, or variations of tag, like Capture the Flag.

"Okay. I'll take your word for it," Ask said.

"Look, all of these games involve strategizing either a way to trick opponents into protecting the wrong thing so your team can maneuver into a position to conquer or using brute strength to force an enemy to capitulate. In both cases, you win once you seize enemy territory." As if to prove her point, the West Fargo quarterback faked a handoff and then threw a fifteen-yard pass to a tight end, who had pretended to block and then quietly slipped into the open. The line of scrimmage moved close to mid-field.

"I see," Ask acknowledged.

"But, why the pads? Shouldn't the players protect themselves through skill and strength, instead of relying on armor? When I played war games with my friends as a child, you were out only when you were unconscious or bleeding. Usually both. We didn't need breastplates and head covers."

"I doubt parents"—Ask nodded toward the stands—"would let their kids play if the game was to the death."

"Pity." Orla shook her head. "How will they learn to be aware of a threat and prepare for combat?"

"Well, our society doesn't work that way. The idea is that everyone lives safe and gets along."

Orla smiled. "You can't fool me. I've seen two world wars and over three dozen regional skirmishes over the centuries. I watched cities burn, soldiers suffocate on chemicals concocted to torment them, and victors pull women and children from their homes on days just like this one to steal away and force into servitude and divvy up as prizes of conquest. Everyone doesn't get along and only some people are safe."

"Okay. Well, I guess we humans hope to move beyond that. We hope to be better than we were."

"Yes," Orla said, a hint of cynicism in her voice. "To the victors, their spoils."

Changing the subject, Ask said, "Look, one of the rituals with this game is consuming food." He didn't know why he was talking to her like she was brand new to Earth. But, in all fairness, despite centuries on this planet, she hadn't actually sat down to watch a single football game. "I'm thinking of getting a hot dog and a Coke. Can I get you anything?"

"Water with lots of ice," she said, turning back to the game. She seemed particularly excited when a running back broke a tackle, or a defensive lineman stood the runner up and pushed him back for no gain. She never verbalized her excitement or made any gestures, but her eyes narrowed into sharp blue points and the edges of her mouth curled into a slight grin.

Food purchased and in hand, Ask watched Orla for a time before ascending the aluminum stadium steps. She leaned forward on her bleacher seat, attention fully devoted to the events unfolding on the field. Since he had spent time training with her, he knew she was assessing the tactics employed by both teams on the field—the attacker and the defender. She had such focus. Her intensity was, in fact, both frightening and mesmerizing. That someone could feel so strongly about something that their entire being buzzed with it. He shook his head and made his way back to his seat.

"Ice water." He handed her a cup.

She looked at the hot dog in his hand, frowned. "How can you eat that?"

Ask fumbled through an explanation, "Well, I don't know. They're not that bad." But he felt ashamed by his poor attempts to rationalize. "What's wrong with hot dogs, anyway?" he accused. *That's right,* he told himself mockingly, *get defensive.*

"Nothing, I guess. I just literally don't understand the concept of hot dogs as food. It's parts of things mushed together in casing that is unnatural or naturally disgusting."

Ask took a big bite. "And it's delicious."

Orla scrunched her nose, shook her head, and said, "I highly doubt that." She turned her attention back to the field, leaning slightly away from the scent of mustard-slathered mystery meat that wafted toward her on the slight autumn breeze.

They sat mostly in silence until halftime. Orla seemed so transfixed by the competition that Ask didn't want to interrupt her viewing. But once play stopped, he said, "You really enjoy this stuff, don't you? The fight, the struggle, the combat."

Orla sounded a bit guarded in her response. "I guess, it's what I know."

"Because of the giants," Ask said.

"Yes, because of the giants." That hint of cynicism again.

Ask was just about to inquire why Orla decided to protect him when he noticed a familiar and disturbing face watching him from across the field. The old man who had stared at him the other day from the street now sat in the visitor's bleachers. His crooked scar, much more visible to Ask from this distance, made a sort of jagged, sideways smile from the right lower edge of his jaw to his upper left temple. His actual lips formed the angriest smile he'd ever seen.

"Don't look now," Ask told Orla. "That man I told you about. He's here. Across the field in the stands."

Ask didn't see Orla look, but she must have done it somehow at some point, quickly, evasively. "I know." She placed a glacial hand on Ask's bare arm and said, "We stay here."

"What does he want?" He couldn't explain why, but he felt compelled to move his lips as little as possible while he spoke and, despite the distance between them, he also whispered. "Is it an intimidation thing?" All the bullies he'd ever known always stared, willing, perhaps, for him to look at them crossly or acknowledge their presence somehow, intent on provocation. A stare, he realized, was a threat; it was a display of power.

"I think you know." Ask felt a little less foolish when Orla responded in hushed tones, under her breath, barely forming words.

He did, in fact, know, but why did he know? In the world he lived in before the convergence and the ax, he would have no reason to suspect malice from a man he'd never met, not even one with that jagged scar across his calloused face. At another time, he may even have smiled at the man, imagined him a hero of some war, the survivor, perhaps, of an accident. *And then he would have me*, Ask thought. *He's waiting for me to drop my guard, to wander unexpectedly into some place dark and forgotten, so he can torture me for the ax and then drain my body of its living energy.*

The game resumed at the fringes of dusk. The sky assumed a calm, purplish hue, which created a touch of dissonance for Ask. In one respect, the evening was comfortable and reminded him of the many early autumn evenings he'd spent reading on the swing attached to the massive elm or sitting on the porch with his parents waiting for the stars, but now it was rendered oddly ominous by this madman staring at him from across the field. He had a difficult time concentrating on the game. He found himself lifting his sight from the field to the man's face and, inevitably, his eyes. He even missed Deonte's best play, a reception of forty yards, which he nearly took into the end zone. He caught the last bit of action when Orla nudged him and pointed.

The hot dog he purchased sat mostly untouched on the ground in front of him.

Orla noticed it as well. "Aren't you going to eat that?"

She was almost too observant sometimes. Frankly, he didn't have the stomach for it any longer. He shook his head.

Orla's expression seemed to ask him why not.

"I'm not hungry."

"I wouldn't be, either, if I were you." She gave an exaggerated glance at the half-eaten hot dog, wrinkled her nose, and pursed her upper lip in an expression of disgust. "It's so unappetizing."

Ask cracked a grin for the first time since noticing the stranger on the bleachers across from them. He was grateful to Orla for lessening the tension. He lifted the hot dog up to her. "You can have it."

She swiped a hand in front of her face. "The stench is horrendous. Get that away from me."

He set the hot dog back on the ground, turned to the scoreboard. At this rate, the Mustangs might pull it off. They were up by ten with only a few minutes left in the fourth. He forced himself to focus on the field, to assign more urgency and importance to the outcome of the game than to the scarred face in the crowd.

"We'll be okay. He's not here to do anything tonight. It's all posturing at this point," Orla reassured him. Ask wondered at what point posturing would evolve into attack.

To distract himself and settle his nerves, he blurted out, "Want to come over for dinner tomorrow evening?"

Orla turned to him. "I suppose you'll be serving hot dogs?"

Ask laughed. "Not really. My mother doesn't like them."

"Smart woman. So, I suppose she will be there as well."

"Well, yeah."

Suddenly, Ask had a new concern to focus on. What could she possibly mean by "I suppose she will be there as well"? Did he just become the biggest nerd in the history of nerdom? What if she thought he was asking her out and then assumed his idea of a date was inviting a girl over to eat with him and his mother? How pathetic. The scariest thing now at the game was the threat of an irreversibly tarnished reputation.

"It was actually her idea," he said, retreating. Did that make things worse?

"Oh? And how does she know about me? Did you tell her about us?" Orla grinned.

He was sweating. What the hell was happening? Now he wished Scarface would gut him right then and there. "Look, she saw you and me training and wanted to get to know you."

Perhaps sensing her advantage, she said, "Mom trying to set us up?"

"No. No. That's not it at all." He didn't hear the final whistle of the game. His face burned with embarrassment.

Orla nudged him. "He's gone."

Ask followed her gaze across the field to the bleachers, to the now-vacant spot where Koerl no longer stared at him.

Then she said, "I don't know about dinner, Ask. That might not go well."

"Look," he clarified, "I'm not asking you out on a date."

She nodded. "I know. I'm teasing you." She did deadpan well. Ask couldn't tell her serious tone from her sarcastic one.

He loosened up a bit but proceeded cautiously. "It was just a thought."

"And a safe one," Orla replied. "I could be anyone. Your mother is right to check on me. It's a tactically sound maneuver." She paused, as if in reflection, and then changed her mind. "Okay, I will have dinner with you and your mother," she concluded.

Though he felt ridiculous, he was also relieved. "Right. Tactically sound," he repeated, as if that explained away the entire awkward conversation.

On the field, they congratulated Deonte. "Did you see that catch?" he asked, mimicking what he imagined was his pose as he caught the ball.

"Your attack was precise and your skill a boon to your battalion," Orla said.

"Okay, maybe you mean my catch was cool and the team is happy. Hey, whatever. I got to hit the locker room. I'll catch up with you later." Deonte jogged off the field toward the south end zone, pausing briefly where he'd made his memorable play.

When Deonte was gone, Ask looked into the darkness where the man had been sitting. "Where do you suppose he went?"

"Back to the others," she said without hesitating. "What you have is important to them. We need to be ready when they come for it."

"But why broadcast their presence? Couldn't they have simply surprised me one day without me knowing who they are?"

"Know thine enemy," Orla said. "He taught me that." She said no more.

Despite spending the evening with her, Ask honestly didn't know where he stood with Orla. She sought him out, trained with him, encouraged him, and even laughed with him. The other day, Ask had stumbled over his own feet, and Orla caught him in her arms. A herculean lumberjack tripping and falling into the arms of a thin girl not even a quarter his size seemed ridiculous to them both. Their laughter was genuine at first and then a way to cover the increasingly uncomfortable fact that Orla was still embracing him. She immediately released him, stopped laughing, and pointed to the ax, as if to say, "Now, back to business."

He often had to remind himself that although she looked like a teenager his age, she was, in fact, many centuries older than him. Plus, what was he, exactly? Too small—despite the massive body he sometimes donned—too immature, too average. He thought about Sheryl Ann and how she could look right past him, even through him, it seemed, if more popular guys were around.

The shame of their exchange about dinner was a lingering reminder of how naïve he must seem to her, confirmation, he imagined, of his ignorance and childishness. No growing ax, regardless of its transforming energy, could change him into a man.

CHAPTER 12

THE AX'S EYE

IN LIGHT OF THEIR ENCOUNTER with the scarred man the night before, Orla insisted they intensify their training. Because Deonte was at football practice, it was just the two of them. She put a blindfold on Ask and told him to sense her movements as she circled him silently. He pivoted to what he imagined were the slight disturbances of her feet against a blade of crackly grass or her boot scuffing lightly against the ground. Every so often, she would poke him with her pike to encourage his concentration. Whenever the sharp reminder landed, he realized that what he assumed were her movements were, in fact, other sounds.

"You have to block out the ambient noise," she instructed him. "See with the ax."

"Now, you're making fun of me," Ask said. "See with the ax? Really?" He knew the top of the ax, where the head and the handle intersected, was called the eye, but that didn't mean it could see anything.

"Ask, the ax has energy that now flows through your veins. You can access that energy to sense your surroundings. When I tell you to see, I don't mean look. I mean, for you to concentrate the energy and feel the disturbances."

Ask thought about his strange new ability to know what his mother felt, or how he could focus his sight like binoculars on objects far away and see details like scars from second-story windows. Was she asking him to further tap into that power? If so, how could he control it? He had been moving while Orla circled him, trying to cover his flank from those nasty jabs. By doing so, he was unable to center himself and concentrate on "seeing." So, he stopped.

Instead of listening for some indication of movement, he tried to feel where she was instead, perhaps latch on to her energy or essence or whatever it was that made his eyes green and hers the whitest blue of an Antarctic iceberg. It was, in fact, her eyes that provided the access he needed. When he imagined her eyes, he soon began to see what she was seeing. Once he realized that he was looking at his massive lumberjack backside, he knew Orla was behind him. In one swift motion, he swung the ax. The eyes widened and then the view tumbled skyward, finding a view of him once more near his left flank. Again, he swung. The view somersaulted. For a moment, he saw himself upside down.

"Very good," Orla commended. "Take off your blindfold."

Ask obeyed.

"What did you see?"

"It was amazing. I saw myself, through you, like I was outside my body but still able to control it." Ask shook his head in amazement.

Orla nodded. "The ax enhances your senses, all of them. With time, you'll be able to see without seeing, to use the ax to anchor your senses. You and the ax will be one."

Ask wasn't sure he liked that idea. Sure, the ax offered some really cool benefits, like transforming him into a colossal warrior, but to turn himself over to it entirely. . . What would he lose in return? What would it cost? Already he had given up so much of the things he loved, not to mention his innocence, his comfortable ignorance. What next? His humanity altogether? Would the ax insist he stay this giant lumberjack forever? Make him hard and calloused?

"What if I don't want to be one with the ax? Have it control me? What if I choose to stay me?" he asked.

Orla was slow to respond. Ask wondered if she would try to convince him it was the only way. Isn't that always what people try to do to get what they want?

"I understand what you are asking me," she finally said. "What I have learned these many centuries is that we always and ultimately surrender our lives to something. We can choose to which measure of good or evil we devote our energy. One way or another, we compromise to a cause, our own or someone else's. The ax is an object of good, pure energy. It will not betray you. So, if its energy brings good, what better cause to dedicate your life?"

A lot of good it did my father, Ask said to himself. "I suppose you've merged with your pike," he said, a hint of teasing in these words.

He didn't expect the serious answer. "No. My weapons are only tools. They don't have a living energy in them. I must manipulate them, give them purpose. Without me, they're immobile, ineffective, dead. Your ax will anticipate your movements, extend your attack, and maximize your strength. It will listen and, if you let it, speak. That's what you must learn. A companionship like that is, well, irreplaceable."

"So, this blindfold thing is really only possible with the ax and its special energy? You're saying I could just go practice in my room by resting my eyes and thinking like an ax or something. Be the ax," he joked.

Again, Orla was serious when she responded. "It doesn't work like that. The training is essential. You must learn each other's movements, respond in thought and action as one. That doesn't come by just picturing the ax in your mind. It comes with repetition, with practice."

"I suppose you could defend yourself with this blindfold on"—he pulled the blindfold over his head and offered it to Orla—"because you've 'trained' to fight that way," he said sarcastically.

He couldn't explain why he teased her in this way. Was he testing to see if she had a sense of humor? Did he hope some levity would decrease his growing anxiety over Orla's prophesied attack? Was he testing her mettle as she tested his? Or was he trying to protect his ego?

Orla grabbed the blindfold and quickly tied it over her eyes. Ask checked to make sure she couldn't peek around curled edges, just as she had done when she secured the blindfold to his face. Once satisfied, Ask began circling Orla, just as she had circled him earlier. He stepped carefully in an attempt to disguise his whereabouts. He stepped left one pace, then right two, repeating this Jacob's ladder-like pattern until he was directly behind Orla. He raised his ax and swiped down toward her head, where he planned to stop inches from impact and delight in his victory. Only, things didn't go that way. As he brought the ax down, Orla dropped, swung her left leg out behind her, sweeping Ask's legs from under him and causing him to fall on his back, Orla's pike blade now hovering just above his neck.

"How did you do that?" He pulled himself to his feet, once unimpeded by Orla's blade.

"Training." She smiled. He thought that smile was a little smug, the sort of I-told-you-so smile Deonte sported when he was right and Ask was wrong.

Orla tossed Ask the blindfold. "Shall we continue?"

Ask pulled the blindfold over his eyes. 'Ready," he yelled, pounding the ax butt against the ground.

For another hour, he practiced sensing Orla's approach with varying levels of success and too many jabs of her pike. By the end of the session, the only sense he seemed able to access was his sense of smell. During one of his most intense efforts to concentrate, he caught a whiff of dinner and that became all he could think about. He convinced Orla they needed to wrap up. He wouldn't be able to continue until he had something to eat.

CHAPTER 13

A GIANT SURPRISE

ORLA ARRIVED PROMPTLY AT 6:00 p.m., allowing Ask fifteen minutes to get home from training before she followed. Ask's mother had laid out quite a feast: broiled chicken, steamed potatoes, cilantro carrots—both ingredients freshly picked from the garden earlier that day—and slices of homemade cottage bread. He dug right in, clearing the potatoes and vegetables in quick order. Orla, on the other hand, picked at the plate, eating a carrot here and there, a bit of potato. Maybe she *didn't* eat. Ask observed her aslant, testing his theory as discreetly as possible.

"So, Orla," his mother said, "you go to school with Ask?"

Ask listened intently, curious about her response. He remembered how difficult it was for him to answer that question a few nights ago.

"That's where I met Ask," she said.

Pressing, his mother next asked, "What's your favorite subject?"

Orla shrugged. "Probably history."

Ask could sense his mother's frustration growing. He knew too well these vague responses didn't sit well with her. He also noticed Heim crouched in a corner, hackles up, issuing low growls in Orla's general direction. Heim never acted that way around anyone.

"Perhaps mythology?" his mother probed.

Orla looked up from her plate. Made eye contact with his mother. "I guess you could say that."

Ask's mother stood up, took Orla's plate, still loaded with potatoes and chicken, and returned with fillets of cold, uncooked fish. "I know you're a giant," she stated flatly, clanging the plate down in front of Orla in one abrupt motion.

"I suspected you would. We had to meet sooner or later," Orla said. She picked up her fork and scooped an impressive portion of fish into her mouth. "I'm here to help," she said between mouthfuls.

"My experience is that your kind doesn't help much unless there's something in it for them. So, what's in it for you?"

This exchange took Ask completely off guard. For the second time in so many days, he found himself wondering what was happening. Wasn't Orla his secret? Of course, his mother would know, and that awareness would be reciprocated. He lost all interest in the remaining chicken cooling on his plate.

"Let's just say we have a common enemy," Orla replied.

Ask's mother laughed. "That's an ironic thing to hear you say. How can you be an enemy to yourself, frost giant? I want to know what you are really doing with my son."

There are moments in which the world you believe as real is turned on its head. Hadn't Orla taught him about the convergence, warned him about and prepared him to protect against the giants? She was the scared girl kidnapped by these monsters, who escaped their captivity and sought revenge for lost years and a murdered friend. What did his mother mean that Orla was a giant herself?

"Preparing him for the inevitable." Orla remained calm, ate her fish.

"An inevitability you no doubt orchestrated. You're planning to lead him to the slaughter, aren't you? You feign friendship, earn his trust, and then take him to your master, signed, sealed, and delivered."

The hand around Orla's fork contracted into a fist. "Never. I hate Hyrrokkin. She is *not* my master. I left years ago. Whether you want to believe it or not, I am trying to protect Ask. He needs to be a warrior if he is to defeat the giantess and her army."

"No good," Ask's mother retorted. "We have been harried by your kind far longer than I can remember. What I do know for sure is that frost giants don't protect anyone, not even their own kind. If you do hate Hyrrokkin, it only means you want to leverage my son for your revenge."

Orla threw her napkin on the table. "I obviously can't convince you of my true intentions."

"No, you clearly haven't told me your true intentions," Ask's mother countered.

"I've told you everything that matters. I mean no harm to you or Ask." Orla stood. "But I see I have outstayed my welcome. I thank you for the fish and your..." She paused, "hospitality." With that, she pivoted and made for the front door. Heim growled at her as she passed. "Not a guardian any longer," she stated without malice but rather with a tinge of melancholy to the dog. Heim stoically lowered his head onto his front paws and whined low.

Ask followed her outside, where stars shone brightly through a clear sky. An owl hooted somewhere in the crisp fall dark. The air was redolent with the scent of fallen leaves. He grabbed for her chilled hand. "You can't just walk away. You're a giant? You made it sound as if you were a victim of giants."

She turned on him abruptly. "I am a victim of giants and of gods and goddesses and of humans, an outcast most would rather see dead. I am tired, Ask, of this interminable war and the hate that turns hearts to stone. Your mother's right, you know. You should stay away from me. I might betray you. Hyrrokkin would welcome me back with open arms if I delivered the ax to her."

Ask nodded. "But you wouldn't do it."

"Are you so sure? Your mother seems to think so. Maybe I need you to carry it to her, because I can't claim it while it's enchanted. Perhaps I've been in contact with Hyrrokkin already. How do you know she didn't send me ahead to find you? Maybe I'm leading you into a trap."

The porchlight glinted brightly against her frost-laden blue eyes.

"By preparing me to fight her? I don't think so. Why are you saying this?"

"Because I want you to be safe. One way to do that is to trust no one," she said.

"But I do trust you," Ask said.

Orla's stance relaxed, and her demeanor softened. "Your trust is both your strength and your weakness, Ask. I will honor your mother's wishes. Goodbye." She dropped his hand and walked quickly down the porch steps, where she stopped.

"What about my training?" Ask called after her.

"Take care of yourself." She turned and bound into the night, her silhouette a dark outline growing larger, not smaller, as she ran down their country road.

Ask's hand burned cold from Orla's touch.

CHAPTER 14

DREAM MEMORIES

ASK WALKED PAST HIS MOTHER without saying a word. Although he didn't look at her, he knew she was pleading silently with him to understand her position. He pulled himself wearily upstairs to his bedroom, shut the door quietly, and dropped onto his bed. Closing his eyes tightly, he tried to sleep so he wouldn't have to think.

Soon asleep, he found himself stomping through a forest, ax in hand, his breath white puffs in the cold night air. He heard screaming in the distance, as he had so many times before. He hurried toward the sound, which emanated from an old pine log cabin. It was similar to images he had seen on the internet of old homesteads or a couple of the historic buildings he toured one summer at Bonanzaville, a frontier museum in West Fargo. Typically, he would wake up at this point, disoriented and shivering, wondering what the dream meant. This time was different. He didn't awake. He approached the cabin door instead and pulled it open. He slid the ax into a sheath strapped to his back, so he could fit through the door, and then he crossed the threshold cautiously.

Inside, the cabin was dark, except for a muted light burning to embers in a fireplace on the other side of the room. The room he entered was sparsely decorated. There were a few chairs surrounding a small round table, a bookcase with a handful of dusty volumes on bowing shelves, a net and fishing pole leaning near the front door, and an iron woodstove below a couple of cabinets. He heard no screaming in the cabin, just a quiet sniffling in a corner between the fireplace and a window. He approached cautiously, his hand hovering just above the ax handle.

As he made his way through the room, and his eyes adjusted to the lesser light, he began to see gouges in the floor and odd markings on the wall that resembled long streaks of. . . was that blood? The scene that came into focus was horrific. Something with large claws had scraped its way across the room, someone or something had been injured, left the telltale signs of a fading life on the walls, perhaps as they fought to get away. And now, the crying in the corner where the light wouldn't reach.

"Hello?" Ask whispered, his voice both stranger and louder than he expected. It wasn't his, he realized. No, but he knew that voice. It was his father's.

The quiet crying stopped. Ask stood uncertain just a few feet from the corner. Some force within himself held him fast in place. "Hello. I'm not here to hurt you. I'm here to help." The feet that were not his propelled him forward.

A small boy sat knees to chin on the hardwood floor. Ask kneeled beside the child. "Where are your parents?"

The boy buried his face deeper into his folded form, reluctant to tell this unfamiliar person anything. He figured his immense size frightened the boy. However, Ask realized, catching sight of his much smaller forearm, he was no longer as massive as he had been in the forest, remembering he had shrunk before he entered the cabin. But he also realized that he wasn't his regular human self either. The low light from the fire illuminated enough that, when he glanced at the windowpane feet away from the child, he saw not his own reflection but his father's. He stumbled back and marveled at the face he hadn't seen in so long.

So unexpected was this vision that he didn't notice right away that the ax blade pulsated green through the sheath, and Ask wondered why the room was suddenly illuminated as if by a stoplight signaling "go." While Ask was distracted, the child slipped stealthily away, leaving Ask's line of sight. The movement in the room brought him back to the moment, where a shadow began growing against the near wall. The child gone, Ask turned around to see a massive form, cold and pale, standing above him, an enormous icicle gripped at the end of a muscular arm. The face staring down at him bore a diagonal scar running from lip to eyebrow. Koerl.

"You're so noble, Paul, such a hero," Koerl said. "All it takes is a child crying, and you come running. Predictably. Like a dog."

He jabbed Ask in the shoulder with the icicle. It penetrated the skin, and pain radiated to his chest and back. He dropped to a knee when Koerl slowly removed the icy blade. From that position, he could see a narrow doorway to another room, where a small arm lay lifeless, blood pooling on the floor.

"Butcher," Ask heard himself say. "You had no right."

"Right? What does right have to do with it? This is a war that will be waged until everyone you protect is dead. Just like these traitors." The giant pointed to the backroom. "No one can hide forever. We will find them all. To the ends of every world."

Ask lifted himself up and retrieved the ax. He grew until he stared Koerl in the eye. "We'll see about that."

"And that"—Koerl pointed at the ax—"will be Hyrrokkin's."

As the ax's energy surged up his arm, Ask felt the wound close and the pain subside. He swung the ax at Koerl's head. The giant dodged the blow and then burst through a wall. Ask followed through the gaping hole to chase after him, but Koerl had vanished. He heard deep, powerful baying. A massive blue ox sidled up to him. He understood the ox say, "The others were here. I tracked Hyrrokkin's wolf to a river, but they got away." This ox, his father's apparent partner, seemed quite familiar to Ask. And then, he knew, somewhere in the recesses of the memories that were not his own, the ox was the goat his father called Babe.

Back in the cabin, Ask approached the still figure lying contorted halfway between the living room and what turned out to be a bedroom. The child had been dead for some time, his little body already seized by rigor mortis. The child

Ask had seen must have been Koerl in disguise, assuming this form, mocking it after discarding it. How do you fight a shapeshifter? A remorseless monster? He peered into the darkness beyond the doorway and, as his eyes adjusted, saw two motionless forms on the bed. Ask realized he knew them, or rather his father knew them: Uffe and Alva, both gods who had found this remote cabin to hide from Hyrrokkin's horde. Their child was called Gabor. He pulled the bedsheet over Uffe and Alva's heads, grabbed a blanket, and did the same for their child.

This time, when he went outside, his face was wet with his father's tears. Ask wanted more than anything to wake up. The pain of this moment lurched in his chest and twisted it into guilt. Why hadn't he arrived in time? He'd been too cautious in the woods when he should have run to their aid, hefting his ax high above his head ready to cleave the evil giant in twain. But he had went his way slowly, perhaps even fearfully, and this hesitation had cost more than even his own death could atone. A voice in his head recited, "You promised to protect them. You promised." Ask couldn't discern whether the words of this internal voice were his own or his father's assigning blame. Either way, this was a memory he would never forget.

Ask awoke with a start, his bedsheets tangled around him. Perspiration matted his hair and trickled down his neck. A muted light from the hallway nightlight cast the objects in his room to shadows against the far wall. It was still late. The dream he dreamed felt too real. Even his left shoulder, where the ice blade had penetrated his father's skin, seared a painful cold-hot. If that weapon could cause such pain and slay refugee gods from Asgard, it must have killed his father, too. Not this time, perhaps, but at some point in the future of the past he witnessed, at which time Koerl's blade must have found purchase in his father's heart. His anger swelled once again.

Orla had said, Ask puzzled, that no giant had slain his father. How could that be when Koerl seemed to have motive to murder him? Why would Ask have been shown this memory if not to reveal how his father died? His mother told him not to trust giants. Maybe she was right. Maybe Orla lied to him to gain his trust. She had said so herself. But why tell him? To confuse and mislead him? Reverse psychology? So many fragments from a past he didn't even know existed five months ago. So much confusion.

Ask, now quite awake, stood and shuffled over to the window. The moon was in its waning stages of the hunter's light, still fat and brilliant. Fall nights were the best for stargazing. His father would call him outside when the sky was particularly clear. Hand on Ask's shoulder, he would point to distant constellations and tell him the stories of the stars in the mythologies of the world.

"And that, son," he remembered his father saying, "is Sextans, named for the instrument that measures the stars, the tool that guided sailors home."

Ask always told himself the stars would bring his father home. That is why he waited late on summer nights for the sky to reveal the map that would guide his father back to him safely. Now, the moon felt like a selfish master and the stars its cruel minions, the lesser light at night a deceptive façade instead of a symbol of hope. He rubbed his shoulder with his right palm and felt his own hope as far away as the dimmest star.

As Ask reached for the curtains to shut out a sky he could no longer look at without feeling the embarrassment of his naïveté and a vague sense of regret, he noticed a large animal among the shorn stems of a newly harvested cornfield. Its breath rose from its snout in steamy tendrils. Atop the creature was an enormous figure gripping an object that reflected the moonlight like metal. No. Like ice.

Consumed by all the injustices he was incapable of redressing in his and his father's past, Ask tore open the window. In one motion, he summoned the ax and called to Babe. A green light struck the grazing animal and transformed him into a massive blue ox. Ask landed as a bulk of muscly flesh, an immense warrior gripping a magical weapon with the strength of the gods. He let out a cacophonous roar and ran toward the distant form, who showed no sign of moving.

Nor did Ask slow down. He thrust his massive body toward the figure. The lithe wolf dodged the attack. Ask slid to a stop and turned around.

"Let's not be too hasty," the giant atop the wolf cautioned. "I have no interest in killing you. I've come to release you of a burden you shouldn't have to bear."

"And I've come to avenge my father," Ask spat between gritted teeth.

Koerl laughed. This unexpected response set Ask a little off balance. "I didn't kill your father. True, he was a pest, devoted to protecting my enemies, but I didn't kill him. The lion doesn't always kill the fawn but lies in wait for the doe."

Chills shot up Ask's spine. Perhaps it was the way Koerl emphasized and drew out the word "doe."

"You really have no need for that ax. It's part of a world and war that doesn't concern you. It's from a time that is dead, a buried civilization. Nothing more than a relic. I promise you my protection if you just hand it over."

Koerl held out his hand.

"It's a weapon of extraordinary power. If I give it to you, you will give it to Hyrrokkin, so she can use it to kill the rest of the gods. Besides, it won't work for you."

"And why is that?" Koerl curled his snarly mouth into a grin, forcing the scar on his temple into an unnaturally jagged line.

"It has already chosen a companion."

Ask knew the minute he said this that he had been seduced into revealing an important secret about the weapon's loyalty, something Hyrrokkin might find useful as she sought to further tame the spear she stole from its warrior protector.

"I see. Perhaps I was too hasty to offer protection. I may yet have to harm you after all." Koerl lifted his ice sword and swung quickly and mightily at Ask's head. Ask ducked the blow, rolled on his side, and then found his footing, lunging immediately for Koerl's unprotected arm. Koerl's wolf stepped aside, and the ax completely missed its target. Koerl swung again, but Ask blocked with the cheek of the ax. As Koerl wound up for another strike, he and his mount were broadsided by a force much heavier than the balance of their weight together. They toppled over, separating them and effectively relieving Koerl of the high ground. Babe stood over them, a beautiful blue tangle of muscle, snorting and tamping the ground with a hoof.

Like his wolf, Koerl was also nimble. He hopped to his feet and lunged forward in one motion. Ask deflected the attack, but the sword still grazed his left shoulder. The familiar sting of the cold-hot ice blade took his breath for a moment, preventing him from an immediate riposte. Before Ask had even registered the first hit, Koerl stabbed him again, this time in the leg. Ask fell to one knee. As he gripped his leg to staunch the searing pain, he glimpsed Babe doing his best to defend against the wolf's gnashing teeth and swiping claws. Despite Babe's immense size, the wolf pushed him back. Blood from gashes, glistening in moonlight, dribbled down the ox's barrel-shaped midsection.

Koerl stood over Ask now. The fight all but done. "Beneath all that magic, you're just a boy. I am sorry to have to take so much from you so early in life. But, you see, I'm on a mission and have been for centuries. It is your misfortune to have come between me and finally fulfilling that mission. Goodbye, young warrior. May you rest well with your failure in the scorched halls of Valhalla."

Ask awaited the final blow, but it never arrived. Instead, Orla, with pike raised high, deflected Koerl's blade. "Ah," Koerl said, too cheerfully, "the apprentice has come to play."

"I am not your apprentice, murderer," Orla said. "And I want blood for what you did to me. . . to Solveig." She pressed a button on the handle of her pike, which released a second blade on the opposite end of the weapon's shaft.

"Oh, there will be blood." Koerl pushed the pike aside and reset his stance, now facing Orla.

Ask had never seen Orla in her giantess form. Her iridescent black hair was long and plaited into a single braid. She was a sleek white-blue, not entirely dissimilar to the pale complexion she exhibited in her human form, with muscles that appeared sculpted out of marble. But unlike marble, her movements were fluid, and her muscles contracted and flexed as she spun and flipped around Koerl, her pike rotating dangerously like the blades of a helicopter. She succeeded in backing Koerl up a few paces.

Ask heaved himself to his feet, gripping his ax with renewed strength, and attacked Koerl from behind. Between Orla's skill and the power of the ax, they drove Koerl further back. As the fight turned to his disfavor, Koerl whistled for his wolf. Disengaging from an intense battle with Babe, the wolf bowled through Ask, which gave Koerl a brief window to escape. Soon, the two were bounding westward across the expanses of shorn fields.

Ask made as if to follow. "Don't," Orla said, placing a hand on his arm. "Others are close by. They want to draw us into a disadvantage. Plus"—she brushed a hand along the wound in his arm—"you're injured."

"You... You came back." Ask allowed Orla to tend his wound.

"No, I didn't," she corrected. "You have to leave in order to come back. I didn't leave. I watched you leap from your window and run headlong into Koerl's trap." She *tsk*ed. "Unwise."

"He would have killed me," Ask admitted to himself as much as to Orla. "He had me beaten, defenseless."

"Koerl is a seasoned warrior. He has been killing for centuries, perhaps for eons. You have been learning to fight for only a few months. This is the danger I warned you about."

Orla cupped her hands around Ask's bicep, where the wound felt like road rash, a red-hot poker, and an intense infection all at once. She closed her eyes, a soothing cold radiated from her hands, and then the pain slowly subsided. "That should help for now."

The ax will do the healing, Ask remembered from the dream.

"What's up with the big cow, by the way?" Orla asked.

Ask shrugged. "It's Babe, my goat. Apparently, he turns into a giant blue ox."

Holy crap, Ask thought, *the goat turns into a giant blue ox.*

In his rush to attack Koerl, adrenaline prompted him to act on instinct. Now that the fight was over, the reality of Babe's transformation surprised him, but it did not shock him. There was something calming and fitting about Babe in his transformed shape, as if they were linked by destiny. Still. A giant blue ox!

"I saw you call to and then point at that goat. How did you know he would transform like you?" Orla held her hand out to Babe, who lumbered over to her, tail swishing, and nuzzled her hand.

"He was in the dream I had right before I saw Koerl out here. I think he can speak, too."

Babe nodded. "I'm glad you finally came to your senses and called on me. By the way," he addressed Orla, "I'm not a cow."

Orla grinned. Apparently, animals that talk are not considered unusual phenomena where Orla came from. "Indeed," she said. "And, mighty Babe, any reason you didn't tell Ask you could transform?"

"Of course. He didn't ask," Babe said. Then, in typical goat fashion, Babe started nosing around the field for anything the harvesters may have missed.

"Tell me about this dream," Orla said.

"It's difficult to explain." Ask paused. Some part of him wanted to keep the intimate details of merging with his father's memories a secret, a special bond that might remain sacred somehow if he didn't tell anyone else about it. Maybe this was all he would ever have of his father from now on. He settled on recounting a modified version of the dream, in which he was only an observer of facts, rather than a participant in the drama of that evening at the cabin.

"Koerl killed this family in the woods," he finally said, "and my father was there to prevent it. Only, he was too late and a family from Asgard died. Well, I mean, Koerl killed them. They fought, my father and Koerl, but Koerl got away. Just like he did tonight. Babe tracked them to the river."

Babe stated then, "Yes, I remember that day well. Your father swore he would protect them, but Koerl found that family somehow and killed them. It wasn't your father's fault, but he took the loss hard. We followed them to the river, but we lost their tracks. It seemed like they'd vanished." Babe nudged Ask. "Do you have apples? Paul always carried apples."

"I'll remember that," Ask said.

"Have you had other dreams like this?" Orla asked.

"Yes. I think my father was standing at a water's edge waiting for a boat to take him somewhere. He had promised he would go to and look after 'her,' but I don't know who 'she' was. It felt like a long time ago, before cars and airplanes and phones and electricity. There really wasn't much to it, and it probably doesn't mean anything."

Orla replied, "I wouldn't say that. Your last dream told you a lot. Follow where these dreams lead you."

"Do you think they'll tell me what happened to my father?" Ask inquired.

"I think they might." Orla didn't hesitate to respond.

CHAPTER 15

A GODDESS'S CONFESSION

When they parted ways, Orla promised Ask she would keep close. It was now late into the night. Ask's breath cut sharp white perforations into the cool autumn air. The sky was clear and bright and full of stars—Vega, Altair, Ursa Major, Polaris—stars he had studied by telescope with his parents on pleasant nights like this.

Ask lumbered down the dirt road toward home. The cares of life before the ax called to him passed numbly through his mind. The chores that had once seemed so tedious were now sweet recollections of a time when life was much simpler. How he longed to trudge unwittingly to the pasture to feed Babe, not knowing the bleating nuisance was really a talking giant blue ox. If only he could pass the time away mindlessly by kicking his soccer ball against the garage wall waiting for Deonte to stop by, so they could spend a lazy summer afternoon fishing or passing a football. If only his father was still alive, he could sleep soundly, unbothered by dreams of memories that were not his own. He could ask his father about the ax and the convergence and what he was supposed to do. Better yet, he could live in ignorance of this weighty responsibility, go to school with only the anxiety of assignment due dates and the awkward insecurities that kept him from talking to Sheryl Ann.

Lost deep in these thoughts, Ask was not prepared when his mother ran out of the house and said, "Paul, is that you? You've come back to us." She was smiling, and her eyes glistened tearfully in the moonlight. She hugged him.

Ask dropped the ax because he hadn't the will any longer to hold it, which caused him to shrink to his small, regular self, not like his father at all.

When Ask's mother saw she was holding Ask and not his father, she held him tighter. "I'm sorry," she whispered. He cried in her arms.

Inside, Ask's mother warmed milk for hot chocolate. He sat at the kitchen table, head slumped in defeat. "I guess Dad and I aren't very good at protecting people." He replayed in his mind the images from his dream earlier that night. Koerl had won then, and he had won again. "It's a wonder I still have the ax."

His mother sat across from him and slid a steaming cup of cocoa in front of him. "Your father was a hero," she said with conviction.

Ask scoffed. "A lost hero who couldn't save the people he swore to protect."

Those bodies lying in their blood in that cabin, his father's legacy, Ask's inheritance. How many others had paid the ultimate price for his blundering? Maybe Koerl was right. Why not skip the futile resistance and just give over the ax? Have it done with for good?

"Ask, I need you to understand something. Your father donned the mantel you now bear and vowed to protect a desperate people from a bloodthirsty horde bent on killing them. It is true he couldn't save them all. But he did all he could to protect them. Right to the end. You see, when the gods and goddesses fell, many became mortal. Their powers faded over time. The reign of the gods had ended. All that remained was Mjölnir. To conceal it from Hyrrokkin, the weapon was split and separated, so its full power could not fall into her hands. The greater of the two weapons, for the power did not split equally, is in the ax your father wielded. The lesser of the weapons, a spear, was sent to another region," his mother explained.

"Yes, yes," Ask said. "I know, and Hyrrokkin killed its protector and claimed its power." Ask felt himself growing impatient.

His mother nodded. If she was surprised he knew about the ax's history, she didn't let on. "But the spear is unreliable in her hands."

"I've heard the story," Ask said. "What does this have to do with Dad?"

"The ax gave your father great strength. It also gave him an extraordinarily long life. He was much older than you can possibly imagine. That wears on a mortal body."

"What are you saying, exactly?" Ask felt as if the world had suddenly tilted several degrees on its axis. "What do you mean a 'mortal body'?"

"Ask, your father was human. He was a man."

This perplexed Ask. "But how could he transform into the protector of the ax if he was mortal?"

"I asked myself the same question. I've spent too many hours trying to figure it out. Here's what I have come to understand—your father was summoned to converge with the ax. It somehow bestowed upon him the power of the gods. It changed him, extended his life, and gave him abilities beyond his mortal limitations. He became lore in the fables of the region and beyond. They described him as a giant lumberjack, accompanied by an enormous blue ox."

"Babe. . . and Paul Banyun."

She nodded. "He was and is a hero to everyone he saved."

"Where is he now?" Ask demanded. "When we need saving. Where is he to protect his own family? From that monster?"

"I can only guess that since the ax called you, he's gone. I don't know where or how it happened. He was here one day and then he wasn't. I last saw him enter the shed, after he'd been out all night performing his duty. I thought he was tinkering around with this bit of wire or dragging that bit of fencing to patch another hole in the pasture before going to bed. A few hours later, I went looking for him. All that was left was the ax and the tools he'd used scattered across the workbench. He'd vanished."

"Where did he go?" Ask paused. He then said, "It's not fair. I can't do what he did. I don't have the strength."

Despite the changes to his body that made him impervious to Deonte's blows, the powerful energy coursing through his veins, the truth was as Koerl exposed it: Ask was just a boy masquerading as a hero.

"You do. The same strength he had, and more," his mother said.

Ask furrowed his brows and shook his head. "No. Koerl almost killed me tonight. He would have too if Orla hadn't showed up. I'm no warrior. I am not Paul Banyun, or Paul Bunyan, or whatever."

Growing up in the upper Midwest, Ask was familiar with the stories of Paul Bunyan. He considered most of those stories absurd, even though he'd experienced the growing ax himself. For instance, Paul Bunyan was said to have been delivered by a giant stork, hauled as a baby in a massive cradle the size of a wagon, and, as an adult, measured sixty-three ax handles tall. His shirt buttons, the legends claimed, were actual wagon wheels. He combed his beard with a pine tree. Of course, Ask knew some truths hide in tall tales. He wondered about the taming of the Whistling River and the quenching of the frozen flames. Perhaps the details of wrestling a river straight and stomping out a forest fire with his gigantic boots were far-fetched, but the idea of controlling the elements and rescuing people seemed right in line with what he'd witnessed in the dream memories of his father. Plus, the ax often factored meaningfully into these stories. At least they got that part right.

He couldn't quite make the connection in his mind between his father and the Paul Bunyan in these ridiculous tales. It was unlikely his father could either. Once, when Ask was young, eight or nine, his parents took him to Bemidji, Minnesota, where a statue had been erected to this lumberjack legend and his blue ox. He remembered his father pondering the statue for a long time in silence, and then he laughed and laughed. The statue featured massive cylindrical limbs painted in red and black for a plaid shirt and blue jeans for pants, which ended high on the ankle, like a pair of floods, just above the top of a pair of boots. The face had a mustache more like a French inspector than a burly lumberjack. Babe stood passive and docile by his side. The ox statue neither portrayed Babe as a partner to Bunyan nor as a particularly intelligent creature.

Plus, Babe was depicted as smaller than Paul. Ask knew Babe to be much larger when both were transformed. In retrospect, he could understand the humor his father found in such an inaccurate rendering of his transformed self and Babe. As far as Ask could recall, there was no ax in sight, another oversight his father might have found especially funny, since he owed everything the legend claimed him to be to the ax. A sign displayed the date of the statue's creation, 1937.

How old *was* his father?

In response to his mentioning almost being killed, an intense expression of worry washed over his mother's face. "Ask. I didn't know. I should have sensed it. Koerl was here?"

He pointed west toward the adjacent field. "Why should you have known? He was as silent as the grave. I saw him only because I was looking out the window." Then he paused. "What do you mean you should have 'sensed it'?"

"There is a reason your father and I have the ax. A reason he protected those fallen gods from Asgard. It's not a coincidence that I know about Orla, the giants, the ax, and your summoning. I took the hammer from Asgard. I cast the spell that separated it into ax and spear. Your father wasn't just protecting random strangers from genocide. He was protecting his family. He was protecting me." She sighed. "I should have been protecting him."

This news disturbed Ask, though he couldn't quite place why. Was it that she had kept her identity, as well as his, a secret from him? Was it because he believed it was her fault that his father was no longer with them? Was it because she, too, could be in danger? What did Koerl imply about lying in wait for the fawn's doe?

"So, everything I know about you, about Dad, and about me is a lie?"

"It's true we didn't tell you everything. We thought keeping our unique family history secret meant you would be safe."

She focused on a clock decorated with various birds on the far wall, deciding, Ask assumed, how best to proceed. The hour hand edged toward three in the morning, where a robin waited in profile, its breast puffed out audaciously.

Posturing, Ask thought. The only chance that bird would have against a predator would be to fly away at the first sign of danger. After his scuffle with Koerl, he empathized with that bird—he might do the same thing if he saw Koerl again.

"You just never know," his mother continued, "how things will work out. It seems that the best-made plans prove us fools in the end. I guess we thought you would grow up and never need to know any of this."

"And that makes it right? You were hoping I would never find out who you are? You were hoping your lie would somehow become our reality?"

"No, of course not. And. . . yes. We made the decision we thought was right," she said.

Ask nodded. He didn't know if he should feel bitter or betrayed. Instead, he just felt exhausted, even though his body coursed with adrenaline, fueled by the power transferred from the ax, and his mind couldn't stop racing. Perhaps the road ahead seemed just too far and too treacherous. He had never considered the summoning, the convergence, or the call to wield the ax a burden. Yet, again, Koerl exposed another truth: sacrifice comes at a significant cost. He wasn't sure, especially now, that he had the—what was it?—fortitude to give the rest of his life over to protecting inhabitants of a world he didn't even know existed until a few short months ago.

He could sense that his mother perceived his uncertainty. "Ask, you are the son of a guardian and a god. You are stronger than your father ever could be. He was the bravest, most caring man I knew, but he was limited to the power of the ax alone. You"—she placed a hand on the side of his face—"you have the power of the gods."

Once the absurdity of the idea subsided, Ask felt a touch of renewed hope in the possibility that he could access powers that may give him the edge in a fight. Then again, he had never actually seen his mother perform an act he would consider godlike.

"What power?" he finally asked.

"It is true the centuries away from Asgard have tempered my powers. I can't quite do what I once could without some time to prepare, but I'll give it a shot." She closed her eyes. "A small demonstration."

She held out her hand palm up and kept her eyes closed. Nothing happened.

A sadness swept over Ask. Although he couldn't articulate the reason, he recognized intuitively that it was either because his mother had seemingly lost a part of herself that connected her to a past gone forever or because she was trying to prove something to him she never actually possessed. Regardless of the reason, watching her concentrate so hard on her cupped hand in the kitchen of a small farmhouse, the fractured memories of a missing father and husband all around them, tugged his shoulders down and forced a tear from one of his green eyes.

"It's okay, Mom," he finally said, taking her hand.

"Wait," she said, pulling her hand from his. "Like I said, it takes time. It's been a while."

So, he waited. Why he could so readily embrace his convergence with the ax, rush into the night to battle the boogeyman from his nightmares, and accept Orla as a giantess vigilante, yet have so little faith in his mother's claim to godly power, he couldn't explain.

Suddenly, a bright light emanated from his mother's palm. The light took shape in the form of an apple. It floated above her hand. She smiled. "See?"

He wondered at this power. Was it an illusion? Was it designed to mesmerize and distract? He reached out his hand and took the apple. It was as real in touch and smell as any he had ever beheld. No, it was not an illusion. Her power was to create.

"Taste it," she encouraged. It was the sweetest, juiciest, crunchiest apple he'd ever bitten into.

He thought about how the now dormant garden flourished in summer and fall. They always had so much yield from his mother's green thumb. Now he understood why. Still, he asked, "To make an apple is nice, but how does it help us fight the giants?"

She replied, "I prefer this power more than the other."

The apple slipped from Ask's fingers and floated back to her palm, where it hovered again above her open hand. She slowly closed her fingers into a fist. The apple rotted to a putrid brown and then turned to ash. He noticed her amber eyes flash dark, almost imperceptibly the change was so brief. "I'm not as proud of this one. This is the kind of power that corrupts."

He couldn't help himself, seeing this ability to vanquish life so definitively by forming a fist, so he asked, "Why don't you do that to the giants? Crush them? Have this war over and done. Stop hiding, afraid, losing the ones you love."

His mother had never aged. She had been in the prime of life since he was born. Nor had she expressed any emotion akin to anger or hate. She always seemed happy. Of course, when his father disappeared, she was quieter, more contemplative at times, took to conversations with herself behind closed doors, but still her smile radiated like the sun, like a goddess.

So, he was surprised and ashamed when she clenched her teeth and narrowed her eyes.

"You would have me deny my life as a creator to kill these pitiable creatures?"

He shrugged, and she softened.

"I'm not ignorant of the role my people played in bringing about Ragnarök. How we trespassed on the frost giants' lands and forced them into battle for pride or sport. How we imprisoned, killed, and disenfranchised tens of thousands of giants for eons. Loki, while certainly not without his ulterior motives, had a legitimate reason to muster an attack. A war was inevitable. Those giants are angry because we gave them good reason to be angry."

Ask replied, "But that was a long time ago. At what point will they stop? They've nearly killed all the remaining gods and goddesses. Still, they continue to hunt down the survivors. If you won't kill them, can't we negotiate, I don't know, some kind of ceasefire?"

His mother smiled a humorless smile. "They've never been very keen on negotiating. We tried. After they returned the third messenger's head on a pike, we stopped sending emissaries to their deaths." She continued after a pause. "Your father also tried. He had convinced a giant by the name of Surtr to meet with him and two other gods. This was quite a feat. You see, Surtr had destroyed many powerful gods and set Asgard on fire. He is part of the reason we can never go back. His fire, from the very depths of the underworld, laid such waste to our world that it will remain a graveyard of ash forever."

"What happened?" Ask felt he might know the answer already but needed to hear it.

"Surtr, like so many of us, had grown tired of the fighting. His thirst for revenge had evidently been quenched. He was ready to return to his homeland to tend his fires. Your father was certain he would agree to speak to the other giants about giving up Hyrrokkin's hunt. Koerl must have suspected Surtr's wavering loyalty. He personally handed your father Surtr's head and told him the fighting would stop when the last god and goddess were dead. He promised that he would kill me while your father watched."

The hatred that had compelled Ask to attack Koerl resurged, pulsing in the veins of his temples and neck like a war drum. "How can you sit here with the power to crush Koerl and allow him to live?"

"Because I won't give up the humanity I've earned these past thousands of years. I swore I would never harm another living creature for the rest of eternity, as penance for my past, for my family's sins. You see, I knew Koerl in the world that was before this one. He was my father's prisoner. Because there were no prisons in Asgard, prisoners of war were kept under house arrest with the highest-ranking warriors until Odin determined their fate. My father fitted Koerl with an enchanted collar that would choke him if he said or did or thought anything that contradicted my father's wishes. He tortured him. And I... I treated him, the whole venture, with indifference. It never occurred to me that his suffering was real, that having no autonomy at all was demeaning and cruel. When the battle began between Loki and the giant hordes and the gods and goddesses of Asgard, Koerl got free of his collar and strangled my father to death with his bare hands. He found me in the hall, weeping over my father's body, whose misshapen head—I remember too clearly—looked like an overripe plum. He could have killed me then, but he didn't. The war had just begun, and he must have remembered the biscuits and fruit I would sneak to him after meals. He must have still felt some measure of compassion because he bowed his head for a moment and then fled. Don't misunderstand. I was not always kind to him. Children rarely are to the creatures their parents teach them to hate. Sometimes you do or say things that are unkind when you're angry or scared." She mused. "Maybe he tolerated me more because he thought I didn't know better. Years later, that compassion diminished, as we met each other on the battlefields of Asgard. He is now driven exclusively by revenge and hate."

Ask struggled to accommodate this unexpected dimension of his mother's and Koerl's intertwined past. Perhaps things weren't as clearly good and bad and right and wrong as he had initially thought. Compounding this confusion was the fact that Koerl had actually told him he didn't want to kill him, until, of course, he realized Ask's death would be the only way he could claim the ax.

"What do we do, then? Hide on the farm for the rest of eternity?" He was surprised at the sarcasm in his voice.

By now, the sun was pulling against the horizon. Some birds twittered around a bird feeder hanging from a maple tree a few paces from the house. The night had run its course and the adrenaline fueling Ask's attack subsided to fatigue tugging at his eyelids.

"We worry about that later. For now, you should get some sleep. I'll call the school," she said. An attempt at defusing the situation by kicking the problem down the road a bit, Ask thought. But he didn't argue.

Ask struggled up the stairs. He fell asleep nearly as quickly as his head hit his pillow.

CHAPTER 16

THE BIRTH OF BJORNEN

IN THE UNCONSCIOUS WORLD HE had come to inhabit in his sleep, Ask stood once again on the shore of a distant, ancient land beneath slopes of verdant pine trees, facing a vast body of water. Next to him, a man dressed in what he could only describe as common Scandinavian traditional garments—the kind he'd seen at festivals held at the Hjemkomst cultural center: a high-collared shirt and vest ornamented with metal buttons, pants that met socks at the knees, and buckled shoes—placed a hand on his shoulder.

"Are you sure about this, Paul?" He pronounced it "Pol."

Another dream memory. Ask as Paul didn't know what to say, but soon the words slipped unprompted from his lips, "As sure as any decision I've ever made."

"It's a treacherous journey by sea. If the sickness doesn't get you, the storms may."

"It's a chance I'm willing to take."

At that moment, Ask's mother, looking exactly the way she did when he last saw her, sidled up to his father. She wore a *bunad* of simple design: a black skirt with a red vest, some embellishments embroidered at the hem and on the bodice.

She pulled him aside. "Do you mean that?" she asked.

"I do. I will follow you to the ends of the world."

"I'm glad to hear that." She smiled. "That's exactly where we're going."

A colonial sailing ship lilted at the end of a wooden dock. Sailors were hard at work loading supplies and stowing equipment. His mother produced two gold coins from a small leather purse and handed them to an attendant near the boarding plank. She kept glancing back at the trees, where the shadows coalesced between the thick bows and tangled in the underbrush. She allowed the attendant to stow their bags but held onto an object wrapped in oiled leather. "I can take that, miss," offered the attendant. Ask thought he looked vaguely familiar. He realized this was, in fact, the ferryman he spoke to during his first dream memory.

"This stays with me," she said. "Thank you."

Though Ask couldn't see the object, its shape was undeniable: a weapon on the end of a thick handle. But it wasn't the ax. No, this weapon was something much more potent. The energy that had surged through Ask's veins when he converged with the ax seemed somehow diluted by the force of this object. Its blunt, squared head gave away the mystery. It was Mjölnir, Thor's mighty hammer. He was certain. He also sensed that his father had no idea what it was at this point.

He was a young man, his father, not long on his own in the world. Ask perceived, from sharing this dream memory with his father, the hope and yearning of a youth who truly believed that the future could be muscled into a shape favorable for his own wishes. He would conquer first the sea, then a distant land, and eventually achieve the full extent of all human happiness.

He thought of his own yearning, as he searched so many nights hoping for his father to return. An indescribable sense of shame swept over him as he thought of his own misguided desires. Watching the horizon by staring down an empty dirt road waiting for the future to materialize into what you wanted it to be, only to realize the future will always only be what it wanted to be all along, unapologetically muscling you into compliance. He thought of the ax, the convergence, and a birthright he never asked for, the father who never returned.

The dream memory seemed to span months as Ask's father sailed across the Atlantic. Passengers suffered from dysentery, scurvy, and seasickness—a putrescence of bodily fluids sloshed uneasily across the ship's wooden belly. At night, Ask watched the light-green glow of the object wrapped in the leather cover, his father unable to sleep, a fortunate distraction from the suffering all around. The glow calmed him, even gave him strength enough to retain his health. At times, he would spend hours lying on his side looking for rhythms in the pulsing light or attempting to make meaning out of the low hum he noticed several weeks into their journey. Ask recognized this as the summoning. He knew all too well the sound that pulsed in the veins like blood, how the synapses consumed it like dopamine. This, he realized, was the beginning of his father's true journey as the legendary Paul Bunyan.

At harbor in New York, his mother purchased two horses, a small wagon, and foodstuffs. She sat on the wagon seat, Mjölnir resting firmly on her lap.

"Where shall we go, Idun?" he heard his father say. She pointed west. They left the city behind, following rolling green hills into open country, the musty smell of the ocean replaced by the sweet scent of trees and flowers. It was summer, so the air was hot and thick with humidity.

They encountered a farmer and his sons at the base of a hill, where the road sloped into a valley full of corn rows on one side and yellowing wheat on the other. The man waved a dirty cocked hat, so they stopped for a quick visit. "Wouldn't go much further," the man said. "It's dangerous. Bandits killed a family two hills yonder." He pointed in the direction their wagon faced. Ask noticed the muskets for the first time.

Calmly, his mother said, "Thank you kindly for the warning." She handed the farmer three apples, one for him and one for each of his sons. "Health and strength to your family." The man nodded and spit tobacco juice on the road beneath their wagon.

Ask felt his father touch the brim of his own hat, and then they were on their way again. Although Ask had understood the man clearly, he realized his father had not. It hadn't occurred to Ask that Paul (or Pol) spoke another language before English. How much he must have relied on Idun those first years in a new country.

The farmer called after them. "May God have mercy on your souls."

Ask's mother replied softly, "Indeed." More quietly, Ask heard her say, "And so she shall."

ASK MUST HAVE SHIFTED IN his sleep, waking for a split second, because when the dream memory came back into focus, he was sitting at a table in a cabin surrounded by the few belongings his parents had brought with them. He glanced out a window that showed massive pines pointing to an intense blue sky like arrows at the ready. He knew his parents would settle in such a place—isolated, verdant, so much like the slope of trees he envisioned at the start of this memory.

He also discovered very quickly that he had joined his father's memory during a rather serious conversation. "What is in that thing you keep so close all the time?" Paul asked.

"It's my responsibility," Idun responded.

"That doesn't tell me what it is, only why you keep it close."

She met his gaze. "A relic from a time long passed. It is the last of its kind."

She pulled back the oilcloth and revealed Thor's hammer, a solid head of metal on a thick wooden handle.

A sudden urge to touch the hammer brought Paul's hand near an inscription engraved on the broad cheek of the weapon's head. It was a language he didn't know. His hand and head throbbed with yearning, the pulse Ask knew too well surging through his veins. So much more powerful was this weapon than the ax that, when he experienced his father touching it, he blacked out, only to find himself staring at the ceiling from the floor, five feet from the table, Idun standing over him.

"The inscription reads, 'Hammer of the Great God Thor, Mjölnir.' It is too powerful for mortals." She smiled sweetly. "It was brave to try."

He returned to his chair at the table. "How did you come into possession of such a weapon?" he heard himself ask.

"I escaped with it to keep it from falling into the hands of giants."

A laugh rose in his throat, though Ask himself didn't find this particularly funny given his recent encounter with Koerl. Nevertheless, he laughed. "You're teasing me," he said.

"If only I were." She stopped smiling.

"But Idun, what are you saying about giants and hammers that belong to gods? Surely these are the things of fairytales. No more real than dragons and monsters. Tell me, now, where did you get it?"

Even in these days of centuries past, a weariness as ancient as the ages shone in her eyes. "Paul, I know what I say sounds impossible, but you must believe me. I am not from Denmark or Sweden, or anywhere else you have heard of in this world. I came from a place where things like this hammer and giants and gods were real. A war with the giants, from whom I rescued this hammer eons ago, destroyed that world. I came here and have been hiding it and myself ever since."

His smile persisted. Playing along with the joke, Ask assumed. "So, why bring it here to this land? What purpose does it serve now?"

"It has no purpose," his mother admitted. "Its purpose died with its keeper. I simply mean to hide it forever. Like I said, it's a relic."

He nudged her playfully. "Should we bury it in the backyard? Perhaps Cronos can do it for us." A sleepy sheepdog lifted his head at the sound of his name, grunted, and then returned to his nap.

His mother considered this more seriously than Paul anticipated. "I don't think burying it will do much good. It will be vulnerable in the ground. The giants will hear it."

"Oh, yes, of course," Paul said. "We must snatch it away to the fairy world and ask the little people to guard it. They take gold, you know?"

Idun hit Paul lightly. "This hammer knocked you off your chair when you touched it. Could you imagine what it might do to your fairy folk? Besides, I have a better plan. I mean to split it in half and hide it in two places."

"Ah. And I suppose you have a stronger, heavier hammer to do the work."

"I'm serious, Paul. And I don't need a hammer, just a bit of magic."

"Well, yes, of course. Magic will do the trick. Should I ready the cauldron, then? Gather the ingredients, you know, toadstools and all of that?" He took her hand. "But, my dear, you are no witch."

"This is true. I am no witch." She laid the hammer on the table.

Ask felt his father marvel at the hammer's immense power. Even if she could, why would his mother destroy such glorious workmanship? What better force to protect the world than this weapon, forged in the heart of a mystical foundry and tested in the hand of the strongest god of them all? Again, Paul was tempted to touch it; perhaps the handle would not resist him. Wasn't war coming between England and America? With such a weapon, he could end battles, command armies, rule countries. The tips of his fingers hovered dangerously close to Mjölnir now.

Idun quickly pulled the hand away. "Remember what happened last time. Let's not repeat that, shall we?"

These temptations, his father's thoughts about using the weapon for political and military gain, surprised Ask. This was not the man he knew the first thirteen years of his life. His reflection on the windowpane brought him the reason: this Paul was young and inexperienced and far removed from the man who raised him some three hundred and fifty years later. He felt his father retract his hand.

"I'm sorry. There is something mesmerizing and wonderful about this hammer. I-I couldn't stop watching it on the ship, sitting next to it on our journey here, or listening to it hum in this house these long months. It seems to speak to me, not with words but with feelings. It fills my head with such stirrings."

"Yes. That is what the giants hear as well. The summoning. It enthralls them. They feel its power, and they want it to destroy their enemies. The hammer is sly, though. It plants thoughts, makes promises, but it does what it wants. The warrior who wields it must learn to partner with it, must find a way to harness its frenzied power into something more disciplined. Become one with it."

She placed her hand on the cheek of the hammer, just below the inscription. She closed her eyes. When she opened them again, one was the golden hue Ask had known his whole life, but the other was ink black, deep, desolate, the flash of darkness he noticed when she turned the apple she created to dust. She chanted lightly, nearly inaudibly. A green and yellow light emanated from the hammer. It resisted at first, but then it gradually gave way to her commands. The hammer shuddered abruptly and then rocked back and forth on the table for several volatile moments. It stopped moving suddenly, and then slowly, the yellow light peeled away from the green light. Two new shapes appeared on the table. One was the long shaft and pointed head of a magnificent spear, which pulsed a dim yellow. The other was the bearded ax, which retained an inscription on the weapon's cheek, and glowed a slightly brighter green.

"But how did you do that?" Paul asked.

"I've been Mjölnir's keeper for a long time. Its discovery grows imminent by the day. I've been dreaming lately about splitting the hammer to better conceal it from the giants. Mjölnir has been directing my thoughts on this matter. It showed me how to split its two power strains, the lesser from the greater, using my ability to channel and redistribute energy."

"I can't believe it, even though I saw it with my own eyes. It speaks, you say, this hammer?" his father said.

"Yes. It is not without its own spirit, you might say. I've known Mjölnir since it was gifted to Thor. A long time ago, I provided eternal youth by tending the garden of the gods. Some called me a goddess of life, of creation."

Ask's father marveled at this revelation. "A goddess?" He grinned. "Yes, I have always considered you so, but to have the power of eternal creation. This is too extraordinary to believe. And yet, I know it's true."

The green pulse of the ax, now sitting separate from the yellow pulse of the spear, intensified in his mind. Paul, as Ask had done himself, felt compelled to touch the ax, even more than he had the hammer.

"We will hide them at opposite ends of this world with the strongest protectors that remain of the old world," Idun explained.

Idun stopped Paul short of touching the ax by taking his hand. "Remember," she said, "Mortals and immortal weapons don't mix very well. Or do I need to remind you?" She looked at the spot on the floor where he fell after touching Mjölnir.

"I'm sorry," he said. "I can't help myself. The ax calls to me. I feel it pulling my hand toward it." So close now to the ax, both Ask and his father, noticed that the symbols on the inscription had changed. He pointed, "What does that say?"

Idun read the inscription, following the notches of its runic symbols with her fingers. "'Bjornen chooses his champion.'"

"Who?" Ask thought and his father responded aloud simultaneously.

"I suspect the ax is called Bjornen." She then put her other hand on his free hand, which had gravitated ever closer to the ax. "Don't test fate, Paul. The ax is too powerful. It is meant to be handled by a god."

"Yes," Paul said. "But I must. I cannot resist this. Perhaps fate calls to me. Maybe Bjornen has chosen."

Worry spread across Idun's face. Unasked questions filled the silence between them: Would the ax yield to a mortal, or would it consume him? Was moral strength the same as physical strength in this fallen world? She let go of Paul's hand, which slowly inched toward the ax once again.

She stopped him once more. "Wait. Try this?" She produced in her palm an apple out of thin air.

Paul was too enthralled to notice, though Ask did. He had seen that very trick not long ago. Not disengaging his eyes from the ax, Paul took the apple and bit into it. Ask recognized the sweet, juicy meat from his taste earlier that day. Then, Ask felt a new power surge through his father's veins. The body he had been occupying, with its perpetual soreness and muscle fatigue from working fields with hoe and with plow, felt light and strong and indestructible. He glanced at the apple, "What is this?"

"A bit of protection from the ax's power," Idun explained.

Paul nodded. He reached down and picked up the ax. The transfer of energy Ask had come to know as the convergence took hold of his father's body. It coursed through his veins and further lent strength to his muscles. Oddly enough, he did not grow, not right away. It was a peculiar sensation. He felt extremely constricted. Ask thought this was how it must feel to be restrained by a straitjacket or wrapped tightly like a mummy. The energy inside was too immense for the flesh that struggled to contain it. In fact, it couldn't. Stuffed inside his father, who was full beyond capacity with Bjornen's power, Ask stumbled through the front door and out onto a bit of lawn below a wooden porch. The sun beating down mercilessly, heat added another level of discomfort. Now, he was reminded of Thanksgiving afternoon, crammed full of three helpings of turkey and all the fixings and two more of pie, sitting in front of the fireplace. It was a sensation of gluttony compounded with heat and exertion.

"I feared this," Idun said from the front door. "No mortal. . ." she began.

And then, Ask could feel both relief and intense pain from a mortal body, despite the help of the protective apple, as his limbs began to enlarge to accommodate the ax's massive energy, growing unnaturally large through the tearing of joints, the ripping of flesh, the instantaneous snapping and re-fusing of bones. Once he was as tall as their house, Paul's pain disappeared because the power that caused the transformation also healed the damage of its expansion. Ask wondered if the transformation was this painful for his father every time he wielded the ax.

His mother was now in front of and below him. "How do you feel?" she asked.

"Better. Very good, actually." His voice boomed a deep, resounding, and resonating bass. "Am I a giant?" he asked, turning this way and that, putting a hand flat on the house's single-story roof.

His mother visibly shuddered at the word "giant," Ask observed. She turned and scanned the hills and the shadows below tall, thick-needled pine trees. "No. You are a person. Just larger than you were. You should shrink now, and we should put the ax somewhere safe." She was wringing her hands.

He noticed the ax was no longer an enormous piece of wood and metal he could barely lift, but a weapon he could easily maneuver in his now massive hand.

"Shrink? How did I grow?" Paul asked.

Idun's mood changed. She smiled. "I warned you, didn't I? Now, you are as big as a house, and you don't know what to do. Why don't you start by putting down the ax?"

Ask felt his grip releasing its hold of the ax. As his fingers disengaged contact with the handle, a nausea began to slosh around in his head. His limbs suddenly retracted jarringly, a sensation unlike any of his previous experiences with reverse transformation. Every bone and joint retracted with sharp, intense pain. The shortening of his muscles a searing pressure. He heard his father howl in agony, as every mortal tissue suffered in its own molecular universe.

When the blinding pain subsided, he found himself doubled over on the ground, looking up at Idun. She came to him with a balm she produced from light in her cupped palms. "I don't think you should ever do that again."

Ask's father considered Idun's suggestion silently, concluding—not surprisingly, since he ultimately became the legendary Paul Bunyan—that the unfulfilled urge to merge with the ax was a greater pain by far than the torture of transformation. Ask wasn't sure he agreed, but he understood. Hadn't he also been summoned? Had he not gone willingly, thirstily, covetously into the shed where the ax pulsated its bright green light and eagerly picked it up? Did he not rush home every evening to take up the ax and train with Orla? Perhaps he, too, would endure that pain if it meant unparalleled relief through the release of convergence.

"We must hide the ax, as I planned. The giants seek it even now, drawn to its call. Now that it has been awakened, we must work quickly."

Idun took the ax in hand and attempted to lift it. It did not budge. She wrapped both hands around the handle and tried again. Nothing.

"What's wrong with this thing? I've carried the hammer these long centuries across the face of this planet. Why does the ax resist me now?" She strained over the ax for some minutes, while Paul watched from a distance.

"Perhaps Bjornen does not want to hide. He's a weapon, not buried treasure for giants to find." Paul walked over and just touched the ax enough to push it over. It yielded to his touch. "As I said, he has chosen his champion."

Idun tried again, but she could not lift the ax off the ground. She fell into a heap next to the ax and put her face in her hands. "You don't know what this means," she said. "This immortal power or the giants, or both, will destroy you."

"What good is a life if it doesn't fulfill its calling? You said you have been running from these giants for a long time. Maybe it's time to resist them, to fight back. I'm not afraid, Idun. Even if it kills me, I will do my part in this."

Ask had never felt so proud of his father. Even though, as his mother predicted, he knew the outcome of this decision years down the line.

Idun nodded. "Let it be so. But I will help you."

She produced a bushel of apples. "These are the apples of the gods. They give eternal life. They also strengthen the body. They will not make you a god, but they will extend your life and, I hope, lessen the pain. You should eat one every day, Paul Bjornen."

CHAPTER 17

NOT FAR FROM THE TREE

A SQUARE OF LIGHT STRETCHING across his bed awaited Ask as he woke up, denoting that day would soon yield to evening. Deonte sat on a recliner in his room, playing a game on his portable gaming system. He paused when Ask sat up.

"So," he started, "you weren't at school today. Your mom said you were sick." He paused for dramatic effect, lowering his head and raising an eyebrow. "I thought to myself, 'Yeah, right. I punch this guy, and he almost breaks my hand. He turns into a giant freaking lumberjack. I don't think he's sick.' So, what's really going on?"

Still groggy, Ask tossed off a tattered old blanket he'd had all his life—several shades of blue lighter than it was when it was new—and got out of bed, disturbing Heim from his slumber in the process, causing the dog to stand, shake, and then leap off the bed. "I've been time-traveling." He yawned.

"Sure," Deonte said, adding, "did you go through a rift in the space-time continuum or astral project yourself?"

"Something like that." Ask grinned.

"You're such a liar."

More serious then, Ask said, "Sort of. I've been having these dreams. About my dad."

"Yeah, me too, from time to time," Deonte sympathized.

"Not like that, though. These aren't dreams about my dad. In these dreams, I am my dad. I see his life, his memories, through his eyes."

"Wait, what? You dream that you are your dad?" Deonte set down the gaming console.

"Not quite. I dream about and experience his life through him. I see his past looking out from his body."

"Are you kidding me? Full of jokes today, huh?" Deonte dismissed this with a wave of his hand and went back to his game.

"I'm not joking. I spent the last several hours seeing the first time he picked up the ax and what happened. It almost killed him." Ask was surprised at how clearly he remembered and felt the events of his dream. That important day in his father's life had somehow become one of *his* memories.

"What happened?" Deonte paused his game.

"It's all so ridiculous and impossible and unbelievable," Ask began.

"Doesn't sound like anything else that's been going on lately," Deonte said facetiously.

Ask pointed Deonte to his laptop. It might make more sense if he showed him a couple of things. "Search for Paul Bunyan." While Deonte opened the internet browser, Ask reached down and scratched Heim's head.

Deonte said. "You want me to do your homework?"

"No. I need you to see something."

Deonte typed in Ask's request and was presented with over nine million hits. "Okay." He directed Deonte to a couple of sites, one on American folklore, another one an encyclopedia. They also watched a brief video that provided commentary on several tales about the iconic frontiersman. "What does this have to do with anything?"

"Isn't it obvious?" Ask said.

"That you're still waking up? That you hit your head the other day training with Orla?" Deonte joked.

"No. A giant lumberjack, carrying a massive ax. Doesn't that sound familiar?"

"Dude. You're not Paul Bunyan. These stories were written like a hundred years ago." Deonte shook his head. "Maybe you should go back to bed."

"No, I'm not. But my father, Paul, was."

"Look, I know parents seem old. . ." Deonte began.

"Not mine," Ask interjected. "They don't seem old at all, but they are. Very old. In my dream, I followed my parents across the ocean on a boat from, like, the 1700s. They traveled west from New York in a wagon. The strange thing is my father didn't seem old when he disappeared and my mother, well, she looked the same in my dream as she does now."

"It was a dream," Deonte reminded him.

"Yes and no. I've had these dream memories before, and they've shown me things that proved to be true. This one was so real. I'm certain it happened." Ask was adamant. If only he could get Deonte to see what he himself was now beginning to understand.

"Look up 'Idun' now." Ask directed Deonte back to the laptop. He spelled the name: "I-D-U-N." He pointed to a site about Norse mythology. They read about Idun, the goddess who protected the apples that gave the gods their immortality and youth. There wasn't much information, other than a reference to Loki conspiring with a giant to steal her away. "That is my mother. She brought the ax—I mean, Thor's hammer—from Asgard after Thor and the other gods had fallen during their great and final war against the giants called Ragnarök."

He remembered the apple she had produced for his father in the dream memory. *Immortality and youth*, he thought. Hadn't Koerl said something about using the child to catch the mother?

"If they're so old, why are you only fifteen? Or are you really like fifteen hundred years old, but you age differently because your mother is a goddess? Does that make your father a god?" Deonte asked excitedly.

"No," Ask answered. "He was mortal. In fact"—Ask rubbed a phantom soreness that twinged in his left shoulder—"his transformation, like I said, almost killed him."

"Then how on Earth could he survive hundreds of years? People's batteries tend to run out in less than one hundred of those years, even with modern medicine, so doctor mom says. He couldn't have lived that long, not as a mortal like you and me."

"It was the apples," Ask said determinedly.

"Apples are healthy snacks, my mother always says so," Deonte added sarcastically. "Really? Apples?"

"No, the apples grown in the magical hands of the goddess Idun. She kept him alive all those years. You know, the apples that gift eternal life and youth." It made sense to him now.

"Ah, I see: a magical apple a day keeps death at bay, right? So, are you like fifteen hundred years old?" Deonte asked again.

Ask was puzzled. "No. I'm fifteen."

"Is it possible you only remember fifteen years of your long life? Like, you know, you reset or something every fifteen hundred years or so," Deonte theorized.

"It can't be. I was a young child for many of those fifteen years."

Ask tucked this small concern into the back of his mind so he might address it later with his mother. He was certain there was an explanation. In fact, after attacking the giant Koerl atop a giant wolf, transforming his goat into a massive blue ox, watching his mother conjure produce out of thin air, and living a portion of his father's life in a dream, Ask was willing to believe just about anything.

"Did. . ." Deonte hesitated before continuing. "Did you find out how your father died? Do you think it was from the transformation?"

Ask remembered the dream memory he had about Koerl's attack in the cabin the night before last. He sensed Paul had learned to control—or the ax had moderated—the transformation so that it no longer caused excruciating pain. He remembered, with a pang of loss, staring through his father's eyes into the reflection in the cabin window and seeing his father's face, not terribly dissimilar to what he remembered before his father disappeared. He didn't, however, remember searing pain when his father transformed that night. That event must have been a long time later.

"I don't think so."

While he was relieved to know his father didn't spend a lifetime of bone-crushing pain growing to accommodate the ax's power, Ask was also saddened to reach another dead end in his search to discover what became of him. None of what Ask saw or experienced revealed what happened to his father. Not Koerl, not his mother, nobody—good or evil—seemed to know what became of Paul, not even Bjornen. Thinking of the two words together brought a smile to his face.

"What is it? Did you figure it out?" asked Deonte.

"Well, I figured something out, just not what happened to my dad. I realized when you say my father's first name Paul next to the name of the ax, Bjornen, it sounds like Paul Bunyan; if you were to Americanize it, that is."

"Well, case closed then," Deonte playfully mocked. "So, now what? You become Ask Bunyan, an apprentice to your father in your dreams, and carry on his legacy? This sounds like a comic book, you realize."

From his bedroom window, Ask stared at the untidy furrows of dirt in the adjacent field that outlined his skirmish with Koerl the previous night. He wondered if he would see him there again tonight. Or would Koerl no longer be content with waiting for Ask to come to him? Would he attack him in his sleep and take his mother away? And then another thought crossed his mind: *Why hadn't Koerl attacked them when he knew what he wanted was within reach, not even locked very securely in the shed?*

"You're doing that thing again," Deonte said.

"What thing?"

"Thinking too dang much."

"There's something else you need to know." Ask realized Deonte hadn't yet heard that Orla was a giant. He himself had just found out the night before. The story she'd told about her capture by, and subsequent escape from, the giants after Ragnarök had imparted only ambiguous details at best about her own heritage.

"Shoot," Deonte said. "I can take it."

Ask had his doubts. He remembered how Deonte responded to his initial transformation. It had almost destroyed their friendship. Because Deonte's opinion of Orla was a little rocky, he feared his friend's reaction would create a chasm of distrust that Ask would not be able to bridge. How would Deonte treat Orla once he knew she was one of the creatures they were preparing to battle?

"Orla," he began and then stopped. He wasn't sure how to continue.

"Okay, yes, what about Orla?" Deonte asked.

Ask grimaced and tried to pass it off as a grin. "She's not exactly what she seems, either."

"You mean the weirdo is weirder? Big surprise. What, does her stare turn people to stone?"

"Look, she's on our side." Ask paused to let this sink in.

"Why would you say that? Is there some reason you think she wouldn't be? What aren't you telling me?" Deonte's teasing smile dropped.

"She's, well, a giant. That's why she knows so much about me. My mother met her the other night. She knew."

"Ask, this is serious. I knew she was just, uh, off a bit. Maybe we *shouldn't* trust her."

Ask quickly interjected, "Her story about Koerl's abuse was true. She's not loyal to them. In fact, she hates them more than we ever could." He added, "I do trust her."

Deonte's next comment surprised Ask: "Okay. If you trust her, so will I. But if she tries anything. . ."

Ask smiled. "What are you going to do?"

"Come up with insults that will embarrass her into the next century." Deonte laughed.

"Come on," Ask said. "We need to find Orla."

CHAPTER 18

THE PLAN

ORLA SAT WITH HER BACK to a lone birch among a copse of maples and elms. Ask watched her for a time before approaching. He thought he knw what loneliness felt like. He convinced himself that living alone with his mother the past couple of years in the country—with only Deonte, and for a time Jepp, over when they weren't required to be at their own homes or in town or practicing for football—meant he knew solitude. But he always had his mother, Heim, and Babe, plus the fairly regular visits from his friends to stem the tide of loneliness. Perhaps he was alone in wanting and waiting for his father to return. But, again, Deonte provided an outlet and made the grief and the yearning a shared experience.

The closest he had come in recent weeks to feeling truly alone was transforming into the ax's champion. The day Deonte had run from him and then the subsequent weeks in which Deonte avoided him at school had been the most solitary, especially when he thought he couldn't talk to his mother about his transformation. When he was in his lowest moments, he wondered how would she believe him? Yet Orla arrived just in time to protect and teach him. So, even though no one else knew what it was to bear the burden of the ax, she knew what it was and how to help him.

So, no, Ask did not truly understand what it meant to be alone. But seeing Orla propped against the tree as shadows pulled the day toward evening, he had a pretty good sense of what it looked like now.

She stood suddenly, pike gripped tightly in hand. "What is it?" she asked.

Ask held up his hand, palm out. "There's no danger. We just came to find you."

Deonte nodded. "Hey, freak."

Ask shifted uneasily at this jab, given he'd shared Orla's secret with Deonte that afternoon.

Orla set her pike on end and retorted flatly, "Oh, you brought bait. Good idea." After a moment, she added, "You really shouldn't be here. Koerl would love to find you, away from home without the ax."

"Why didn't he attack me in my sleep the other night?" Ask replied. "He waited for me to come to him."

Orla nodded. "Your mother. There's something you don't know about her."

"I know a lot more than I did," Ask said.

"She's like a goddess of apples or something," Deonte added, nodding to Ask, as if to say, "I've got your back."

"She told you then?" Orla asked.

"Not exactly," said Ask. "She told me a few things. Gave me a magic apple. But I saw most of what and who she is in a dream."

"Dreams are powerful," Orla agreed. "They are portals through time and space."

"I told you," Deonte chimed in. "Space-time continuum."

Orla furrowed her brows. "Space-time continuum? What do you mean?"

"My dreams," Ask clarified, "are unique. I don't dream as myself, but as my father, years ago, in other times and places."

"The energy in the ax transferred his memories to you. Now that you are one with the ax, that energy is inside of you, and so his memories are now your memories. What you see in your dreams are the shadows of his life."

"I know my mother split Mjölnir into two weapons, a spear and the ax. I also know that she was its keeper, until Bjornen chose my father, that is," Ask began.

"She escaped with Mjölnir before Hyrrokkin and her armies could take it," Orla finished Ask's thought. "Koerl can't cross the line of your farmstead because your mother created a sort of energy shield that blocks giants from entering."

Ask was confused by this. "But then, how were you able to cross that barrier?"

Orla glanced at Deonte and then back at Ask as if to say, "I guess that cat's out of the bag."

"Yeah, yeah, you're a giant. Big deal. Whatever. Though I bet you cast some kind of dark magic, some bad juju on this place," Deonte cut in.

"Well, you invited me," Orla said to Ask. "If you tell me to go, I won't be able to come back unless you invite me once more."

"Then get out of here," Deonte said.

Orla didn't move.

"I don't think she's telling the truth," Deonte said.

"No, I think she doesn't have to go because you don't live here," Ask explained. "Besides, we can't send her away."

"Why not?"

"She saved my life. What we need instead is a plan. I'm not going to sit here night after night and watch Koerl watch me until I slip up or until he figures out how to get through this barrier to me, or my mother. It's clear he doesn't plan on giving up until he takes the ax. Frankly, I don't plan on giving it to him. He alone may not be a match for Orla, me, and Babe. . ."

"Wait, what? Babe? Your goat?" Deonte asked.

"Well, he does turn into a giant blue ox." Ask smiled and shrugged.

"The goat?" Deonte repeated.

"Of course," Ask said. "You know, Paul Bunyan and his big blue ox."

All three looked through the trees to the pasture where Babe chewed contentedly and nosed around for the greenest tufts of grass to chew. He seemed the least fearsome creature anyone could imagine. They gaped a moment in collective disbelief and silence.

"Like I was saying, I doubt he'll come by himself next time. Now that he's tested our strength," Ask continued.

Orla nodded, a small grin tugging at the corners of her mouth, as if the proud teacher approved of her pupil's surprisingly astute assessment. "What do you propose we do?"

"We get the spear back," Ask said without hesitating.

The slight grin on Orla's face disappeared altogether. "You can't just take the spear back. Koerl is strong and cruel, but he can't defeat us both on his own. Hyrrokkin is different. She is the most powerful giant I've ever encountered. Not even our combined strength would be a match for her. Plus, she keeps the spear with her at all times. How would we ever get close enough to take it on the off chance she sets it down?"

These were logistical challenges Ask anticipated. "I disguise myself as a giant, and you alter your appearance a bit to resemble another giant, one in her circle. We hang around the troop until the opportunity arises. Then, we take the spear and escape."

"Disguise ourselves? Like wear plastic glasses with mustaches attached?" Orla asked in disbelief.

Deonte laughed. "You *have* been hanging out at the high school too much," he said. "Sassy. I love it." And then he looked away with what Ask recognized as embarrassment, a rare reaction for his friend.

"Nothing so crude," Ask said. "You can change shape, correct?"

"Yes, but how do you know that?"

"Well, Koerl looks like a regular-sized old man, and you look like a teenager. Plus, in one of my dream memories, Koerl transformed into a child he killed." He looked away, as if Orla might take offense, as if he were accusing her of wrongdoing by association.

Instead, she nodded, sadly. "That is one of his favorite tactics." After a pause, she said, "So, who do I turn into?"

"Who does Hyrrokkin trust more than anyone else among her horde?" he asked.

Orla thought for a moment. "Besides Koerl? Probably Grior. She is a nasty giantess full of avarice, ambition, and hatred. She follows Hyrrokkin's every command because she wants her power, or at least to share in it."

"How do we lure her away from Hyrrokkin?" Ask wondered aloud.

"We entice her with something she can't resist," Orla said.

"What do you have in mind?" Ask said.

Orla smiled broadly, her jaws clenched. "Leave that to me."

Ask nodded and then summarized: "We get Grior out of the way, we change our appearance, we get in close, and we take the spear."

"What do I do?" Deonte chimed in excitedly.

Ask had actually worried about this question for some time as he'd pondered delivering this plan. Deonte had always protected him. In fact, until Ask's transformation, Deonte was often the only thing keeping Ask safe from bullies. Ask had the reputation of an intellect. He read voraciously and answered questions willingly in classes. For his trouble, some of his classmates knocked books out of his hands, tripped him as he ascended stairs, and teased him. Deonte was always around to push back, pick him up, and raise his spirits. It came as no surprise that Deonte wanted to protect him in this as well. But this situation was different. This time, Ask had to protect Deonte. He didn't know how exactly to let his friend down easy. As he contemplated ways to lessen the blow that Deonte couldn't help this time, Orla blurted out, "Sorry, friend. This is going to be tricky enough without a human to babysit. You can help by staying out of the way."

Deonte gave Ask a conspiratorial eyebrow lift, as if to say, "Can you believe what she just said? Babysit me?"

Now Ask was in a tough spot. He knew Orla was right, but he didn't want to exclude Deonte, who had taken some time coming around to the idea that Ask could transform into a huge lumberjack. He found himself walking a rhetorical tightrope.

"These giants aren't going to go easy on you if we get caught," Ask said. "Orla is one of them. And I—well, I'm protected by the ax. Maybe you can stay at my place and keep my mom safe."

"You mean, stand behind the energy field that no giant can cross? Your mom's a goddess. I doubt she needs my protection. I'm going with you." In an effort to press his argument and sweeten the deal, he offered, "My dad has a couple of rifles and some ammo we used for deer hunting. I haven't been shooting much—well, at all since he left—but giants make for big targets. We could light them up before they even know what hit them."

Ask hadn't even considered arming himself with a gun. He, too, had a rifle for hunting. Would that work? Could they shoot the giants and be done with them? Attacking from a distance would simplify things significantly.

"No good," Orla interjected. "Giants are impervious to weapons in this world. The bullets won't penetrate their thick hides and dense, hard bones. You'll just make them angrier and become an even more appealing mark for them yourself. Weapons to defeat giants must be forged in Asgard, out of Asgardian metals."

Deonte adjusted his argument. "I'm small," he added, "and can move around without drawing attention. They won't expect it."

Deonte actually made a very good point about the giants not expecting a human moving among their ranks, Ask thought. He paced between the trees, finger on lips and thumb on chin. Could he somehow incorporate Deonte into the plan?

A couple of squirrels chittered and then scrambled across branches overhead. How long the squirrels had been skittering about above them was unclear. You just didn't pay much attention, he realized, to the ambient sounds of wildlife that pose no threat.

"Okay. This can work to our advantage," he finally said. "But no guns."

He imagined Deonte grazing a foot or bullets ricocheting off giants to create friendly fire. More to the point, he feared the implications of what bringing a gun to a battle with immortals might convey. Hyrrokkin would know right away that Ask and Deonte had no idea what they were doing and any deception they attempted would be over in short order. Their chances were slim enough. They didn't need to tip their hands to reveal how vulnerable they truly were.

"What are you thinking, Ask? You can't be serious," Orla said. "Look, Hyrrokkin will kill him if she catches him. She won't care that he's human or that he possesses. . ." Orla paused and then proceeded carefully, "no old-world powers. She'll tear his spine out of his back or squeeze his neck until his head pops off."

"Graphic much?" Deonte asked.

"My point is, giants don't show compassion. They respect strength and lead with violence. They take joy in destroying those who are weaker than they are. They are what your mother said they are—ruthless, compassionless, soulless."

"That can't be entirely true," Ask said.

"Of course it is. I've seen it with my own eyes. I. . ." She hesitated. "I was part of it for many years."

"But, Orla, you changed. You aren't like that now. That tells me not every giant is bad, and, like you, perhaps some of them aren't happy about living in fear under Hyrrokkin's rule. I've been thinking," Ask elaborated, "we can't beat them all. What if we convince some of them to turn on Hyrrokkin? What if we break up the band, so to speak?"

Orla turned away. Deonte looked at Ask and shrugged.

"My motives aren't necessarily good, Ask. Yes, I escaped Hyrrokkin's control, but you have to understand I am still a giant, the natural enemy to some."

"Like my mother," Ask added.

"Yes, her especially. I don't exactly fit in here or with Hyrrokkin. In fact, I don't really belong anywhere anymore. I may look human, but it is not who I am."

That distant, melancholic look he recognized when she left his home the other night returned to her pale blue eyes. He wondered how many miles and years she crossed recalling the landscape of her lonely past.

Ask put his hand on her shoulder and endured the searing heat of the cold emanating from her glacial flesh. "You're wrong. You belong with us."

He shrugged at Deonte, as if to say, "Do you have my back now?"

Deonte didn't disappoint. He said, "Yeah, you may be a freak, but you're our cold-blooded freak."

This made Orla smile like Ask hadn't seen her smile before. It was broad and genuine and made her starkly pale skin glow brilliantly. He removed his numb hand from her shoulder and said, "We can do this. Hyrrokkin's reign is about to come to an end."

In the distance, Babe bleated.

CHAPTER 19

MJÖLNIR'S LAMENT

THE DREAM MEMORIES OCCURRED MORE frequently now, consisting of vignettes from his father's life, a sampling Ask had come to anticipate with some measure of excitement. True, some of the memories were painful, others confusing, but in all of them, Ask grew closer to his father.

His dream memory on this night traced his father through hills and woods to a clearing surrounded by thick birches. The still air lingered, undisturbed by the ambient sounds Ask had acclimated to in his world—the whooshing of a car on a nearby road, the rumble of a jet engine far overhead, the mechanical churnings of tractors working a field. In this dream sequence, the only sounds were chittering squirrels, clicking cicadas, whistling birds, and the rustling of leaves caught in occasional breezes. He guessed a time before modern technologies and conveniences.

A quick scan of his hands showed Ask that his father was already in his transformed state. A shadow confirmed his mass. His father stretched his arms above his head and then out to the sides. He settled into a crouching position, ax gripped with both hands and poised for swinging. For an hour, he witnessed his father step, maneuver, and slice the air with the ax. These movements, seemingly rudimentary at first, exhibited a certain grace through repetition. Ask also realized that by repeatedly swinging the ax, his grip felt more secure, his control of the weapon and himself more profound.

In a final dramatic exertion, Ask's father threw the ax at a large, thick cottonwood. The bit lodged deep into the trunk's heart, nearly splitting it in twain. By releasing the ax, his father returned to normal size, with some degree of pain, and fell back onto a patch of creeping thyme interspersed with moss and redolent of musky clover. The sky was a brilliant blue and the moss cool beneath him. Soon, lulled by the soft sounds surrounding him, Ask's father, and therefore Ask, fell asleep.

Ask remained fully aware that he was in a dream inside a dream recounting a memory. Transported to this new dreamscape, Ask wobbled with disorientation. The environment in which he found himself was cobbled with stone roads and sculpted with white marble buildings. Vines trellised above arches and hung from window ledges. A water fountain extolled a muscular figure gripping a massive serpent by the neck and a powerful hammer in the other. *A statue of Thor*, Ask thought.

The city to which these wonders belonged consisted of tall ageless solid structures surrounding the courtyard, where the fountain stood sentry. Ask thought it was odd that the streets seemed abandoned, particularly at such an hour. It must have been about two o'clock in the afternoon, judging by the angle of the sun, and he hadn't seen a single person. Not one person was even working. Such conditions made Ask shiver, and then he realized that, seeing this vision through his father, the shiver was Paul's. *What happened here?* passed through their shared mind.

A closer inspection of their surroundings showed a city already in significant disrepair. The marble buildings, which at first seemed undamaged, were riddled with deep gouges, or were missing entire sections of decorative cornices or friezes. Some of the arches had been reduced to partial frowns—entire sections dislodged like missing teeth. Many of the roofs bowed into buildings as if smashed from above by some powerful impact. The city was empty, Ask realized, because it was a war zone.

At that moment, an enormous mass of building, the shape and proportion of a colossal ceiling joist, landed on a nearby roof, causing an implosion, followed by a cloud of debris forcing its way through what remained of ornate stained-glass windows. The subsequent explosion exhaled through every orifice not sturdy enough to contain the blast. Only the solid oak door remained in place. Ask involuntarily turned away from the ensuing dust and covered his eyes. Just moments after the devastation, a giant walked by swinging a tree-sized club at anything in his path, including the statue of Thor. He jubilantly decapitated the hero with a single powerful stroke. "Dead and dead," the giant declared. Before the giant could relish in his victory, a spear gored him through the chest. Several warriors clad in winged helmets and thick metal armor materialized from alleys and dark doorways to hack at the giant's thick legs and slit his trunk-like throat.

Ask turned away from the grotesque scene as the blood pooled beneath the inert giant's body. Having disposed of their enemy, the warriors moved further into the city, where the clanging of swords composed a discordant music like many angry cymbals. His father decided to move away from the violence, pausing only briefly to stare at Thor's empty marble eyes seeking solace in the vastness of the skies.

Outside the city, the landscape was verdant with pine trees and intersected with streams and rivers. Log bridges offered access into the deeper reaches of the woods, where his father felt compelled to travel. In that unspoken compulsion, Ask felt the summoning of the ax again, but this time more potent, more powerful. He knew his father felt it, too. Despite walking for hours, his father pressed on without deviating from his course, sometimes fording shallow rivers to keep a true line toward the voiceless call that urged him on.

Just beyond the densest part of the woods, where the thickets grew in tangled masses that tore at his clothes and scratched his flesh and where the bushes, trees, and grasses formed a nearly impenetrable wall, there was a meadow upon which nestled a makeshift village. Several log homes had been hastily constructed, and dozens of villagers were in various stages of preparing for battle.

One enormous bearded man stood at an anvil and pounded pliable steel into a growing pile of stabbing weapons. Ask stared in marvel at the blue-white sparks that emanated from the blacksmith's hammer as it contacted the metal. He also puzzled over the fact that there was no foundry to heat the metal. Where was the blacksmith's fire to supply his labor? The blacksmith exposed the mystery when he grabbed a piece of metal and squeezed it until it glowed white-hot. He was producing the heat himself. These were the gods of his mother's story, the war of Orla's sadness, the Ragnarök of mythical legend. It was not, however, the Asgard Ask had imagined as a child.

Because he was evidently invisible to the inhabitants in this dream world, having failed to engage anyone in conversation, he meandered unimpeded from cabin to cabin, tent to tent, until he found the source of the energy that had brought him to this secluded place in the woods, where the depleting armies of the gods mustered their remaining forces, hidden by the gnarly vegetation of Asgardian wilderness. At the entryway, he stopped and listened, both at the pulse coursing through his veins and a heated discussion he happened upon, already in mid-debate.

"We can't let her have it," a tall, sleek god demanded passionately. His armor bore the crest of a howling wolf. A fresh wound slithered a jagged red course from forearm to wrist. "We all know what Thor had to do to get it back from her before." Mjölnir lay humming on the table in front of him.

"The devastation," someone in the back offered. "Laying waste to our cities. Murdering our kin."

"No one wants that." Ask recognized his mother's voice. She sat a few feet from the table. Next to her sat a cloaked figure wearing a low hanging hood, which prevented Ask from seeing a face. "We must take the hammer away," his mother continued. "We can't allow the lives lost in rescuing Mjölnir from Thor's tomb to mean nothing."

"And where do you propose we take such a powerful weapon? We can't hide it from her. It calls to that beast, and she will stop at nothing to reclaim it," the tall god with the wolf crest insisted. "Even now, she harries our army at the edge of the woods. And if she succeeds. . ."

"If she succeeds, we all know the outcome. That is why we must take it somewhere Hyrrokkin's connection to the hammer will be diluted," Ask's mother insisted.

"If only such a place existed. We could bury it in the ocean, and still, she would find it," the tall god contested.

The cloaked figure whispered, "To the human world."

An uncomfortable silence settled in the room. Finally, a short, stocky warrior with a blond beard said, "But that means we would no longer have its protection." He paused. "It means we've lost."

The cloaked figure laughed. "Look around, Dagr. We *have* lost. Now, we must survive. We send the hammer to Earth, and then we follow."

"Never," the tall god exclaimed. "We fight until we destroy them all."

"Your queen has spoken," the cloaked figure said.

"Tyr, noble warrior god, we are outnumbered," Ask's mother tried to reason. "Look around. All we have left is here at this camp. The cities are destroyed. The fields." She paused. "My beautiful orchard. There is nothing left for us here." She added, "If Hyrrokkin finds that hammer, she will finish off the few of us who remain. We have no choice."

Tyr nodded slowly, defeated, it appeared, in so many ways. In a voice only the weary and vanquished truly understand, he said, "We take Mjölnir to the human world. As the queen commands." He touched the weapon, as if in farewell, as if parting from an old friend, one he planned never to see again.

Idun wrapped the hammer in oilskin and pulled it close to her chest. It yielded to her willingly. "We should get out now while we still can."

"Go," Tyr said. "I will hold them off."

The cloaked figure quickly replied, "And I will stay with you."

Tyr shook his head. "No, my queen, you know what must be done. Go with Idun. You must survive."

"I will kill them all," the cloaked figure declared, slowly bringing her hand into a feeble fist. "Someday. When my powers restore." Idun hooked her arm around the queen's and assisted her out of the tent, inches from Ask. Somehow, his mother looked younger, the same but younger. Perhaps it was her eyes. They shone a bright gold, despite the circumstances that would send her away from her home forever.

While Ask felt the weight and poignancy of these vicarious partings profoundly, he realized the dream sequence with which he had accompanied his father was not primarily about these people, not Tyr, Dagr, Idun, or the queen. The stirrings from the hammer's energy proved as much. In all of Ask's personal encounters with the ax and his dream memories of his father's contact with Mjölnir, the energy had bolstered and empowered him. Not this time. As Idun passed with the hammer, the energy actually diminished, withdrawing it from, rather than depositing it, into Ask's essence. He grabbed a tent pole to steady himself as some of the energy left his body. He didn't have to read his father's mind to know, because they both experienced the same thing—that Mjölnir mourned. Like the crash after an adrenaline-filled training sequence, Ask was exhausted.

As Ask waited for the feeling to pass, he realized that this was not one of his father's own memories. It was of a time and place well before his father was even born. He would have no knowledge of the Asgard that was. No. This was something different. His father must also have experienced dream memories from time to time. This revelation made Ask feel closer to his father. But if it wasn't his father's memory, then whose was it? His mother's? Had she also connected with the hammer? That couldn't be. She was the bearer of the hammer, not its companion. He puzzled over this as he, following his father in this dream, stumbled after the hammer.

Suddenly it dawned on him: This was Mjölnir's memory. He knew because the sadness was ancient and the lament powerful. The hammer mourned for

Thor and also for the world he would never see again. After a few more steps, the woods around him began to blur until a brightness blotted everything out. He found himself staring at the sky in the field where his father had fallen asleep, sunlight blazing in his eyes.

Before Ask had time to fully readjust to the original dream memory of his father training with Bjornen, a loud voice called, "Awake just in time for me to take off your head, tiny human." Ask's father sat up to find a giant he knew by the name of Creskep trying to dislodge the ax still stuck in the cottonwood. "The last thing you will see is your ax slicing your neck." Creskep tugged and tugged at the ax, but it wouldn't come loose.

Ask felt the corners of his father's mouth curl into a smile. "Would you like me to help?"

"You can help by dying." Creskep grunted as he yanked with all the force he could muster, even placing a foot against the trunk for leverage.

"Is this going to take much longer?" his father goaded. "I can't loiter about in this field all day. Say, how long have you been going at that ax?"

Creskep snarled. "Almost long enough." He gave a tremendous tug, but the ax remained fixed in place.

One of the least endearing qualities of Creskep is that he wore a belt laced with the skulls of the gods and goddesses he'd killed over the centuries. His current count numbered about thirty. Despite the fun he was having with Creskep, Paul knew, and Ask perceived, the giant would soon lose interest in the irony of killing him with the ax and just use his own scimitar, an elongated blade with both edges of the crescent worked to a deadly sharpness.

As if on cue, Creskep released hold of the ax handle and drew his scimitar. "I suppose it makes little difference how you die, just as long as you're dead."

"Well, if you're through with it, I think I'll use my ax to defend myself." Paul held out his hand, and the ax came to him immediately.

This further infuriated Creskep. "Enjoy your little victory, small man," he said, despite Paul now standing nearly eye to eye with him. "It's the last one you'll have."

Creskep swung the scimitar at Paul's head. Just as he'd done in practice, Paul crouched, dipping low to avoid the blade. In one fluid motion, Paul parried with an upward swing of the ax, which connected with Creskep's chin. The giant stepped back, nearly falling. His arms flailed, and, in that split second, Paul flipped his grip and brought the ax down, slicing a gouge from Creskep's throat to his bellybutton, severing the belt and releasing skulls from their prolonged and profane imprisonment at the giant's waist. As Creskep teetered back out of Paul's reach, Paul returned to a crouch, bringing his ax to his right side, both hands on the handle, the cheek close to his own.

Creskep howled. "This isn't over." The blood pouring from his gut suggested otherwise. Hands gripping his torn clothes in an effort to staunch the flow, Creskep ran off into the woods. Ask tried telling his father to press his advantage, to finish the filthy giant. But even as he thought it, he knew it would be wrong. The energy of the ax told Ask to be patient, not to kill unless absolutely necessary. But Ask had never been very good at patience, and wasn't killing giants the point?

CHAPTER 20

GOAT WISDOM

ASK HAD NEVER HANDLED WAITING very well. His recent dream memory hadn't changed that. He thought about the final week of classes before summer break, how the clock hands seemed stuck in place and the days stretched on endlessly. He experienced similar trials in awaiting the mornings of Yule and Winter Nights for the feasts and gatherings of friends, or for family trips to Itasca or Rushmore, places where he could spend time with his parents and see new things. Conversely, so had he struggled with waiting for other kinds of things—a high stakes exam, a presentation like the one he delivered in Astronomy on the elemental compositions of stars last year, and the first few days scanning the horizon for his father to return after he disappeared. Waiting, on either end of the anxiety/excitement spectrum, was never fun and never easy.

He was certain that waiting for Orla to complete the first phase of their plan fell somewhere in between fear and excitement. Orla would be risking her life to tempt away a giantess who never left Hyrrokkin's side. The tricky part wasn't necessarily luring Grior away—Orla knew well what she desired and would set her trap accordingly—rather, it was Hyrrokkin recognizing her absence for a short time, while Orla secured Grior and assumed her identity. Plus, what if Hyrrokkin didn't fall for it? While Ask hadn't met Hyrrokkin face to face, he had heard many stories about her, none of which suggested she was stupid or easily manipulated. Orla would have to pull off Grior's appearance, her voice, and her attitude to make it work. But riskier than all of this was Orla's mission to plant doubts in some of the giants' heads. She would need to recognize those most disillusioned by Hyrrokkin's never-ending mission, isolate them from the pack, allude to troubles, real or perceived, and then convince them to leave. As Ask ruminated deeply about this plan, the more anxious he felt and the more doubtful he became of its success.

He wandered the halls at school in a daze, mind elsewhere, accompanied by second thoughts and what-ifs.

Maybe Deonte was right, he thought, *I think too much and do very little.*

By the end of the school day, he had all but convinced himself that the plan would fail and that he had sent Orla to certain death. As they deliberated the day after solidifying the plan, Deonte had told him he should scrap the idea and go on the offensive. "You don't win a football game by kneeling the ball every play and focusing on defense. Coach always says the best defense is a good offense." At the time, Ask countered that infiltrating the giants' lair and turning them against one another was a pretty bold offensive move. "But your plan is indirect and depends on one person. It's like standing around while one player does all the work. What happens if that player fumbles the ball or gets knocked out of the game?" Ask now conceded that point. Perhaps he should take the fight directly up Hyrrokkin's throat and hope she chokes instead of swallowing them whole.

To make matters worse, the fall sky was blanketed by low clouds that released misty rain that made everything wet, cold, and uncomfortable. Perfect conditions, Ask pondered, for Orla, and that sent his mind looping back to berating himself for his misguided decisions. Lowering himself from the school bus, he trudged the long dirt road to his house like a condemned man approaching his execution. The elm at the intersection of his driveway and the dirt road below it reminded him a bit of a gallows straight out of the old West. If Orla died on account of his foolish plan, he deserved no better.

He stopped at the pasture fence next to Babe. He held out his hand, and Babe nudged it. "I think I really screwed up," he said. "I don't know if Orla will make it out alive. All I'm doing is sitting here waiting. What if she fails?"

Ask didn't expect a response. He thought Babe could talk only when transformed by the ax's energy, so he was surprised when Babe stopped pulling up clumps of grass and said, "She's been fighting this war for a long time. If she agreed to your plan, she must have thought it could work. You have to trust she'll do her part and be there for her when it's time to do ours."

This made a lot of sense to Ask. "Have you been able to talk the whole time, even before I found the ax?"

Babe bleated, and it sounded like laughter. "What do you think?"

Ask nodded and forced a smile. He then asked Babe, "What would my father have done?" Ask hoped the answer to making the plan work might reveal itself through his father, as so many answers to the curious puzzle of the past few months had.

"Your father didn't have all the answers," Babe said. "He fought Hyrrokkin for a long time. Centuries, in fact. At first, he thought he could reason with the giants. He even convinced one to give up the fight. Koerl killed him. Next, he tried to anticipate their attacks and protect those in their path. Sometimes this worked. Sometimes it didn't. He also tried a direct assault. He barely escaped with his life. For the last couple of decades, he kept mostly to the farm, hidden, responding only when Hyrrokkin discovered one of the gods or goddesses."

"Do you know what happened to him? Why he disappeared?" Ask hoped Babe was there when it happened and could make the final few details of this mystery clear.

"We returned from a sort of skirmish with the giants. We had to escape a rather hairy situation. When we got home, Paul put the ax in the shed. We both shrunk to our normal size. He started toward the house and then went back to the shed for something. I have not seen him since," Babe said.

More to himself, trying to cobble together an explanation, Ask said, "Does this mean he vanished into thin air or was pulled into some portal to another dimension?"

Babe bleated again. This time, it did not sound like laughter but like a lament. "I have no idea. I was grazing, so he could have slipped away while I ate."

Ask nodded. He placed a hand on Babe's head and rubbed between the nubby horns. Babe lifted a back leg and kicked at the air. Sweet spot. "Did you know him well?"

The dreams in which Ask witnessed the world through his father's eyes made him realize he had known almost nothing about the man. Even watching some of the events of his father's life play out as memories taught him very little of Paul's character, of his true self.

"He awakened me from an animal stupor some hundred years ago or so. He never explained why, or maybe I couldn't understand the reason at first, but it became clear to me that he needed a companion, a strong being to join the fight against the giants. He always treated me as an equal, not as an object or a pet, but a friend. He came to me like you have today to seek my advice." Then he added, "A little to the left," and leaned into Ask's hand.

Ask smiled. That sounded like his father. Again, to himself, he asked aloud, "I wonder how he'd feel about our chances to defeat Hyrrokkin?"

"Your father was unable to do it," Babe said. "But he was Paul, and you are Ask. You have help, something he didn't have. Your plan is as good as or better than anything Paul tried. I'd say your chances are better than if you do nothing."

Ask stopped rubbing. "That's your wisdom, Babe?" he said with uncertainty. "Doing something is better than nothing?"

"I can't predict the future if that's what you're after. I only know what Paul and I tried and what you and your friends plan to try. There is no certainty in this world—that is the only truth I know for certain. But, if you trust each other, take care of each other, and fight for one another, your chances of defeating the giantess increase considerably."

Ask felt oddly comforted by this. If the future, as Babe suggested, was entirely unknown, a blank slate on which to write, then why couldn't they defeat Hyrrokkin? Why couldn't Orla set in motion the first phase of the plan and prepare the way for them to win? The weight of imminent failure suddenly lifted from his mind.

Before he went inside to see his mother, he said, "Thanks." A few more paces, and Ask stopped. "Say," he called back over his shoulder. "Why blue, though? When you transform, why do you turn blue?"

After a long bleat that must be laughter, Babe said, "Wouldn't you like to know?"

CHAPTER 21

TALES OF HYRROKKIN

That night Ask dreamed a new memory of his father. The setting was familiar. His father left the North Dakota farmstead of Ask's childhood as night swallowed the shadows of evening. He tramped through cornfields, only thigh-deep in his transformed shape. The moon was large and bright, either just waxing toward or waning away from its brightest stage of the month. Wetness pervaded the air from lingering humidity. The crops' tassels gathered silvery dew, brilliant shimmers in the moonlight. It must be late July or August, Ask assumed. Babe tromped behind him, his massive mouth scooping up rows of the corn as he went, his jaws moving in a rhythm Ask found reassuring, even peaceful. He had not felt so relaxed in a long time. Yet stirring deep within him was an anxiety he was unable to explain. That gnawing anxiety of waiting that had pursued him all day tugged uncomfortably at his guts. He wasn't sure if this was an emotion he brought with him to the memory or something his father felt about this journey.

As he traveled farther into the countryside, his father crouched more and more, and Babe quieted his chewing. There were fires up ahead, sputtering amidst trees, whose trunks and leaf-laden branches cast dark silhouettes beneath the moon, sporadically muting the firelight as Ask advanced. At a massive cottonwood on the opposite side of the fires, Ask's father stopped. He glanced quickly around the trunk. The view through Paul's eyes brought the reason for the anxiety. There, huddled around the fire, sat, stood, or lay several giants. None were disguised as humans. Each was less than an arm's distance from some kind of weapon. One giant turned a cow on a spit over the largest fire pit. Three dozen fish flopped in death throes on a tarp.

"Hurry up," one of the giants said, "I'm starving."

The supposed cook replied, "Eat some fish while you wait. It's better than this nasty cow flesh, anyway."

"This heat," another giant chimed in, "will melt us all."

"Stop your bellyaching," a giantess interjected in a deep, resonant voice. "You eat when the meal is ready. We eat what's available to survive. We are on the hunt. Your whining for creature comforts is a coward's lament. Be warriors."

Ask had never seen Hyrrokkin nor heard her voice, but he knew it was she who spoke, because when she did everyone listened, and the complaining stopped. A low growl emanated near her. The wolf, Ask remembered. If Koerl's mount was so powerful and lithe, as he recalled from their fight, he wondered how much more dangerous Hyrrokkin's wolf would be—the alpha of the pack.

When Paul's father stepped into a clearing near the tree, a move Ask didn't quite understand since it put him completely at the mercy of the giant horde, he was able to see Hyrrokkin for the first time. She was larger than the other giants. Her dark hair was braided tightly to her skull to resemble, Ask conjectured, the vertebrae of a spine. Pale gray arms each the diameter of two large men standing back-to-back, she was muscle and girth with a gnarled disposition manifested in a perpetual scowl. She bore a couple of tattoos, one that encircled the bicep of her left arm in the design of barbed wire and the other a sickle under her right eye. Her face was pocked with what Ask could only imagine battle scars from weapons that didn't cut deeply enough. On the ground at her feet lay her albino wolf with its own array of scars from snout to tail. It fixed its gaze on Ask's father as if he were prey. Hyrrokkin held the spear in her right hand. A dull yellow light pulsed along its shaft and glinted in pale winks across its sharp steel tip.

"What have we here?" boomed a voice Ask recognized immediately. Koerl stood a few feet left of Hyrrokkin, his snarly wolf mount baring its teeth. "Come to surrender?"

"No," his father said. "I've come to talk."

"You've come to die, ax wielder." Koerl stepped forward, posing for attack.

Hyrrokkin held up a hand. Koerl, now brandishing his ice sword, lowered his arm.

"I'm not interested in palavering, unnatural spawn of the ax," Hyrrokkin said. "I expect you to hand over that weapon so I may reunite it with the spear."

Hyrrokkin stood at least a head taller than all the other giants, nearly twice as tall as Ask's father transformed. Despite his situation, Ask couldn't help but watch the dim yellow energy pulses of the spear slowly but certainly fade. What would become of Bjornen or Mjölnir if Hyrrokkin succeeded in conquering them?

"I'm here to do no such thing. I came to reason with you, Hyrrokkin. This fight has gone on long enough. Revenge, you must realize by now, is an empty quest, one that will carry on forever if you let it and will never provide a fulfilling resolution. Revenge can't fix the past."

"Child." Hyrrokkin shook her head. "You know nothing of revenge or immortality. You think of endings because you are always moving toward one. Mortality produces morals because you fear death and imagine some great judgment. You know your end begins the moment you are born. I'm not interested in making nice to indulge your fleeting notions of right and wrong because you fear death. I want to rid the future of a race of fallen gods who imprisoned and hurt my people for eons. I carry on this fight for a future without gods, a future for giants."

"And then what? You live happily ever after? You set aside your swords and live in peace with humans? Till these fields, perhaps? Fish these rivers? Lounge about recalling your glory days?" Paul challenged.

Hyrrokkin laughed. "I said nothing about happiness, nor of peace. Like us, war is eternal."

Several of the giants sniggered at Hyrrokkin's bold confession. Ask shuddered. So, his father wasn't just protecting his family and mother's friends; he was protecting all of humankind. His mother and Orla were right about giants: They only knew how to kill.

"So, give me the ax, and I'll promise a swift end to your miserable existence," Hyrrokkin concluded. The albino wolf leapt to its feet and began to circle.

"Idun warned me. She said you haven't the capacity to see rationally, to forgive, to move past the old hatreds. I now concede her point."

At that, Paul swung the ax mightily against the base of a tall, thick pine tree. The massive branches crashed down on the makeshift camp, driving the cow into coals and giants into each other. Hyrrokkin boomed a command, and the giants tore at heavy pine branches to jostle themselves free. By the time the tree was rent into shreds and needles, Paul was miles away, riding Babe, who was surprisingly fast for a big, stout blue ox. Ask wasn't sure if his own adrenaline surged, or if it was his father's, as Babe topped hills in broad leaps beneath the silvery moon, but he found himself smiling widely. He tipped his head back and shouted victoriously.

The moment soon passed, however, and Ask found himself contemplating the seriousness of Hyrrokkin's declarations. She was more dangerous than he could ever have imagined. It was one thing to hear Orla talk vaguely about the terrible things she had seen Hyrrokkin do. It was another altogether to see and hear and feel that evil himself. A fear for Orla's safety resurfaced in his mind, followed very quickly by a fear of her success. Fighting Koerl alone made the idea of fighting an entire horde of giants that much more frightening. Even in this dream memory, where the consequences had already come to pass, he worried for everyone's safety. Yet, despite the increasing weight of what he knew was coming, Ask was grateful for the dream. He now understood who he was dealing with.

Ask was surprised how far his father had gone to find the giants' camp. He and Babe didn't return until just before dawn, as an orange sliver of light spread across the horizon. Babe transformed back to a goat and nuzzled the grass in the pasture, while his father shrunk to his normal size, having replaced the ax in the shed. Ask noticed that the pain he experienced in the dream memory of his father's first transformation had returned. It wasn't nearly as pronounced, but he gritted his teeth through the popping and pulling of joints and bones. A dull ache persisted. His father staggered toward the house, tired from the long night and aching from the transformation, longing for the comfort of a mattress and pillow. Just as he reached the front door, a whisper called to him from the shed. The sound was not audible but transmitted as a pulse coursing through his body, the sort of biological Morse code he experienced during the summoning. He wondered how long it had been since his father had felt that pull, heard that call. He immediately turned back to the shed and made his way hastily to the ax.

This series of events, Ask realized, matched what Babe had told him. His father put the ax away and made his weary way to the house, only to return to the shed moments later. He was finally going to find out what happened. Before entering the shed, his father turned back to the house and paused his gaze on Ask's bedroom window. There was a recognition in that lingering look. He knew something Ask couldn't fully make out. Just as Paul entered the shed, Ask awoke.

"No!" he yelled, sitting up. "Take me back. I need to know what happened," he pleaded. But he was wide awake, and the dream was over.

His mother rushed into his room. "What is it, Ask? What's going on?"

"I saw it. I was Dad the day he disappeared. I was about to see what happened, but then I woke up before. . ."

"Before what?" His mother was holding him.

"Before I saw him go," Ask said. "He looked at my window before he went into the shed. It's like he knew he wouldn't be coming back."

His mother comforted him. "Even if we never learn the truth about what happened to your father, we know he loved us. Everything he did, Ask, was for you and me. I know I haven't told you this—in all fairness, there is a great deal I haven't told you until now—but we couldn't have children for a very long time, centuries, in fact. We always suspected it was because he was mortal, and I was not. Over time, the energy in the ax changed him in many ways. Not only could he transform, and not only was his life extended, but he began to show signs of an immortal. One of those signs was you."

His first inclination, which he voiced aloud, was to say, "Gross," and then he said, "Am I fifteen or older?"

"What?" his mother asked.

"Am I fifteen years old or a hundred and fifty?"

"You're fifteen," she said.

"I'm sure the apples helped keep him alive," he replied, returning to her initial comments.

"What are you talking about?"

"Your apples. The ones that keep the gods young forever," Ask said.

"What do you know about those apples?"

He backtracked a bit. "You made one and gave it to me."

"Yes, but I don't recall saying anything about what the apples do or what they're for. How did you know?"

"The ax tells me things. In my sleep. I dream memories." He paused. "Dad's memories. I saw you separate the ax. I felt him lift it for the first time, felt the fullness of the energy force his body up and out, and I felt his pain. . ." He paused again. "You gave him an apple to help."

She grimaced at the mention of Paul's pain.

"Oh, and then I looked up myths on the internet," Ask added.

"Clever," she said. "Those myths aren't always true, you know."

"Were they right about the apples?" he asked

She smiled. "Sometimes they get lucky."

Ask nodded and then looked out the window. He thought about his father's close call in Hyrrokkin's camp. A quick decision and the fortunate fall of a massive tree were all that stood between his father and failure. What if Ask didn't have the same good fortune?

"What is it?" his mother asked.

"What?" Ask said, distracted. He hesitated before asking, "What do you know about Hyrrokkin?"

She sat silently on the edge of his bed, thinking. "That's a difficult question to answer. Hyrrokkin is unusually large and strong, even for a giant. She has always been cruel. She once took Mjölnir but lost him again to Thor. She is intelligent and, one could argue, charismatic. She commands respect and rules absolutely. As you have probably guessed, she does not permit herself to lose. She has and will continue to chase me to the ends of the world. But for all that power and persistence, she has never been able to persuade the magical weapons of Asgard to yield to her demands." She looked intently at Ask, perhaps having discerned his intentions for asking. "She's dangerous. You need to stay away from her."

"You said it yourself," Ask began, "she will never give up this relentless hunt. Something has to be done. We have to confront her."

Idun looked down. "That's what your father said the night before he disappeared. 'We have to confront her.' I don't think that's the wise course of action."

"But we need to *take* action. You said she doesn't control the weapons of Asgard. Orla told me the spear she stole is unruly. It may be the advantage we have to defeat her."

What he didn't say was, "I'm going to get it back." At some point, yes, he would need to tell her, particularly if the ax and spear were to be reunited. But he would cross that bridge when he got to it.

Without a word, his mother stood, pivoted toward the door, and left the room. She returned moments later with a square-cut amethyst gem on a leather necklace. The thin leather straps were worn with age. "This torc is from the old kingdom. It protects the worthy wearer by deflecting weapons wielded by hate." She slipped it over his head. "The energy of the ax is powerful, but the amulet magnifies that power. The fullness of its power, however, depends entirely on how you use it. I want you to have it in case Hyrrokkin finds you."

Later, as Ask was preparing for school, he touched the torc, running the smooth amulet between his fingers. He tucked it under the tunic he now wore unfailingly beneath his shirt. He wished he had one to give to Orla. In two nights, he would know if the first stage of their plan had worked.

CHAPTER 22

PREPARATIONS

Ask and Deonte used to play a game they called War. In this game, they would dress up in fatigues and move about the wooded area near Ask's house as stealthily as possible. The idea was that the two boys were soldiers caught behind enemy lines. The only way they would survive was to sneak back to safety, usually delineated by a single line of pines on the other side of Ask's house. The challenge, always, was to crawl, roll, run, and take cover to avoid detection in the open spaces between the wooded area and the pines. In this space lay the pasture containing Babe, who always seemed to bleat if they came too close. If they crossed the space on the other side of the opening, they risked Ask's mother, who they consistently referred to as an enemy government agent, calling out to them or waving, effectively blowing their concealment and alerting the enemy army. Of course, punishment from his mother wasn't so bad. She typically brought them a bowl of grapes or cherries to refresh them from the hot afternoon sun. The best way to reach the tree line successfully, especially in late summer, was to cross from the trees to the field, where corn, alfalfa, or soybeans grew. Among the tall stalks or beneath the thick leaves, they could hunch or crawl to the pine trees, leaving only a short distance of ten feet to cross in the open. Of course, there was an actual risk in taking to the fields. If the farmer who owned the fields saw them "messing around in his crops," he would tell his parents, and Ask would be punished. Come to think of it, Ask and Deonte rarely won this game. Why did he have to remember this particular memory now?

The realization of his failed attempts at a game called War sat heavily on his mind as he ate lunch, or at least tried to eat lunch, while attempting to convince Deonte to stay home tonight. They had selected a Friday night for the secret rendezvous with Orla and subsequent attack on the giant horde. Deonte had a Saturday football game, so he said there was nothing standing in the way of his helping. They had worked out a time and spot to meet a few miles south of his parents' farm, where two dirt roads met at an intersection. Because the corn had already been harvested, there would be no concealment, no way to cross open fields without being seen, no hunching among corn stalks or crawling through alfalfa. Ask and Deonte would have to rely on dark clothing and clouds to obscure the three-quarter moon they were certain to encounter.

Ask pushed his tray away. He knew what they were facing, and his stomach wouldn't let him forget it. Deonte, on the other hand, did not let the graphic description Ask had provided of his dream memory of Hyrrokkin deter him from eating. In fact, once he had wolfed down his own soybean-enhanced hamburger and processed cheese, he motioned to Ask. "You gonna eat that?"

Ask shook his head. He wondered what Orla would have thought of their menu that day. Deonte tucked right in, finishing not only Ask's burger but his excessively oily tater tots as well.

"Why do you let this bother you so much?" Deonte asked as he scooped up a remaining glob of ketchup with the final oily tot. "Orla is a freaking giant. You grow into this ginormous lumberjack, carry a huge ax, and are basically indestructible. If that's not impressive enough, you have me. I juke, rat-a-tat, and do all that," Deonte said, imitating a sports announcer Ask recognized.

Despite himself, Ask laughed. Then, serious again, he said, "Hyrrokkin is not Greely Hempstead, okay?" Greely Hempstead was Fargo South's star linebacker. Colleges were already recruiting him, even though he was still only a junior. Deonte had half-joked, half-bragged once that he could run circles around Greely if the coach just put him in the varsity lineup. Ask had reminded him that he wasn't a running back, so the coach would not even consider it. Of Hyrrokkin, Ask said, "She's the largest giant I've ever seen. . ."

Deonte cut in. "I know, arms as big as Hummers and ugly as sin. Look, my friend, the bigger they are, the harder they fall."

"Or the more quickly they squash you." Ask couldn't help himself. A persistent and nagging pessimism filled the stomach he hadn't filled with food.

"No way, man. I'm wearing my cleats tonight. You know, game night. I'm coming ready to play."

"This is all a big joke to you, isn't it?" Ask accused, becoming suddenly angry. "I didn't tell you this, but that night my father left Hyrrokkin's encampment, he disappeared. I could sense in him, even as large as he was wielding the ax, fear. He walked into the lion's den, and only by luck and quick thinking did he make it out alive." He paused before continuing. "Just hours later, he stumbled into our shed and never came out again."

Deonte lowered his head. "I'm sorry, man. I'm just trying to lighten the mood. No sane person wouldn't be afraid of doing what we're going to do. I just want you to know you can trust me. I know I don't have a power like you and Orla, but I can help. They won't be expecting me. You, yes. Orla, for sure. Not me. I'm your wildcard."

Ask nodded. "I won't let anything happen to you."

"Wrong," Deonte said. "I won't let anything happen to you."

They both laughed.

AT THE END OF THE school day, the friends walked slowly toward Deonte's house. They were hours from their rendezvous with Orla. Ask didn't feel the need to rush. He wanted to enjoy a few lingering moments of what he'd considered his normal life while it lasted.

"You're quiet," Deonte said. "You okay?"

"It's cold early this year," Ask responded. He pulled his light jacket closer around his neck and tucked his arms into his sides. "I should have worn my parka."

"It might snow tonight," Deonte confirmed. "Saw it on the news this morning."

Ask didn't know if the storm would prove an advantage for them or not, though he did remember how Orla seemed to thrive in the cold. Since Hyrrokkin was a giant, like Orla, the cold would give her the advantage.

They walked south out of town, following a long road into a neighborhood nestled beneath tall elms and cottonwoods. Deonte's house was at the end of a cul-de-sac. It was the oldest house around. Deonte claimed it was built in the late 1800s, at least that's what his parents told him. He said all the modern portions of the house were additions, expanded as technologies provided such luxuries as plumbing and electricity. He even claimed he knew where the outhouse had been. Ask was skeptical, but he had no proof to contradict this claim, so he just went along with it. Still, he didn't miss a chance to tell Deonte he thought his theory was crap.

Inside, the varying stages of renovations to the home gave it a peculiar layout. For one, you could get downstairs from two separate sets of stairs at opposite ends of the house. One led into a family room and the other into a cellar. The cellar was not accessible from the family room side of the basement. Deonte explained he was not allowed to go in the cellar because his mother stored food there that she didn't want him eating. This made sense to Ask, who regularly watched in awe as Deonte ate an entire pizza, both a foot long and a half sub sandwich, or an entire large box of cereal in one sitting. He imagined Deonte's mother had her reasons for making the food off-limits.

The strangest design of all, however, was a circular room, almost like a turret or tower at the back of the house. It was the only room with a second level. The entire structure was stone and reminded Ask of a castle. The room itself contained an enormous library with books in cases that spanned from floor to ceiling. He had never been to the second floor of this room because,

Deonte explained, there had always been and always would be a lock on the thick wooden trap door in the ceiling. The locked door had been a mysterious object of speculation for the friends over the years. That interest, however, diminished with time, and the mystery dulled. Now, the door was just another fixture in the room.

The purpose of the visit to Deonte's home was rather strategic in nature. So neither of them would be missed, each boy planned to ask his mother if he could stay the night at the other's house. That old lie that everybody at one point or another think they alone have devised and believe wholeheartedly in its flawless execution.

Deonte called from the foyer, "Mom?"

No lights on in the house. No sound from the kitchen or the library, except a few creaks and moans as the structure's old bones shifted and settled. They checked the rooms but still found no sign of Deonte's mother. He shrugged. "Probably visiting a friend. She'll be back soon."

They raided the refrigerator and cupboards. Deonte gathered sliced ham and turkey, tomatoes, lettuce, a bag of bread, and mustard and mayo. He set to constructing sandwiches, two for himself and one for Ask. Ask shook his head. The thought of eating still set his stomach to somersaults. Deonte shrugged and kept making the three sandwiches.

In an hour, after Deonte had polished off the sandwiches and the two boys finished their second round of *Mario Kart*, Deonte called out to his mother again. No answer. "This isn't like her," he said. "Something's wrong. It's supposed to be her day off."

Ask heard Deonte talk, but he couldn't process the words. He stared, instead, at the door to the library, where a new sort of energy similar to but different from the ax emanated. He'd never noticed it before converging with the ax. The energy wasn't necessarily calling to him, but he could sense it palpably. He stood, padded over to the library on his sock-laden feet, and opened the door. The drowsy light of a sunny fall afternoon streamed across the floor and climbed up and over a desk. The stairs leading to the locked trap door in the ceiling remained in shadows.

Deonte whispered in his ear, "What is it?" Ask started at Deonte's sudden appearance at his side. "That door," Deonte said, "is locked, and I don't have a key. Remember?"

Ask made a fist. "We could get in if we wanted to."

"But, why? We've tried for years. You know the door won't budge. What's the urgency now?" Deonte asked.

It's true. For as long as Ask could remember, he and Deonte had plotted ways to force that door to satiate a curiosity formed from its interminable inaccessibility and from lack of a sufficient explanation. Still, they'd given up that quest long ago.

"To know what's there. I feel something." Ask instinctively touched the amulet around his neck.

Deonte motioned consent with his hand. Ask ascended the iron circular stairs until he was within striking distance of the door. Drawing back slightly, he punched. To his surprise, the door remained locked. In fact, it didn't budge at all. He pulled his arm back further and really laid into it. Nothing.

"Go on, then," Deonte urged. "Give it a good one."

Ask put both hands up and pushed with all his might, channeling, he felt, all of the energy the ax had transferred to him. Still, the door remained locked and shut tight.

"What's going on in here?"

Both boys swung around to see Deonte's mother and, surprisingly, Ask's mother standing in the entryway to the library.

"Deonte, I thought I told you that room was off-limits."

"Yes, Mom. I'm sorry. We were just curious." He did not say that Ask felt compelled to reveal its secrets. Ask imagined that Deonte hadn't said much at all to his mother about Ask's new power. Any human who hadn't seen it for themselves wouldn't believe it anyway. In fact, Deonte *had* seen it with his own eyes and still hadn't come to terms with it for a couple of weeks.

Calmly and without sternness, Ask's mother said, "Son, you won't be able to force that door. It's protected by energy as strong as yours." She walked over, set her hand below the trapdoor, and closed her eyes. The lock clicked, and the door sagged wearily on old hinges. A child could now kick it in. "Come away from there," she told Ask. "What's in that room isn't for you."

Ask was both puzzled and intrigued. Why was his mother speaking so openly about his power in front of Deonte's mom, and why had she used her power so publicly?

But most confusing of all was this: If the room that so distinctly called to him moments ago wasn't calling him, to whom was it calling? *Of course*, Ask thought, *Deonte*. And even without knowing why the energy called for Deonte, Ask knew it was true.

CHAPTER 23

DEONTE'S GIFT

ASK KNEW VERY LITTLE ABOUT Deonte's father. Sure, his parents and Deonte's parents had been friends as long as Ask could remember, but the man, though gentle and patient, kept to himself and generally said no more than a few words each visit.

Ask assumed a lot of things when he was a child. He thought, for one, that his own parents were ordinary people, unusually talented to him in terms of growing bounteous gardens and talking to fish, but more or less just like everyone else's parents. He guessed the same about Deonte's parents—that they were special in ways Deonte knew but also much like other parents.

Ask had not considered that the friendship between their parents might extend far, far back, to a time before, in a world beyond this one. Was it possible that he and Deonte were more alike than he knew? Deonte's mom, after all, didn't seem shocked or surprised that Idun could unlock a door with the wave of a hand.

The four of them stood in the turret-shaped library beneath the door that may as well have been an elephant hanging from the ceiling because no one could ignore any longer that the mystery once kept hidden from Deonte was now made available to him. Plus, it had required magic to open. Why was no one surprised by this? Ask waited for an explanation in speechless astonishment.

Everyone looked at Deonte. His mother finally spoke. "How do I begin?" she asked herself aloud. "Idun knew your father. Neither of them is from *here.*" Then she clarified. "He was from another place, another time. He escaped when a war between gods and giants destroyed their world, and the gods had all but been wiped out."

Deonte nodded blankly. He and Ask had heard and talked about this story before. Of course, she didn't know that. But to hear his mother confirm the story in her own words, as if she were part of it too, must have felt surreal, even a little disorienting. Ask thought of his own mother's confession and how she produced an apple out of nothing. The world seemed topsy-turvy for a while. No doubt, this was a lot for Deonte to process. Ask's friend remained silent.

She continued. "When I met your father about fifteen years ago, he had been running from the giants who followed the survivors of that war here, to Earth. He was known during his time in Asgard as Threjald, gifted with speed and strength. He gave himself the name of John, something indistinct, general enough that he could hide in plain sight. He took a family name from a man who he met centuries ago called Henry."

Ask wondered why that name sounded so familiar.

"It's ironic, really," she continued, "that your father, despite trying to keep a low profile, actually became a bit of a legend. That strength and speed earned him a certain reputation in the railroad industry."

That's it, thought Ask. Yes, John Henry allegedly raced a steam-engine machine to clear a tunnel for trains in West Virginia or somewhere back east. Ask had come across this legend several times as he searched for information about Paul Bunyan. Their stories did have some intriguing parallels.

Aloud Ask said, "But I thought John Henry—the legend, I mean—died like a hundred years ago, a burst heart from racing a steam drill."

Deonte's mom nodded. "It was at that time he had to leave. His fame had placed an unintended target on him. The giants, he told me, took talk of legends very seriously. Any word of a human performing superhuman feats, they suspected, must not be human at all, but a god from the old world. He soon saw signs of their scouts investigating. He made his way west to Minnesota. He worked in Minneapolis for a time at the railyard. Kept his powers in check. Eventually, I met him, and we married. That"—she pointed to the room above them—"is your father's study. Idun used her power to seal the room when. . ." She couldn't say the rest. Instead, she added, "To keep it safe."

She motioned for Deonte to climb the steps and take a look. With the ceiling within reach, Deonte pushed the door open. Before going inside, he motioned for Ask to follow with a wave of his hand. The light had faded, so the objects in the room appeared as shadows. Ask could make out a worn trunk along one side of the curved wall, a desk and chair along another side, an antique wardrobe along another, and a circular rug on the floor in the middle of the room. Deonte felt along the wall until he found a light switch. The room was, actually, quite stark, but the energy inside was potent. Ask could hear and feel it hum.

Deonte went immediately to the wardrobe, as if the voiceless impulse called him there directly. No lock prevented him from opening the doors, though Ask was certain that if he'd tried the handles would have resisted him. Before it revealed its contents, Ask wondered if this wardrobe might be a portal to another land filled with magical and mystical creatures, a sort of C.S. Lewis transportation device. However, no pine trees appeared behind rows of fur coats when the doors were spread wide for all to see. Inside was an old, oil-stained pair of striped overalls dangling from a hanger, a robe made from a cloth that resembled velvet but felt entirely unlike velvet to the touch, and a pair of crusty old work boots. Deonte pushed the clothing aside and grabbed the boots. In his hand, they emitted a purplish glow, barely visible, but Ask knew its meaning. It was a different strand of the energy he had seen in the ax and the spear.

"Yes, Deonte," his mother said. She and Idun had joined them in the study. "That is your birthright. Those boots make you fast and give you strength. Your father explained it to me. He used them to help others, like Ask's father."

Deonte had been quiet the entire time while his mother revealed his father's secret. "How did he die?"

Silence. The room suddenly felt like a tomb. Ask understood this was the right question. It was, even after the surprising details of his father's life, the only question that really mattered.

"Well. . ." Dr. Henry sat down on the trunk. "After you were born, he stopped running from the giants. He felt his responsibility to you, to us, meant he needed to fight back. He and Paul sometimes worked together, sometimes separately, to stop the giants from their genocidal attacks on Asgardians and their friends and families. I was told that one night he followed some of Hyrrokkin's scouts into a massive ravine somewhere in the badlands. The entire horde awaited. Because he was fast, he knew he could outrun them. Paul told me he found him miles from the encampment the next night, a small hole in his chest where he believed a spear had mortally wounded him. Paul performed the Asgard funeral rite and sent his ashes back to the energy. He brought the boots here for safekeeping."

Deonte's jaw set and his fist clenched around the collar of the boots. Ask knew what Deonte was thinking, how he was feeling. When Ask believed Koerl had killed his father, he felt the same way. Seeing the rage growing in Deonte's eyes now made Ask realize that knowing what happened to his own father might not bring him the closure or peace he thought it would.

"Son, I'm sorry I never told you. Please understand that his death wouldn't have made any sense without knowing about his life. It would have been for you, at the time, an unbelievable tale. I wanted to spare you the weight of all of this."

"I might have surprised you," Deonte mumbled.

"The situation was complicated, and I didn't know how to tell you or what to say. You were so young. When Mrs. Banyun—Idun—told me about Ask and how you knew and were helping him, I realized it was time."

"Time to end my suffering from not knowing? Of thinking Dad simply disappeared? Time to stop lying?" Deonte challenged.

This last criticism must have affected Deonte's mother deeply; she closed her eyes and brushed an errant tear aside. "Yes, to fully explain what happened to your father. I never intended for my not telling you what happened to become a lie. But, I suppose you are right: A lie, for any reason, is still a lie." She paused. "I guess I felt that if I didn't say the words out loud, he wouldn't really be gone, that he might just show up again, as he had so many times before. I know it doesn't make sense to keep it from you. I did it mostly for me, and that was selfish. I'm sorry." With conviction, then, she continued, "But the truth is your father died a hero, Deonte. He sacrificed all for us, for the protection of the family he made here and those he fought beside in Asgard."

Ask wasn't entirely sure what Deonte was thinking, but his friend seemed to come to terms with something because he nodded and dropped the boots on the floor. As Deonte slipped them on and began to lace them up, Ask kept thinking the boots looked terribly uncomfortable. He remembered trying on a pair of boots at a thrift store that had already conformed to someone else's feet. The folds and stretches were in all the wrong places. He knew if he wore them for too long, he would get blisters all over. "How do they fit?" he asked.

Deonte stepped lightly on each booted foot and then walked around the room. "Fine," he said. "You know, these are the most comfortable boots I've ever worn." And it was clear to Ask that Deonte wasn't exaggerating. He moved lithely, each step accepting, even aiding his stride. "They feel like Air Jordans," Deonte added. "My favorite pair. The ones Dad bought me years ago." Ask knew the shoes Deonte compared them to. They were Jordan 4 Retros, black and gray with red accents. Deonte's father had been a huge fan of Michael Jordan. Deonte wore the Jordans every day for years, until he finally had to discard them because the sole was separating from the toe box, partly from wear and partly from Deonte outgrowing them.

Then, something miraculous happened that neither Ask nor Deonte expected. The old work boots transformed into the pair of Jordans Deonte mentioned, except they appeared new, no signs of the wear and tear that prompted Deonte to finally dispose of the pair they resembled.

"Did you see that?!" Deonte shouted. A purple spark shone in his eye. "Check this out."

Between blinks, Deonte was gone. Ask heard a loud crash near the front entryway. He rushed down the stairs and out of the study to see what happened. Moving so quickly, Deonte hadn't been able to open the solid wood door before running into it. He lay on the floor, hand pressed against his forehead and laughing. He stood up, opened the door, and disappeared only to reappear a few seconds later.

"Where did you go?" Ask said.

"I went for a run down the street and back." He picked a few leaves and a small branch from his hair. "Got into a little tussle with a lilac bush." He shrugged.

"Cool!"

As Ask and Deonte marveled at the boots-turned-Jordans that endowed the wearer with super-speed, Ask's mother cleared her throat. The boys looked up from the shoes.

"This is not the only reason I came by," she said. "So, Orla sent a message," his mother began. "It sounds like things are going as planned. Can you tell me what that means?"

So much for the sleeping-at-each-other's-houses tactic, Ask realized. He wondered how his mother got ahold of a message meant for him. He also knew she'd disapprove if he told her the whole truth, so he filtered the plan a bit. "Well, Orla is spying on Hyrrokkin, so we know what she's up to."

"And where does the attack on the horde to reclaim the spear come in?" his mother asked.

Ask sighed. "Look, we have to act. Koerl has been waiting to attack for weeks. Hyrrokkin's anger is growing. She won't stop once she's killed all of the gods and goddesses. She told Dad humankind was next. Instead of waiting for that to happen, we're going to take the fight to her."

"You're just like your father," she said. Ask wasn't sure if this was meant as a compliment or an accusation. He remembered his mother pleading with his father not to pick up the ax. He recalled a more recent interaction in which his mother told him the same thing.

Deonte added, "It's now up to us to stop her."

"You're in on this too? Pot and kettle," Deonte's mother pointed out. "And when were you going to tell me?"

Deonte looked down, as if studying the stitching of his new shoes.

"I know this is dangerous," Ask began, "but *you know* that Hyrrokkin will kill us if she gets the chance. She wants the ax and, chances are, she wouldn't mind getting her hands on Deonte's Jordans. Koerl nearly killed me the other night. I suspect he'll try again. Our best chance is to go on the offensive. We need that spear."

"You're just children," Idun said. "This is my responsibility. I will go to Hyrrokkin and face her. I will clean up the mess my people started."

"Mom. You can't do it alone. *We* need to do this. The plan is already in motion. There's no going back at this point."

Idun sat contemplatively for a time, silent. Then she said, "Ask, you lost your father, but I lost a husband. If I lose you too, our child. . ."

"You won't," Ask cut in. "The plan is solid. We are just going after the spear. Orla is already at the giants' camp. Now, what was the message she sent?" Ask knew this tactic was designed to distract his mother from canceling the mission, but she was, as always, too focused, too determined to give ground.

"Ask. It's not that I don't trust you. I do. The ax chose you for a reason. You have to remember, though, Hyrrokkin has killed many gods and goddesses with powers much greater than yours over millennia. She is a strategist and a killer. No plan is foolproof against her. You should have talked to me about this before putting this plan into action." She paused. "Orla texted that she's removed Grior from Hyrrokkin's side and has convinced at least two giants to give up Hyrrokkin's archaic quest. She says she still plans to meet tonight." Idun raised an eyebrow. "Tonight?"

"How did you get her text?" he asked.

Idun handed him his phone. *So stupid,* Ask thought. *How did I leave my cell phone home today?* He shot a glance at Deonte, who was shaking his head in disbelief.

"We will meet Orla tonight," Idun said. "Then, we can decide the next course of action."

Resigned to being ousted as leader, Ask nodded. At least the plan would move forward.

Deonte said, "Alright. We got this."

Deonte's mother replied, "Excuse me? What do you mean '*we* got this'? You have homework, chores, and a curfew. There is no 'we' in this situation that involves you."

"Come on, Mom. I can't let my best friend down when he needs me the most. Plus," he said and pointed to his shoes, "I'm part of the plan."

She shook her head. "This is against all better judgment," she said. Finally, she conceded. "Well, you sure aren't going by yourself," adding the condition, "I'm coming tonight, then, too."

A general hush settled in the room. Deonte was the first to speak, "Mom. . ." he began, but the look she gave him—that go-to-your-room, watch-your-mouth, I-taught-you-better-than-this look—meant the decision was made, and it was final.

CHAPTER 24

ORLA'S PRISONER

STANDING AT THE INTERSECTION OF potholed dirt roads a couple of miles south of his home with his mother, Deonte, and Dr. Henry was not how Ask envisioned the rendezvous going with Orla. Yes, he realized, he may have romanticized the espionage and intrigue aspects of the clandestine meeting, but this reality was disappointing and counterintuitive to his plan: For starters, there were too many people involved. They would never be able to carry out a quiet incursion into enemy territory. Then, he saw himself as leading the plan, not deferring to an adult like a child. Why didn't his mother just let him protect the family, like his father, and trust that he could handle himself? Idun stood hugging herself for warmth half a dozen feet away. He knew he should understand her insistence to join them, but all he felt now was the resentment of wounded pride.

Fortunately, the moon was partly obscured by clouds, so they didn't quite stick out like four sore thumbs, waiting awkwardly, not to mention suspiciously, in barren fields in the middle of the night. It was cold too, as Ask and Deonte had discussed earlier that day. Ask kicked a rock off the road. *Nothing works out*, he thought, *because nothing ever goes as planned.*

A slight rumble in the distance caused the ground to shift at intervals. Giant footsteps, Ask determined. Soon, Orla was standing in front of them, her true giant size, with another giant tied around the wrists and waist with a thick rope that reminded Ask of the ropes used to moor boats. This second giant—Grior, Ask guessed—was also gagged. He had never seen before so much hatred in a set of eyes or anger in a scowl.

"I'd remove the gag," Orla said, "but I doubt you'll want to hear what she has to say."

"You did it," Ask replied.

"Did you think I wouldn't?" Orla asked icily.

As Ask fumbled for the right thing to say, Orla winked. "It wasn't easy. But Grior here can be persuaded."

Grior growled in protest beneath her gag.

"Let's take this someplace a little more private," Idun said.

Orla nodded, but Ask wondered if she was confused and a little concerned by this change of plans. Without another word, Orla plodded after Idun, who led the way home. There was a moment of hesitation just outside the borders of their property. Idun had to hold up her hand and utter a few ancient words Ask couldn't make out before Grior was allowed to enter. As she did, the giant automatically shrunk to the size of a human. As she did so, the ropes slid off and the gag fell to her feet.

"What did you do to me, Asgardian witch?" Grior snarled.

"Just a little assurance. Don't try to enlarge or to escape. You can now do neither," Idun responded. She then waved Orla in, who remained just outside the magical barrier. "You're welcome here," remembering, perhaps, that she had sent Orla away the last time they met.

"When they come for me," Grior threatened, "I will use your blood to wash my face."

"No one's coming for you, Grior. They believe you're hunting. When I return, in your disgusting image, they won't be the wiser that you're gone," Orla said.

"And you." Grior pointed to Orla. "Siding with these insignificant vermin. You traitor. Koerl will freeze your heart with his blade when he figures it out. And he will figure it out."

"Let's find someplace comfortable for you to wait this out, Grior," Idun said. She led Grior to a rarely used barn that Ask was told never to play in because it was dilapidated to the point of falling in on itself. Thus, to Ask, the barn had become part of the scenery of his childhood and not a space for function or frivolity. Inside, Idun held her hand out to the floor. A thick wood door shuddered and then dropped open. Below, Ask saw a cement basement with a few scattered chairs, a table, and a light dangling from the center of the room.

"I know it's not five stars, but you'll get fed three times a day while we sort this out," Idun told Grior.

"You should kill me now if you know what's good for you," Grior said as an expression of gratitude.

Idun nodded. "I do know, Grior. Not that you'll care to understand, but killing isn't always strength, and compassion isn't always weakness."

Grior hopped down into the cellar. "Spare me your pacifist philosophies. Power renders your wisdom moot. I've seen many of your kind mistake compassion for claiming to care for their giant prisoners. You can't fool me, and you can't fool yourself."

Idun shut the door and sealed it with an energy field.

Deonte's mother asked, "Why would she implicate you in something so unethical as keeping giants as prisoners?"

Idun didn't hesitate. "Many eons ago, my family, most of the families I knew, took giants as prisoners after battles. Battles we often began out of bravado or pride. It was wrong, and, truthfully, those arrogant battles started this war. I was a child when our giant prisoners escaped. We never took another. Grior won't forgive my people." She hesitated. "I don't blame her. She's right. It's hypocritical to take the moral high ground from such a degraded position."

"I see," said Dr. Henry.

Orla spoke up, "Sometimes, vengeance is all you have, once your dignity has been stripped from you and all you cared about destroyed."

Idun finished the thought. "The war—over the freedoms Grior said giants were denied—destroyed most everything, including our home world, including nearly everyone I knew and loved. This was true for giants as well."

"And," Orla added, "they turned on themselves. All that's left of that world are the bitter survivors who have nothing left but their hate."

Dr. Henry gave an understanding nod.

Idun led them into her home. When Orla paused just outside the doorway, Idun smiled. "Please, come in. I'm sorry I doubted your intentions before." Then she added, "And thank you for saving my son's life."

Once seated around the kitchen table, beneath the clock that imitated different bird calls on the hour, Idun began to interrogate Ask, Deonte, and Orla—at least that's how it felt to Ask. She probed into every nook and cranny of their plan, testing the thoroughness of its design and the logic of its phases. Finally, she concluded, "It's not bad, at least the part about separating Hyrrokkin from the spear. We have a better chance of defeating her without it." Then she said, "No use talking to Hyrrokkin to just give it up and let bygones be bygones, I don't suppose."

All four, Ask noticed, sat with the same jaw-dropped expression.

"No, of course not. Paul tried that. Okay, well, Orla returns to Hyrrokkin within the hour disguised as Grior," Idun ordered.

"That was the plan," Ask said, a little too sarcastically.

"And," Idun continued, "I follow. When the giants are all sleeping, I will take the spear."

Ask could feel the situation slipping through his fingers. He never would have recognized it as jealousy, but he murmured in his mind, *That's my opportunity to prove myself a hero. I devised this plan. I should be the one to carry it out.* He thought about the restrictions his mother put on him after his father was gone. He could only go into town on a bus, with her, or accompanied by someone else's parent. He had to ask permission to stop at a friend's house after school. These "boundaries" as she called them suddenly felt like unfair burdens designed to subject him to her will. Just as he tested those boundaries, he challenged Idun's revised approach. "I don't like your plan," he blurted.

Idun waited. When he didn't elaborate, she asked, "Why not? What am I missing?"

"Me," he said, and then pointed to Deonte—strength in numbers. "Us."

A little less patiently than usual, Idun said, "It's too dangerous." Dr. Henry nodded in agreement.

Ask stumbled onto another excuse, or another reason, as he rationalized with himself: "You might not be able to pick up the spear. The ax resisted you, remember? What if you try to take the spear, and it won't let you? You'll be standing in the middle of a bunch of angry giants with no backup to help."

"It will let me. The ax only resisted because. . ." She stopped midsentence. "How do you know about that?"

"Uh, well, I saw it in a dream. It doesn't matter. Facts are facts. You need me—"

Deonte cleared his throat.

"I mean, you need *us* there."

"Ask, I lost Paul. I can't lose you, too." She placed a hand on the side of his face. "I know you miss your father. But that loss, that grief, pales in comparison to losing a child. You're mine to protect. I couldn't live if something happened to you, especially if I could have prevented it. Your being here is a miracle in and of itself. I won't squander that gift."

His anger subsiding, Ask changed tactics. "But we'll be there together," he said. "What safer place in the world is there for me?"

"Nice try," she said. "Here." She pointed to the kitchen, to the house protected by energy. "Here is safer for you." Turning from Ask, Idun said, "Okay, Orla, before you go—tell us what you know."

Orla nodded. "There are about fifteen of them altogether. It looks like all the teams Hyrrokkin had dispatched to scout the globe have returned. Koerl is there and some of his captains, like Urgaard and Fein. Only two, maybe three, are tired of Hyrrokkin's vengeance and may run instead of fight in the event of an attack. Overall, they look strong and ready." Orla paused. "In fact, they are so ready. . ." A scar slowly began to materialize on her face. She reached out and grabbed Idun around the throat. "They may have caught Orla and set up a bit of a trap."

Orla transformed then into Koerl, the human-sized version of himself, scar fully visible on his face. "I missed my chance to rid the world of you, Idun, many, many years ago. I won't make that mistake again." He drew back his free hand and brought it down in a fist against Idun's head, rendering her unconscious.

At first Ask didn't move. He was stunned; things were moving so fast. How did Koerl so completely and thoroughly trick them? His mother's unconscious head bobbing in Koerl's grasp brought him to his feet. He quaked with anger. "Let go of her!" Ask shouted.

The ax was in the shed. Summoning it, he realized, could be a problem, if it crashed through walls and endangered a room full of people seated all around him. He couldn't chance collateral damage.

"I will, boy, as soon as you bring me the ax. We're camped twenty miles south, southwest of here. The ax for your mother."

Ask gritted his teeth. "What about Orla?" he demanded.

"Why, she's a hero. She infiltrated the enemy's home base, earned their trust, and has now set in motion the events that will bring our quest to a successful conclusion. You know, I misspoke. We didn't so much as catch her as welcome her back." Koerl smiled menacingly.

"You're a liar. What have you done with her?" Ask demanded between gritted teeth.

"Tomorrow night," Koerl insisted, and then he backed out of the house and vanished into the darkness with long giant strides, Idun slung over a shoulder.

CHAPTER 25

THINGS FALL APART

Ask, Deonte, and Dr. Henry sat staring dejectedly at the kitchen table. Not only had things not gone to plan, but they had actually gone badly awry. Not only had Koerl outmaneuvered them and kidnapped Ask's mother, but Ask was left wondering if Orla truly had betrayed them. He didn't want to believe it, yet anything was possible. He thought about his mother's suspicions of Orla. Neither were around to confirm or deny accusations. The clock struck four to the sound of a wood thrush whistling four times in sequence, shaking Ask out of his reverie. He sighed deeply. It was obvious that a new plan had to be made and quickly. Only this time, Ask didn't have Orla or his mother to guide or help execute that plan.

"What if we just run in there and take her back? I could do it before they even know what hit them," Deonte offered.

"Sure, that might catch them off guard for a moment, but we don't know enough about where they're keeping her or if there are energy fields or guards. Then, we're not sure if carrying someone will slow you down. Plus, you haven't even begun to understand your gift. What if something goes wrong? What if you lose a shoe or run into a rock?" Ask wanted to say it's hopeless. He settled on, "Maybe we just give them the ax. It's what they want. They let my mom go, and we come back here and regroup."

"An hour ago, you were begging your mom to let us go," Deonte reminded him. "Now you want to give up? We hand Hyrrokkin the ax, we'll wind up winning the battle but losing the war. There has to be another way."

Deonte's mother, who had been quiet since the abduction occurred, said, "Ask, they won't let your mother go, even if you give them the ax. They need her to reunite the spear and the ax, and then they will kill her. It's the whole reason they're here. I'm sorry, but we owe it to your mother to find another way."

The stakes too high, Ask couldn't think. He kept replaying impossible scenarios in his head. They all ended the same way—Ask losing the ax and his mother dead. When he added Orla to the equation, his thoughts fluttered into chaos. How could he save his mother and keep the ax? Would Orla also fight against them? And then, he had a breakthrough.

"Deonte," he said. "Do you have an ax at home?"

"Yeah. Why?" Deonte asked.

"We're going to need it."

Koerl's comment about Orla had created enough doubt that Deonte asked the question Ask didn't have the heart to ask himself: "What about Orla? Do you think she was a spy for Hyrrokkin?"

"I don't know."

He wished he would wake up from one of his dreams and find a different reality waiting for him. If only he had some way to figure it all out—an ace in his pocket to give him some sort of edge.

CHAPTER 26

SEEKING LEVERAGE

IT DIDN'T TAKE ASK AND Deonte long to realize they had some leverage after all. Grior was still sealed in the barn cellar. Perhaps Hyrrokkin could be persuaded to make a trade? Of course, Ask thought this was a longshot. Hyrrokkin didn't strike him as the sentimental type. She could, he guessed, just as easily leave Grior to rot as to welcome her back to the giants' ranks. Nevertheless, the two boys didn't discount the possibility of strong bonds between war buddies. They stood above the door to the cellar as the morning sun filled the empty corners with soft light.

First, Ask thought, *we have to figure out a way to release the energy that's barring our entrance to the giant.*

As they scuffled about on the sagging floor, making the creaky floor joists moan, Grior called up, "Do you have my breakfast? I'm starved. Course, I'd be happy to eat one of you since mommy isn't here to protect you."

Ask wondered if Grior was just a prisoner used to pull off Koerl's deception or if she was part of some twisted trap Koerl had set for them. She came willingly with Koerl and expected, Ask was certain, that she would be rescued once his mother was dead. Orla's complicit involvement seemed more and more likely. Still, none of it added up.

"Sorry," Ask called down, "no food today. Unless, that is, you can answer a few questions."

"Save it, boy. I'll eat mice and hold my tongue," Grior said.

"How about a bouquet of freshly caught fish?" Ask said.

Ask could almost hear her salivating. "Fish, you say? Throw one down so I can see."

He didn't tell her he didn't have any fish, nor that he couldn't "throw one down" even if he did because of the energy field. Instead, he led her on a bit. "What good is giving you this cold, fresh walleye—wasn't it bucking twenty minutes ago, Deonte?—if you don't give us some information first? That would be," he paused, "childish of us."

What began as a growl below their feet quickly evolved into loud guffaws. "You are clever, child. You had old Grior tricked for a moment. But I spent the night kicking at that door, so I know you can't open it. Your mother's the only one with that power. So, you might as well run along. I'll be free by sunrise tomorrow. You know, I think ol' Grior will feast on your raw flesh and suck the marrow from your bones for supper."

Getting nowhere with Grior, Ask went back outside, where Deonte leaned against the barn wall near the door. He said, "Well, that didn't go very well."

Ask shook his head. "We'll have to think of another way." He kicked the side of the barn. A weathered board sighed.

One small bit of leverage right here, Ask thought, *and I can't even use it.*

Deonte nodded. "You know, I'm missing a home game for this."

Ask chuckled. "They do better without you." He nudged his friend.

"Not with these." Deonte pointed at the enchanted boots now resembling Jordans. "I'd be juking tonight."

Deonte and Ask made their way back to the front porch, where Deonte's mother sat deep in thought. Some moments after they joined her, she said,

"How can I help?" A pause and then, "Asking you two to face those giants alone is too much."

"Because we're kids?" Deonte said accusatorily.

"Partly. And because those giants are monsters and will kill you. I don't like this," she added.

Ask held up the ax. "We have this, Deonte's shoes, and Babe," he said. "If worse comes to worst, we give up the plan and run."

"Look, Mom, we'll be fine. Ask is right—first sign of trouble, and we're gone." Deonte pointed to his superfast shoes as if they were proof of his promise.

Deonte's mother nodded wearily, as if she'd heard that promise before. "First sign of trouble."

In this way, the boys convinced Deonte's mother to go home and wait for them. Deonte accompanied her home and then rejoined Ask, materializing suddenly from a puff of dirt at the end of Ask's driveway, carrying the ax Ask had requested.

After their failed attempt to trick information out of Grior, Deonte raced around the pasture, eyes on the ground while dodging small piles of Babe's excrement, practicing controlling his movements at high velocities, while Ask sat with his back against a tree and rubbed mud all over the ax Deonte brought from his garage. Ask knew he had to make the ax look as much like Bjornen as possible for his plan to work. The mud dulled the yellowish tint of the lacquered wood handle just enough that dim light and enough distance would likely render the ax indistinguishable from Bjornen.

Both parents gone, Ask said silently to himself.

He leaned the ax against the tree. He tried not to think too deeply about his mother, this predicament, because his courage was shallow and could easily wash away. Any disruption to this brave façade, and his true scared self would surface, at which point he wasn't sure he'd be able to go through with the rescue attempt.

He never needed his father more than at this moment.

He hadn't slept a wink since Koerl stole his mother away. The fall day was also quite comfortable, with a light cool breeze, few bugs, and a bit of what his father called the wisp of the fairy. First, Ask's eyes grew heavy, next he lay back against the tree, and then he drifted off to sleep.

Once again, Ask found himself transformed by the ax as his father some years ago. He'd grown not only accustomed to seeing the world through his father's eyes in dream memories, but he'd also come to feel quite comfortable with and comforted by these visits, even if they were shadows of the past, even if he couldn't change what was lost and gone. To see his father in these contexts, to walk moments of his life in his shoes, created a connection Ask knew he would never have achieved if his father hadn't disappeared, leaving Ask the ax and its powerful and magical legacy.

In this dream memory sequence, Ask, as his father, walked next to his mother a couple of miles from the house Ask had lived in his whole life, but he could sense this was before his time. It was dark, early morning, Ask judged, by the thin line of purple rimming the horizon. His father's arms were weary. He could barely heft the ax leaning heavily against his aching shoulder. His mother also dragged a bit, it seemed, visibly overexerted and forcing every step.

"That was close," she said.

"Too close," his father said.

"Maybe now Frieda and Ro will find a new place to hide. We warned them they were too exposed," his mother reprimanded.

"They won't," Ask heard his father say. "They're tired of running. They'll stay, regardless of the risk."

"That can't be true. It's only a matter of time now. They need to leave," Idun insisted.

"And go where, Idun? They've been running for so long. They will stay, and they will fight."

"Then, they will lose, and they will die." Idun thumbed an amulet on a torc around her neck. Ask could just make out a wink of amethyst sparkle between her fingers.

Of course, Ask recognized the amulet immediately. He now wore it around his neck, her gift to him just a few days ago.

Even in this dream memory, his stomach wrenched at the thought of her tied up at the giants' camp. How Koerl had seized her by the neck, which was no longer adorned by the protection of the torc, and punched her unconscious gripped him in a sudden fury. So much so, in fact, that he nearly forced his father to form a fist. He could feel the hand tensing, the fingers curling in toward one another, almost but not quite coming together. His father's attention, oblivious to Ask's expression of anger, remained on the amulet. He asked, "What is that?"

His mother stopped fiddling with the amulet and quickly tucked it back into her shirt. "Insurance," she said but didn't elaborate.

Ask felt a grin spread across his face. "Insurance from what?"

Idun didn't seem interested in explaining, so she tried to explain it away. "Oh, you know, from evil, from things designed to do harm."

"It's magic?" Paul asked.

"Old magic. Energy, actually," Idun clarified.

Ask was intrigued. He remembered his mother telling him the amulet would deflect weapons wielded by hate and that it would enhance the energy the ax already produced, but he wasn't aware that it possessed potent and ancient energy itself.

"I'm sorry to pry. I meant no disrespect. I'm just curious why you wear it," his father said.

"It was my mother's. I found it tonight," Idun said.

"Tonight?" Paul asked.

"Yes, on that giant you slew. Girgor. He and Koerl killed my family."

"His death was vengeance as well as protection, then. Two birds," Paul said, "one ax."

They limped on toward home in silence for some time. An owl hooted in the thinning darkness overhead on its way from hunting the fields, racing the sun to its perch in the hollow of some massive tree or some farmer's barn. The silhouette of their house grew larger and larger as the sky lightened to the pale grays and deep reds indicative of sunrise.

Idun broke the silence. "If anything happens to me, I want you to take this torc. It's imbued with the same energy from which I draw my powers. There's just enough in the amulet to block an enemy attack or to counteract some spell. It won't produce the apples of life, but it can prolong your mortality some years."

Startled by the thought of his mother's potential demise, Ask nodded in his mind when his father asked, "Why do you tell me this? You have lived a long time and will continue to live long after I'm gone. I will have no need of that necklace."

"Paul, as long as the giants pursue my people, as long as I am alive, they will keep coming until they have accomplished the task. It's foolish not to face the possibility."

Ask felt the ax lifting in his arm. "Do you see this, Idun? Bjornen and I will not let that happen. If they won't stop coming, then we have to kill them first. They can't pursue you if they are all dead."

Idun tittered. "Now you sound like them. Must it be that they must die for us to live? That philosophy has destroyed lives for eons and has resulted in this stalemate. You must understand that your weapon wasn't forged to kill mercilessly. It will betray you if you wield it with hatred or anger or vengeance."

This admonition must have led to Paul's efforts to negotiate peace. Ask remembered his father's determination to persuade the giant Surtr to give up the fight and how he approached the giants' camp to offer a treaty. Ask thought about his mother's explanation of the ax as well. Would he have been able to slay Koerl if he had overcome him the night they fought, or would the ax have prohibited it since Ask was enraged? Was the spear a similar weapon? Did it reject Hyrrokkin because she attempted to use it to kill? Did this limitation constitute some kind of advantage, or did it mean he would never be able to harm the giants because he hated them so much?

"Besides," Idun continued, "I need to know you will be here for our child if I don't survive."

"Child?" Paul said, genuinely astonished. "But we could never have a child. All those years?"

"I can't explain it, Paul. Perhaps as you grow more connected with the ax and I become more distanced from Asgard, we become more compatible."

Paul dropped the ax, transformed to his usual size, and hugged Idun. For a moment, they enjoyed some measure of joy at the end of a long night, one of many that demanded their time and energy for centuries.

CHAPTER 27

THE AMULET'S ENERGY

ASK AWOKE IN THE LATE afternoon, his neck sore from leaning oddly against the tree trunk that had served as an unintended pillow. His head throbbed a bit from pressure.

Deonte called from across the yard, "Check this out." One moment he was standing near the pasture, and the next he was above Ask in a tree. "I ran up the tree! How cool is that?"

Ask called back flatly, "Amazing." He slipped his hand down the front of his shirt and touched the amulet.

"It only took me, like, ten tries. By the way, don't run headfirst into a tree trunk. It *will* leave a mark," he added. "What's that?" Deonte asked, suddenly standing next to Ask.

Ask involuntarily flinched. "I think I liked it better before you put those shoes on." He pulled out the amulet so Deonte could see it better. "It's something my mother gave me, an amulet. I believe I can use it to reverse the energy field around the barn cellar."

"Seriously? So, maybe we do have some leverage after all."

Ask patted the amulet. "Perhaps. If I can figure out how to do it, that is."

The stretching shadows across the lawn reminded Ask that time was running out. He hurried over to the barn. Inside, he held the amulet to the trap door in the floor leading to the cellar, confining Grior inside.

"That you, boy?" Grior called from below. "What are you up to?"

He tried focusing his mind on releasing the door, but nothing happened. Not even a shudder to suggest he was making progress. He told Deonte to kick the door while he concentrated on the energy field's release. He even told Deonte to try a running start. Still, nothing, except for a deep bellowing laugh from below. "Sealed up tight, young fellow. Nothing a little runt like you can crack."

"Should we try 'open sesame'?" Deonte asked facetiously.

Ask shook his head and paced the length of the barn. Neither the power of thought nor magic words seemed to have much effect on the amulet. Ask shook the torc. *How do you get this thing to work?*

More laughing from below. "What's the matter? This door too much for a little boy to open?"

Wait, thought Ask, what had Grior just called him? Little boy? *Little*? That's it!

He held up his arm, and the ax flew into his hand. The amulet, his mother told him, enhanced the energy of the ax. The torc alone wasn't enough. The amulet magnified existing power. It needed a conduit. It needed the ax.

At first, Ask thought he would bring the ax crashing down on the floor to dash the energy field to pieces. Years of parental guidance, however, whispered a warning not to destroy what didn't need to be destroyed. So, instead, he simply touched the ax to the door. When nothing happened, he placed the amulet against the ax blade. Following an abrupt, luminescent purple spark, the cellar door released, revealing Grior sitting back against the wall and staring spitefully up at them. Ask was grateful he had transformed before Grior was, for all intents and purposes, free.

"Well, now, aren't we full of surprises?" Grior stayed seated on the earthen floor, a few mouse hides and bones scattered around her.

"Get up," Ask commanded.

"I don't think so, false little god. I'll wait for Koerl as instructed," Grior said.

Something bothered Ask about her cavalier response and her desire to stay in captivity. "As instructed? Why did Koerl bring you here and then leave you?"

"The ruse, of course." She laughed, her voice scratchy and deep like gravel bouncing in a concrete mixer.

Ask reviewed the events of the previous night. Once Koerl had been allowed entrance to their home, he could have attacked Idun at any point, even before she had imprisoned Grior. Something didn't add up. "I don't think you understood me. You're coming with us."

"I will do no such thing. I don't take orders from a child masquerading as a giant."

Ask, until that day, had never seen such a sinister grin, not even from Koerl, but that is what spread disturbingly across Grior's face.

Because her hands were tied together, and as far as Ask knew, unable to grow into the giant version of herself, Ask jumped into the cellar and grabbed her by an arm. She shook and swung at Ask in an effort to slip out of his grasp. Finally, frustrated by the scuffle, Ask threw her out of the cellar. She landed with a thud a few feet from Deonte. She launched herself from the ground, her tied arms reaching for Deonte's throat. He quickly evaded the lunge and, in a flash, was behind her. He delivered a swift kick to her backside, sending her sprawling to the ground once again.

"You'll pay for that," Grior threatened. By then, Ask was out of the cellar and standing over her. He pointed the ax at Babe, who enlarged immediately into his form of a massive blue ox. "I will stay here," Grior declared, as if the decision was final.

Why the insistence when she could be reunited with the giants sooner rather than later? For some reason, she wanted to stay. Was it fear Hyrrokkin might see her as weak if she reappeared before they rescued her? That couldn't be it. They let her get captured. She was part of their plan. They wanted her here. Ask had always relied on Orla and, more recently, his mother to determine motives of creatures he didn't understand, or even knew existed a few months ago. Now it was up to him and Deonte to make sense out of Grior's peculiar and unsettling desire to stay.

Ask remembered they had checked her for weapons, but they had mostly trusted that Orla—well, Koerl—had already conducted a thorough pat-down, as it were. What damage could she do if she stayed behind, especially before they released the energy seal above the barn cellar? Did she have a weapon concealed somewhere?

"Why are you so set on staying?" he asked Grior.

She didn't answer right away, but then, cunningly, said, "Because you want to take me."

"So, you mean to be contrary? You're so insistent because you aim to do exactly the opposite of what we want you to do?"

"Such wisdom," Grior mocked.

"No way," Deonte chimed in. "Ask, this sounds just like Jepp when he's about to do something nasty. It's lies, deceit, and misdirection." He turned to Grior. "So, what is it that you want to do when we're gone?"

Again, a delayed response. "I don't answer to you, tiny human."

"Answer the question," Ask said, his voice booming.

She said no more.

"I'll make her talk," Deonte said. He formed a fist.

"No. Not like that." Ask put a hand on Deonte's shoulder. "If she won't tell us, we'll just have to search for what she's hiding."

Grior's smile turned to a scowl. "Touch me and die, child."

Ask reached down with his free hand, grabbed one of Grior's legs, and flipped her upside down. A few items fell from loose pockets: coins, a rabbit skull, some oddly shaped rocks.

Wait. Ask stopped shaking Grior and set her back on her feet. Those weren't rocks. In the research he'd conducted about his father and mother, he had come across a variety of related topics; one of those topics was rune stones. Grior tried to snatch them up, but Deonte was quicker. He held the oddly shaped stones in his hand., leaving Grior to grip only air. "What are these symbols?"

Ask couldn't have made them out if he wanted to. He was no scholar, and despite his newly discovered genealogy, had never learned anything about reading runes. Because of his connection to the ax and convergence with its energy, however, he had become quite attuned to the energy emissions from powerful relics. These runes, he could feel, emitted a dark force and glowed dimly of a sickly sinister essence.

"Those are mine," Grior snarled. "Give them back."

"What are they for?" Ask inquired.

"Trinkets. Babbles. Reminders of the old world, nothing more. More valuable to me than to you," she insisted.

"You know what, I think we'll keep these for now. You can have them back later," Ask said.

Grior's scowl bore into him. She gritted her teeth and rushed at Ask. He held out his hand and forced her to sit. Her attack was futile since she didn't have the girth her giant stature would typically afford her. *That kind of reaction for a trinket*? Ask wondered.

"I think we discovered part of their plan," Ask told Deonte. "I'm not sure what these are, but we better hold on to them." He planned to find a thick bag in which to stow the runes until they had more time, and hopefully the expertise of his mother, to investigate their meaning and power. In the meantime, he slipped the stones into his pocket.

As Grior sat powerless at his feet, dozens of leaves gathering around her in the autumn breeze, Ask knew he had to ask, even if Grior was unreliable. "Did Orla betray us?"

He didn't doubt Orla was capable of such a strategic move, but it seemed so out of character for the Orla he had come to know, who had protected him, who he saw sitting so alone beneath that tree the night they sketched out their plan. Didn't the cold blue of her eyes seem to soften as she searched outside and inside herself for answers with which to reconcile the losses of her past? Hadn't there been genuine effort in preparing him so thoroughly to defend himself against creatures like Grior?

As if in response to her name in his thoughts, that scratchy, guttural, almost victorious guffaw burst from Grior's lips. "You think it surprising that a giantess could outsmart two little boys? Did you ever ask the question, 'why is she helping me'? As you trained, she learned. As you fought, she studied. As you plotted, she spied. She didn't betray you. She was simply loyal to us."

Because he was angry and needed to lash out, Ask clarified, "You mean, she was loyal to Hyrrokkin."

Grior stopped grinning.

"That's right. Not to you. You mean about as much to them as a hyena scrounging around a pride of lions. Is that why they sent you to be a captive? It's the only thing you're good for?" Ask said.

"Watch your tongue, little one, or I will yank it from your mouth and swallow it whole."

Ask raised the ax as his anger grew. Maybe Grior's life was threat enough. He could stop this ruse with one clean stroke, put an end to that hatefully smug grin.

Deonte pulled Ask aside. "Pull it together. What's the matter with you?"

His jaw set, Ask said, "How could she do this to us?"

"Who? Orla? You're going to take *her* word for it? Need I remind you this piece of crap has lied to us at least a dozen times since we dragged her sorry butt out of that cellar?"

This had occurred to Ask. Grior could be lying. Why wouldn't she? He entertained this notion only briefly, however. He couldn't look past the facts. For instance, how had Koerl known about the rendezvous place, the intel Orla was supposed to gather, Orla's main objective to distance Grior from Hyrrokkin, so she could assume her form and act as their informant? No, the lying angle didn't seem to line up. All the evidence suggested Orla had betrayed them.

"Not this time. She's at least partly telling the truth. Orla has betrayed us. That's the only explanation for Koerl's success. He knew all the things Orla was supposed to do. Only Orla revealing the plan could so thoroughly prepare him."

Deonte shook his head. "I just don't believe she would do it, at least not willingly."

"You think she was forced to tell our plan?" Ask hoped this was the case.

Deonte elaborated. "She might have been captured, coerced, tortured even. She may have had no choice."

Ask was surprised Deonte would advocate so hard for someone with whom his relationship was, well, complicated. "Even so, it doesn't mean she didn't betray us, torture or not."

"That's pretty harsh, Ask. Maybe she had no choice. None. They could have tricked her, drugged her, beat her. . . We just don't know what happened," Deonte said.

Even though he felt ashamed for wishing Orla's betrayal had been coerced, perhaps by painful means, Ask replied, "We do know that Koerl was invited into my home and took my mother. This was a result of Orla's betrayal, intentional or not."

"Okay," Deonte relented. "Look. Let's focus on getting your mom back."

As evening descended over the fields around them, Ask and Deonte discussed what they had to work with. There was, of course, Grior to employ as a bargaining piece to trade for his mother, though Ask doubted Hyrrokkin would care one way or another about her missing giant. He expected that offer to fall flat. They had the ax, not to mention a bit of a diversion with the ax Deonte had retrieved from his house that Ask had carefully worked to resemble the original Bjornen. This, too, was a long shot. What they did have was Deonte's speed. He hadn't demonstrated that skill when Koerl arrived as Orla. The real Orla wouldn't know about that discovery either. Yes, that could catch them off guard.

As Ask considered the implications of these things in relation to their impending visit to the giant camp later that night, he happened to catch a glimpse of Grior, watching him. She smirked at him, her lips curling into that malicious grin.

CHAPTER 28

THE TENUOUS JOURNEY

Ask stood guard by Grior as Deonte went into the shed to tie the ax securely around his torso against his back. He wore a thick black hoodie to better conceal the ax, so neither Grior nor any other giant he encountered could see it. He gave Ask a thumbs up once the deed was done. Then, in Grior's full view, Deonte tied the ax he retrieved from his house to Babe's back. He then strung a thick rope around Babe's large blue neck and attached it to Grior's tied hands. Ask and Deonte had discussed slinging Grior over Babe's back but decided having her walk would wear her out and, perhaps, remove her from any fighting that might occur.

This is how they would approach the camp when the time arrived: Deonte would speed ahead and hide in whatever form of concealment he could find—bush, copse, riverbank, shallow embankment. From there, he would watch and wait. If the opportunity presented itself, he would rush in and extricate Idun.

In the meantime, Ask would walk behind Grior with a knife his father had given him for camping trips. It was a bowie knife with a wood handle and a stainless-steel blade. While its purpose was to gut and clean fish or segment rope for lashing branches for shelter, it could, for all intents and purposes, also be employed to encourage a lagging giant to keep moving if necessary.

Because Deonte had the real ax, Ask hoped the decoy ax would act as enough of a deterrent to keep Grior from attempting to escape. This part of the plan was dangerous. At any moment, Grior might decide to make a play for the ax and, if successful, realize it was not the ax the giants were looking for. If it came down to it, Ask doubted his little knife would do much against Grior. Fortunately, the convergence had left Ask strong and difficult to harm. The knife served best, he thought, as a display of power instead of the power itself.

For the first time in his life, Ask was the weapon, not the little boy who needed protection.

"Well," Deonte said, "see you on the other side."

Ask wasn't sure what Deonte meant by "the other side," but he nodded anyway, despite the phrase's potentially ill-omened undertones. Regardless of the outcome, he supposed, they would be past something, emerging somewhere other than where they were at this moment. He hoped the intensity of his look conveyed to Deonte the importance of every decision from now until they reunited at his house before dawn. And then Deonte disappeared.

"Come on, Babe," he said, and the big blue ox lumbered forward in slow but massive strides. As the rope stretched tautly, Grior was pulled forward into a quick walk. Ask followed closely behind, but not too close. He had grown accustomed to the deceptions and tricks of Hyrrokkin's horde. Grior would take advantage of any little mistake.

He knew their walk would be relatively slow. If he needed to make up time, he could always hop up on Babe's back and run him for a few minutes. This he would do only if necessary. He wanted to give Deonte plenty of time to scout out the situation. His friend would provide a report a few miles from the giants' camp.

It was dark. The full moon had been waning for several days, which meant the remaining light reflected off a little less than half its mass. Autumn clouds scuttled in long, thin wisps across the sky, blotting out the moon and further reducing the light. Fortunately, Ask's heightened sense of vision, one of the benefits of his convergence with the ax's energy, brought the landscape into relatively sharp focus. He could make out brush in ditches along the barren fields and even saw the slinking outline of a fox making its quiet way across the dirt road ahead of them. Even though they were still miles from the camp, when he concentrated on the horizon, he saw the flicker of fires on the open prairie, a stretch of untamed land situated between agricultural acreage. While there were no trees or large rocks to hide behind, the grass was still quite tall. He had spent summers battling the pervasive growth of weeds and grass when told to pluck the invaders from his mother's garden. He despised the interminable task, knees in the mud, back hunched, fingers pressed against the dirt to extricate deep enough to jostle the roots free from the fertile soil. But now, he was grateful for grass that grew and grew and grew, until it reached his chest when untended.

Of course, he thought, *they expect me to come fully transformed. They think the grass of little consequence. Another slight advantage.*

"Boy, I will slice that smile of yours all the way around your head," Grior said.

Ask had been waiting to gag Grior because he could imagine how uncomfortable it must feel to have one's mouth cinched tightly shut. He didn't want to hurt her. However, he also wasn't above inflicting some measure of discomfort on the giantess, especially if it meant she couldn't warn her friends and, bonus, he didn't have to listen to her anymore. As they neared the camp with every step, he knew he couldn't wait any longer. "Babe," he said, "hold up."

The ox stopped and looked back.

"I need your help," Ask said.

"What can I do?" Babe asked.

"Well, I need you to hold Grior down on the ground so she can't use her arms or legs."

Grior's eyes grew wide.

Babe took a step back. Grior tried to pull away, but Babe, much larger, not to mention much more agile than one might think a big blue ox could be, turned and pinned Grior to the ground with his front hoof.

"I am sorry about this." Ask pulled a roll of duct tape from a backpack he was wearing. The backpack, a last-minute decision, served as a utility bag of sorts, not exactly like but in the ballpark of a superhero's utility belt—at least that was the comparison Deonte made. He wrapped the tape around Grior's mouth and head twice before tearing it free from the roll. "Now," he added, "we can all finish this trip in peace."

Just as Babe removed his hoof from Grior's chest and Grior returned to her feet, Deonte was suddenly standing beside Ask. Ask jumped when Deonte said, "It's pretty flat and open at the giants' campsite."

"A little warning next time would help. Scared the crap out of me." Ask held a hand to his chest.

Deonte smiled. "Sorry, man. Trying to be stealthy."

"Mission accomplished. Did you see my mother?"

Deonte nodded. "She looks okay, but it's not going to be easy. They have her chained to a cage."

Ask made a fist, clenched his jaw. "You mean, chained *like some animal* in a cage?"

Babe, who had been grazing on corn kernels that had likely been jostled free of a harvester while it bounced down the dirt road, turned to Ask. "Animals should never be chained."

Ask said, "What are you talking about, Babe? My mother needs us to free her."

The ox nodded slowly, wisely. "Yes, Ask, but you must understand that animals should not be chained up or caged, either. Paul and I had this discussion often. He said that animals cause a lot of damage if left to their own devices. Chaining them up, he argued, keeps them under control. I would remind him that no living thing needs to be or should be controlled. Humans often think of themselves as the masters of everything, which means they don't give a second thought to chaining up whatever, whenever, or whomever they feel like. They believe, falsely I might add, in their right to control. But life is unpredictable. Chains give the illusion of control. But they are cruel and take away free will."

Ask thought about his mother confessing that giants had been prisoners of the gods prior to Ragnarök. The collars that controlled them. To keep them from wreaking havoc. He looked over at Grior, whose eyes bore murderous traces into his skull, and felt suddenly ashamed.

How do you win, he wondered, *when what must be done comes at the expense of the good you try to do, what you try to be?*

No hero, he realized, would use chains, threats, or brutality. He understood, now, why his mother could not crush the giants by closing her hand. Yes, it would be simple. She had the power. But what would it cost? *Don't such creatures deserve to be locked up?* he silently argued with himself. Yet, try as he might, he couldn't fully dissociate the brutality of the giants' imprisonment from the brutality of their freedom. *Which came first?* he wondered. Did war create the hatred that produced brutality, or were the giants always and forever hard and unforgiving and determined to conquer or be conquered?

And then, he thought about Orla. Her capacity for tenderness. The depth of mourning for her friend Solveig, murdered so many centuries ago. Even if she had betrayed them, didn't her conduct suggest the potential for redemption?

A little defeated by his tenuous conclusion, he said, "You're right, Babe. Nothing should be chained up. It's inhumane. I will think of a better comparison in the future."

Babe snorted approval and went back to the pile of corn kernels gathered in rutty troughs created by wide truck tires.

"What just happened?" Deonte asked. "We're not going to chain up those monsters. We're going to kill them if we can. Better yet, we get your mom and the spear, and we get out of there, like we planned."

Ask nodded. "Go back to the camp and wait for us. We're about an hour out." Before Deonte zipped off, he added, "Did you see Orla?"

Deonte pursed his lips. "Yes, but I can't make sense of it."

"What do you mean?"

"She's there, not tied up or anything, but she doesn't appear to belong. I watched most of the giants joke and fight and curse at each other. She sat away from the fire, almost in the shadows, and kept to herself. I don't want to get your hopes up. I don't have any proof that she didn't betray us. All I know is that she seems out of place."

"And the spear?"

"In Hyrrokkin's hand," Deonte said.

"Okay. See you in an hour."

As Deonte disappeared into the night, a swirl of dust occupying the spot in the road where he had stood, Ask told Babe their break was over. The ox lumbered forward, pulling Grior once again into a quick walk. She scowled at Ask as she passed. Some inexplicable compassion stirred in him, and he felt sorry for her.

CHAPTER 29

THE EXCHANGE

THERE WAS NOTHING FRIENDLY OR welcoming about the fires scattered about the giants' camp.

Ask's family were avid campers. Every year, he, his father, and his mother would spend at least a week exploring the vast forests of Minnesota, Michigan, or Montana. His favorite part of their campouts was the campfire. His father would tell stories, mostly myths Ask believed were fictitious, though recent experience had proven these to be more like oral histories or even memories. His mother would make the most delicious food, cooked in tinfoil or in a small Dutch oven his father insisted on hiking into their campsites, which tended to be miles from a road. In retrospect, he never recalled his mother ever saying she didn't have an ingredient or that she forgot something. The chicken and potatoes were always perfectly seasoned, the vegetables diverse and overflowing, and the s'mores always rich and marshmallowy. Of course, in hindsight, this preparation made perfect sense. What, with having a goddess for a mother who could create matter in the palm of her hand. As for his father, if he'd known about the side effects of the ax's energy and the transfer of power through the convergence, then he would have understood carrying additional weight, like a Dutch oven, wouldn't have bothered him at all.

Those trips were among the happiest of his life. How he wished to recapture those carefree days now, to close his eyes and find himself sitting by a fire with his parents, no fear threatening to claw its way out of his heart through his rib cage or his throat. He longed to feel, again, the comfort of not knowing the cruelties in the world.

He fought himself to stay focused on the task at hand. There was no time for nostalgia. He must put this plan into motion and save his mother.

As he knelt in the tall grass a quarter of a mile outside the giants' camp, next to Babe with Grior gagged and tied to the ox's waist, Ask made a curious, albeit unrelated connection. His father always had the ax with him on those camping trips. He wondered how many of those nights, after he'd fallen asleep, his father would rush off to some bit of rescuing, some hero work that had prompted their trip in the first place. He remembered his father telling Ask to chop wood with the ax. He never felt its power, never experienced even a tinkling of energy course through him in those early encounters with the ax. Not until his father had gone. He now wondered why he could lift the ax when his mother could not. A memory he acquired during one of his dreams resurfaced, reminding him that Bjornen chooses his champion. If that was the case, perhaps Ask had been chosen early for this calling. Perhaps his mother knew all along that Ask had been destined to succeed his father. That would explain her concern when she learned of his summoning.

Taking a deep breath for courage, he motioned Babe forward. Two sentries called to Hyrrokkin as they approached the outer edge of the camp. "He's here." He noticed them snigger and point at Grior.

"Well, if it isn't Paul's pup. You were wise, boy, to bring me the ax and my," Hyrrokkin paused, "warrior. Leave these things and be on your way."

Ask shifted his weight, forcing himself to stand his ground, though his hands shook fiercely. The stench of rotting fish and unwashed flesh permeated the camp. Massive faces, bulbous and mishappen, dull blue-gray and scar-pocked, stared menacingly at him. Slowly they hemmed him into the center of the camp.

"There's the matter of a trade," he managed to say only above a whisper.

Hyrrokkin rose from a massive stump upon which she had been seated and said, "I made no such bargain." Standing, she was immense.

A couple of sniggers issued behind him. A giant the shape of a lopsided bowling ball on short stubby legs with a spiked club balancing on a shoulder spat at Ask's feet. Ask looked around, taking in the scene. He was surrounded by the monsters of childhood nightmares. They were gigantic, menacing, unforgiving. His pulse raced.

Of course, Ask didn't expect that Hyrrokkin would accept Koerl's terms. Despite his growing fear, he steeled himself and tried to posture the best he could for the next step of the plan. As confident as he believed his father would have been, Ask said, "I give you Grior as an expression of good faith." He cut the rope from her wrists, and Babe nudged her forward with his back leg. "I will not give up the ax until my mother is free."

Once within reach, Hyrrokkin kicked Grior hard on the backside. When Grior scowled and grumbled beneath the duct tape still covering her mouth, Hyrrokkin added, "I suppose you wanted a hero's welcome," and laughed. A chorus of laughter followed. Hyrrokkin held up a hand. The laughing stopped abruptly. "Be grateful you still have your life." Grior bowed and shrunk back to her place next to the stump.

Hyrrokkin turned her attention back to Ask. "It's brave of you, tiny human, to come marching into my camp like a feisty stray and make demands. I'm sure you understand that I have need of your mother yet. Your ax and my spear." She pointed vaguely behind her. Ask peered around her. He could see no spear. Hyrrokkin could sense general confusion as giants also squinted in the lesser light behind her. She turned. "My spear. Where is my spear?"

"You," she said, pointing at Ask. "You've a bit of the witch in you as well. Return my spear and give me the ax, or your mother dies." She unsheathed a massive sword curved like a scimitar and ground to sharp edges on both sides. A quick motion of the arm, and the blade was millimeters from his mother's neck.

"Wait!" Ask yelled. "I don't have your spear. But the ax, yes, please take the ax."

He pointed to Babe. A burly, barrel-shaped giant yanked it free from its makeshift tie-downs. He delivered it gently to Hyrrokkin, as if it were the holiest of grails.

Hyrrokkin put away her sword and took up the ax in her hand. As she inspected the ax, a series of events transpired very quickly. First, there was a spark by the cage to which Idun was chained. Idun, Ask noticed, was there one moment and gone the next. At that same instant, Grior had pried the duct tape from her mouth and yelled, "Majesty, the ax you hold is a fake."

She must have noticed after all, Ask thought.

Hyrrokkin, seemingly puzzled, rubbed at splotches of yellow on the ax handle that Ask was unable to cover, confirming Grior's pronouncement. She then glanced behind her to see Idun missing. She boomed a command, "Kill that boy!" and she threw the decoy ax at Ask.

In that same moment, Ask was suddenly holding the real ax, Bjornen—thanks to Deonte, who none of the giants had yet seen or heard—and immediately transformed. Ask deflected the decoy and began swinging the massive ax at giants as they amassed to attack. As he fought, creating space by pivoting on his right foot with the ax extended at arm's length, Ask heard Hyrrokkin yell, "Find the other boy."

It wasn't long into the fight that Ask realized he was outnumbered and surrounded. The ranks were quickly closing in on him. He hoped Deonte was on his way home with his mother. Ask caught a glimpse of Grior searching the perimeter of the camp by stabbing the darkness with a long pike, in case Deonte was still around, attempting to strike his friend as he ran by. As the horde crowded around him, Ask saw Babe bowl through several giants, head down and horns set to impale. Before he could clear a path of escape for Ask, however, several of the giants' wolf mounts nipped at Babe's legs and launched themselves at his neck and back. Babe disengaged from the giants to defend against the onslaught of gnashing teeth and blade-like claws. Ask would have to do this alone or die trying.

Despite the discipline Orla had tried to instill in Ask, his training began to fail him. He had never been presented with so many attackers all at once, each the size and strength of Orla in her regular giantess state. He overcame two giants by sheer will, lashing out like a cornered animal, but the burst of adrenaline cost him future moments of endurance. Even transformed, Ask had to press his muscles to the verge of exhaustion, something his training with Orla never prepared him for.

As he shed two more giants and a small path to freedom lay ahead of him, Koerl stepped in his way. "This would have gone much easier for you," he said, "if you had left the ax and gone away. You had a choice."

Ask's strength all but spent, he lowered his ax. "Is that the same choice you give everyone you kill? Do what I say or die? How many weren't given even that option?"

Koerl grinned. "It really doesn't matter now. You are going to die, little guardian."

Koerl raised his ice sword above his head for a final deathblow. Ask couldn't force his arms up to block the attack. He closed his eyes and waited. When the blow didn't land, he peeked at Koerl. The giant gasped for breath; spittle and blood sprayed from his mouth. Ask noticed the tip of a pike sticking out of Koerl's chest. Orla emerged from behind Koerl as he fell forward onto the ground.

"Enough!" screamed Hyrrokkin. The giants paused their advance. Orla turned and stepped protectively back toward Ask. "You"—Hyrrokkin pointed at Orla—"I gave you a chance to make amends for helping and training this boy, and this is how you repay your people? By killing your teacher?"

"He was no teacher. He was a murderer."

"Well, yes, of course, you obviously missed the point of the lessons. You will pay for this with your life." She turned to Ask. "You now have three things I want—my spear, the ax, and your mother. I expect them returned to me immediately."

"Never," Ask said, as he felt his body surging with renewed strength. "You need to go away and never come back."

"Is that a threat?" Hyrrokkin spat and then began to laugh.

"It's no threat." Ask, suddenly emboldened, continued, "It's what will happen if we don't work this out. We'll just keep on fighting, forever. If we don't negotiate a truce, nobody wins."

Hyrrokkin wrapped her fingers around the hilt of her sword. "You sound like your father. Negotiate peace! I will agree to your terms once you're all dead."

Up close, her sword boasted a massive steel blade nearly half Ax's transformed size. Despite being extremely old, the sword appeared clean and well-tended. Sharp. He wondered how much blood had oiled that weapon over the centuries.

Orla whispered to Ask, "I told you—giants don't negotiate. They only understand this." She raised her pike and shook it.

"I'm sorry," he said loudly, surprising even himself.

"Oh, it's a little late for that now, boy," Hyrrokkin replied.

"I'm sorry my mother's people captured and chained you up," he said to the other giants. "I'm sorry they treated you with such disrespect. It was wrong of them. I understand your anger. And you, Hyrrokkin, you deserved better than to be corralled in a forest you couldn't leave. That, too, was wrong of them. But it was also many lifetimes ago. The gods who did those terrible things are gone. This fight is old and worn out, brittle pages in a book nearly crumbled to dust."

"As fresh in my memory as Koerl's blood on Orla's pike." Hyrrokkin and a few giants slowly crept toward them. But, to Ask's surprise, several did not.

Orla nudged the back of his elbow. "Keep talking."

"My father believed there could be another way, a way we could live here, all of us, and put the past behind us, bury the old hatreds. No more war, no more meaningless death." More were listening now. "We don't have to live together, but we can coexist. We can have peace."

"Oh, I will have peace. When the last body is laid in the last hole of the last graveyard of the gods. When every last soul mourns in the dead halls of Valhalla. Then, I will have my peace." Hyrrokkin was quite close now. "I want my spear and ax. If you won't retrieve them for me, you have outlived your usefulness." She swung the sword from right to left. Ask jumped awkwardly out of the blade's path.

"Looks like we fight our way out." Orla held the blade end of her pike toward the advancing giants. Neither of them said so, but Ask knew, pending a miracle, they wouldn't make it out alive.

Suddenly, several of the giants fell down. Deonte appeared between Ask and Orla. "I leave for one minute, and you get yourselves in trouble."

Grior grimaced several feet away. "There you are, little fishy. Come meet my hook."

"What in the hell does that mean?" Deonte said. He disappeared just briefly. When he returned, he was brandishing Grior's large pike. The giantess looked around perplexed. Even with increased strength as a result of his enchanted boots, the pike—the size of the high school's flagpole—wobbled precariously in his grip. As the giants who had paused their attack during Ask's small speech, no longer dissuaded, regrouped and continued their advance, Ask realized they would soon be blocked in, and Deonte's movement would be limited.

"You've got to get out of here, Deonte."

Before Ask could recount the many reasons for Deonte to leave, Deonte was no longer standing by him. Instead, some general confusion arose behind the horde. Several giants turned to block the pike Deonte swung wildly over his head. He connected with a few knees and thighs but could affect no significant damage. Plus, the pike was so large it set him off balance and detracted from his speed, which made him vulnerable to counterattacks. He couldn't hold up the distraction for long.

Orla paced in a slow orbit around Ask. She spun her pike in impressive circles, causing enough concern that several giants stopped in their tracks. "Now's your chance," she yelled over her shoulder. "Get out of here."

Everything they planned that fateful afternoon, what felt so long ago, had fallen apart. Ask stood like a giant toddler surrounded by angry adults. He wanted to pull himself into a ball, close his eyes, and will away the clattering of swords and the incessant vitriol in the voices around him. For a moment, he pictured himself, Deonte, and Orla laid out in a row, lifeless on the frosty morning grass, fires extinguished and giants gone, scavengers of the air pecking at the most tender morsels on their bones, tugging at the soft meats of their flesh. At that moment, he knew they would not leave the giants' camp alive, not this way.

As he readied his ax for his final stand, a voice—no, not *a* voice, *the* voice of the ax, Bjornen—spoke to him but not with words at first. He felt in his veins the gathering energy that surged as pulses through his arm, in his heart, and up to his brain. And the impression of impulses he heard gathering in his mind coalesced, forming actual words for the first time, and the voice associated with those words sounded just like his father.

"Wrap the amulet around the ax face. I'll do the rest."

Also at that moment, Ask knew what happened to his father: His father had been with him all along, in his hand, mercifully preserved by and in the ax.

There was no question that he would comply. Ask tore the torc from his neck and tied the loose, broken straps around the eye and the heel of the ax head, cinching the amulet tightly against the cheek. The green energy that had first compelled him to pick up the ax now illuminated both ax and amulet. Before he knew what he was doing, he lifted the ax high over his head. Sensing the trajectory and impact of the blow he was about to strike, he commanded, in a voice more powerful than his own, "Run! Now!"

Orla instinctively obeyed, jumping through a brief gap between two rows of giants. Deonte threw Grior's pike and disappeared. Babe tossed aside the wolf he had been gouging with his horns and took massive steps away from the horde now crowding more densely around Ask.

Ask heard Hyrrokkin yell, "I will have that ax!"

"Yes, you will," Ask said. He brought down the ax head with all his might, so powerfully that the bit clove deeply into the ground, up to the beard, creating a small chasm over which he straddled, his legs separated widely.

When he looked up, to his great surprise, all of the giants were gone. He looked down into the massive crevice below him, but he neither saw movement nor heard any groans. The giants were just gone.

Deonte and Orla reappeared, weapons at the ready. Ask readied the ax in case the now empty field was one of Hyrrokkin's tricks. Puzzled, Ask yelled, "What happened?"

"Dude, I was going to ask you the same thing. What did you do?" Deonte studied the rift Ask created from an arm's length away. "That's deep as hell."

Ask looked at Orla pleadingly. Without forming words, he tried to convey the question, *What is this? What did I do?*

Orla just shook her head. "I've never seen anything like it." He noticed that she wouldn't look him in the eyes.

Ask wandered around searching for some evidence of the giants—a shirt sleeve, a buckle, even an ear. But he found nothing. It was as if they had simply vanished. He resisted asking the question at first, because he was afraid of the answer, but he had to know.

"Did I kill them?"

"No," Babe interjected. He, too, had returned. "They are far from here, but they are not dead. You somehow transported them away. Paul managed only a minor transportation once. This was, well, much more."

THEY LINGERED IN A SORT of after-battle stupor for some time. Orla stood off a distance from the rest of them, Koerl's deception and Orla's alleged complicity forming another kind of chasm between them. When Deonte mentioned the sun would be up in a couple of hours, Ask suddenly found himself toeing the edge of that chasm. First, he said, "We'd better ride Babe." He holstered the ax, so he would be less of a burden to his blue friend. Orla also reduced to human dimensions.

Deonte said, "I'll go ahead and let your mother know everything's okay." And, like that, he was gone, which left Ask and Orla quite close to each other on Babe's back with a rather lengthy journey ahead of them.

Once they were both settled, and Babe was trotting north toward home, Ask said, "We don't have to talk about it if you don't want to."

Silence.

"I'm just glad you're okay."

Then, Ask stopped talking. As the adrenaline left his body, a weariness found him like nothing he'd ever experienced before, not after a long hike or an intense soccer game. Every ounce of him ached for sleep. He closed his eyes.

After a while, the early stirrings of morning peeked out over the horizon. Orla's voice awoke him from a deep, dreamless slumber. "It's all my fault," she said. "I almost single-handedly brought us to ruin. Everything was going to plan. I had lured Grior away from Hyrrokkin, tied her up someplace no one would find her, and spent two days at Hyrrokkin's side."

Cautiously, tenderly, he asked, "What happened?"

"Koerl. He was suspicious. My mannerisms didn't quite match Grior's. She sneers constantly, randomly hits the other giants, so they know and acknowledge her place in the horde. I guess I wasn't cruel enough often enough in the right ways. He watched me all the time. The day before our rendezvous, he found me out. They tied me up and told me they would kill you if I tried to run. I- I couldn't warn you. I'm sorry."

"It's not your fault," Ask reassured her. "Any number of things could have gone wrong and, well, everything did. But here we are. All of us made it out alive. And we got the spear. I guess that means we won."

"Yes, but you also had to rescue your mother. That was an unnecessary risk that wouldn't have happened if I'd pulled off my deception."

"And she's okay, too," Ask said, reassuring her.

Despite his talk of winning and everyone being okay, Ask knew he had not seen the last of Hyrrokkin. In fact, the idea of winning didn't feel right at all. If anything, the encounter constituted at best a Hail Mary kind of draw that merely bought them some time. Without the ax and its guidance, the outcome, he knew, would have been much different. Next time—and he knew there would be a next time—he would have to be ready, truly ready. He would talk to Orla later about further training. That is, if he could truly trust her. He didn't blame her, but trust was something else, something more. Nothing felt as certain to him as it once did. In the meantime, on the journey home after a hard-fought night, he would tell himself they were victorious and everyone and everything was fine, and he would do his best to believe it.

CHAPTER 30

PAUL'S DESTINY

ASK LINGERED IN THE SHED while Deonte delivered the play-by-play of their victory to their mothers. Laughter at his reenactment through hand gestures and exaggerated expressions, his sudden appearance as three different people in three different places in the blink of an eye, made Ask feel tired and lonely for some reason, as if the joy from this temporary victory couldn't quite make up for what was yet to come, what Ask still must do. Instead of joining the fun, he stared at the ax he had just set against the wall where he'd first found it, perhaps willing it to speak to him once more, to soothe an ache that continued to strike his heart at unpredictable intervals. Orla, who had once again been forgiven and invited into Ask's home, stood just outside the open door.

"It's funny," he said without turning. "My mother told me I would learn what happened to my father if I opened the shed. I didn't believe her because I didn't know what I was looking for."

Orla didn't respond.

"You know, my father told me once that things aren't always what they seem. He used to talk to fish—did I tell you that? I thought he was teasing me. One day, his face grew serious as he held a fish to his ear, and then, he let it go. I wonder what it whispered to him, where it led him that night."

"Fish carry powerful secrets," Orla finally offered.

"Yes, I believe that's true. Now. I couldn't believe, then, that what shouldn't speak could. What shouldn't be is. Even after the ax summoned me, and the history of the war between gods and giants became, well, painfully real, there were things I wasn't ready to accept."

"Like how a father can walk into a shed and just disappear?" Orla asked.

"Exactly." He allowed his fingers to hover over the ax handle without touching it.

"You know now, don't you?" Orla said.

Ask nodded. "I don't know how exactly. I only know what happened and where he is." He paused before saying, "Bjornen absorbed him."

"Come again?" Orla asked. She was standing next to him now.

"I thought the same thing when Bjornen spoke to me last night. For a split second, I saw the whole thing in my mind, because the energy—his energy—is in me too. You see, my father, a mortal, lived far longer than his body could handle. It began to break down. Bjornen couldn't keep him alive any longer. Even the magic apples my mother fed him couldn't give immortality to a mortal, only extend his life, which it did for a long time, much longer than any human can live. As my father's body weakened, Bjornen did what he considered merciful to such a faithful companion. He absorbed my father's energy."

"But how?"

He thought about this for a moment. He'd been asking himself the same thing for hours. "All matter, even this"—he pinched the skin on the back of his hand—"is energy. As energy, it can be changed and redistributed. He," Ask said, pointing to the ax, "transferred my father's knowledge, a portion of his essence, the parts of his memory that are essential to protect the ax and its mission, to me. I think that's why I can live his past, through his eyes, in my dreams."

"So, your father didn't die or leave. He's been here all along?" Orla marveled at the ax. Ask noticed her expression soften, and he perceived in the light blue of her irises something like the white-blue mornings of deep January, when the temperatures plummet to forty below and newly fallen snow glistens like stardust. "So, when you joined the power of the ax with the amulet. . ." Orla began.

"That was my father's voice guiding me."

"You have to tell your mother," Orla insisted.

"I suspect she already knows, even if she hasn't fully accepted it," Ask said.

"Yes, she knows now." Ask's mother was standing in the doorway. Ask didn't know how long she'd been there. "No, she doesn't want to accept it." A sad smile tugged at her lips. "We knew something was changing nearly sixteen years ago, about a year before you were born. It was, as I've told you, impossible for us to have children before that. But, you see, the apples weren't working any longer. The ax's energy became too intense for him to handle from time to time. When he transformed, it was painful, not quite like the first time it happened before the convergence, but achy and persistent, like arthritis deep in the bones. But from that rejection and deterioration came new life."

"Me." Ask knew too well the dull ache of his father's painful transformations from his most recent dream memories. He felt that pain now, which amplified the other pain pressing into his chest and trying to push its way through into his throat and out of his eyes.

"Ask, I had an inkling of an idea of what happened to your father, but I didn't know exactly what or why it happened. I'm starting to understand it now." After a pause, she asked, "What did he say to you?"

"It's not what he told me," Ask replied. "It was what he showed me. A sort of conscious dream memory."

He recounted the moment his father's voice resounded in his head as the giants pressed in all around him. At first, he described the surge of energy pressing into his mind, the impression to combine the torc with the ax to boost its power, and then the flash of an image that somehow showed him much more than he should have been able to see. As he explained it now, the impossibility of that flash surprised him. While pulling the torc free from his neck, tying it to the ax, and raising the ax for the blow that transported the giants to some distant place, he found himself standing, as his father, in the shed the day he disappeared. He felt his father's weariness as he ran his hand over the eye of Bjornen.

In the solitude of that shed, he heard his father say, "Well, I'm about spent," a sadness in his voice. "It seems you're never quite ready to let go."

Bjornen moaned with a depth of grief Ask couldn't imagine any object, living or inanimate, capable of. In his father's heart, he felt peace as the ax whispered without words, "I will take care of them. Let me now be the protector. You can let go."

"If it were only so easy," his father said. "I just can't *let go*. People hold on until their grip fails, until their hands must be pried from life."

"Let me ease your passing. Let me extend your time the only way I can," the ax answered, the sensation in his body one of compassion, one of love.

Paul fell to his knees, the body he had willed to continue living long past its mortal expiration pressing him toward the earth, back to dust. "As you must," he puffed between breaths harder to command with each exhale.

"Take my handle once more." As Paul did so, the green energy began to leave his body and, with it, Paul's body transformed one last time—not into the giant of the lumberjack warrior made legendary over the centuries, but into the green energy being absorbed from his body, now indistinguishable from his flesh, drawn into the ax.

"Idun, my love," he whispered.

"I will keep her safe," the ax promised.

"My son," Paul called out before he disappeared completely. "Ask."

"You will speak to him again," said Bjornen.

Ask felt tears coursing down his cheeks. "He did," Ask managed to say. "The last thing the voice told me was 'I'm here with you, son. I love you.'" And this love, he remembered, gave him the strength to banish the giants to some distant land.

Orla lowered her head, perhaps remembering her own losses over too many years to count and stayed silent.

Idun went to her son. Ask could sense within her the profound pang of loss but also the relief of finally knowing what had become of her husband: a release, a closure. They held each other. Ask watched the ax over her shoulder and swore he saw a quick green wink issue from the metal.

CHAPTER 31

THE RUNES

ASK FOUND HIMSELF AT SCHOOL on Monday morning feeling much older than he did before his journey on Friday. He sat silently at his homeroom desk, thinking about a battle he couldn't win, learning how his father died, and contemplating how mortality does not spring eternal, not even for those blessed by the gods. The image of his father eviscerated by age, knees collapsing from unstable bone density, finally to dissolve into green flecks of energy to be sucked into the metal head of a sentient ax weighed heavily on his mind. If even for a moment, Ask experienced his father's death vicariously; the memory of a seething cry of agony where there was no mouth to scream seared Ask's heart. A sharp exhale pushed from his lungs. He coughed to cover the peculiar and plaintive sound.

As others arrived to claim their seats in class, Ask realized that he'd been unwittingly rattling stones in his pocket as he tried to suppress the ever-intensifying memory of the painful finale to his father's life. At first, he couldn't remember why he had stones in his pocket. Perhaps he'd picked them up on the road to Hyrrokkin's camp, a reflex from youth, something he and his father would do when they found a particularly unique specimen. He kept a jar with dozens of all kinds of rocks on the windowsill in his room—agates, dacites, obsidian, to name just a few. But that couldn't be. He'd been preoccupied ensuring Grior would not escape. The rocks did have something to do with Grior, though. That much he remembered.

He moved them around until he had all of them in his hand and pulled them out, revealing, in his open palm, the runes. He'd completely forgotten he had them. He looked at the symbols engraved in the stones. One of the stones bore symbols that resembled a straight vertical line, something that could pass for an *h*, or half a church building with an exceptionally tall steeple, and what looked exactly like the capital letter *M*. Another stone had a symbol that resembled either a mask with sideburns or two flags kissing. A third stone showed an angular *R* and something like a pitchfork standing on its tines. The other stones bore odd shapes that sort of represented crosses, animals, and a black moon, almost the exact inverse of a black ball in pool. The rune was roundish and white with this black dot centered on one side. None of the other symbols affected him much, but this black dot made him uneasy. He shifted in his chair. His hand holding the rune shook slightly. *What were you planning, Grior?* he asked silently.

He managed to sit impatiently through class, although he was anxious to discuss the stones with Deonte. When the bell rang, he launched himself from his chair and out into the hallway. The halls filled quickly with people, but he couldn't see Deonte. He did, however, run into Jepp, literally. Still adjusting to his strength post-convergence, Ask accidentally knocked Jepp into the lockers, rather solidly.

Jepp turned toward him, both startled and angry. "What the hell do you think you're doing?"

Ask, always the diplomat, said, "Oh, hey, Jepp, I'm sorry. I didn't mean to run into you."

"Run into me? You pushed me. On purpose. And I'm going to show you what happens when you push people, nerd."

"I wouldn't do that, Jepp. Really. It's in your best interest to—" Ask started to say.

Jepp swung his right fist, the one he used to throw touchdowns and win games, upon which his talent and fame relied, against Ask's chin. A loud crack and Jepp's scream brought curious passersby to a stop. As Jepp held the wrist connected to the hand now curled into an *S* shape that could only loosely be called a fist, Ask started to apologize. "Jepp, look, I'm sorry."

Jepp skirted past him, whispering as he went, "Freak." Suddenly, Jepp's pants were around his ankles, and he tripped. Not having both hands to brace himself, he went down on a shoulder and rolled onto his back, the little smiling dolphins on his boxers seeming to laugh with everyone else around. Sheryl Ann walked past Jepp and smiled at Ask.

A light hand on his shoulder, and Ask knew Deonte stood next to him. "Nice touch," he said. "First, you push him, and then you break his hand on your face. Dude deserves it."

"Wearing your 'new shoes' to school today, I see," Ask said.

"Well, you know. Gotta break 'em in." Deonte grinned.

A little more seriously, Ask said, "He didn't deserve it."

"No? He punched you," Deonte said.

"Yes, but it didn't hurt me. It hurt him. We need to be careful with our," he paused, stealing a quick glance around, "special talents. As Jepp just proved, we could really hurt people."

"Yeah, alright. Be careful. Got it. Even if the jerk deserves it," Deonte grumbled.

"Ask?" It was Sheryl Ann. "That was brave of you," she said, "standing up to Jepp like that."

"Yeah, well, it wasn't intentional," Ask said, his voice cracking.

Deonte raised an eyebrow, as if to say, "Don't screw up your chances this time."

"Well, he's always been a little jealous of you," she continued.

"Of me? Why?"

"Because you're smart. He talks about you like you're the competition." She blushed.

"Sure. That's because. . ." He stopped in midsentence, realizing he was about to say, *he knows I like you too*, but instead he settled with, "we used to be friends."

Sheryl Ann nodded. "I know. He told me. Look, things aren't that good between me and Jepp; haven't been for a while. I guess I'm trying to ask"—she laughed at the play on Ask's name in the verb—"if you want to hang out sometime."

Deonte's smile was so big Ask could feel it next to him.

"Sure, sometime. I've got some things going on right now I need to focus on, but we'll work something out."

Sheryl Ann's smile diminished a bit. Ask realized too late that he had just brushed her off. "Okay," she said. "I'll. . . I'll see you around." Books pressed tight against her chest, she lowered her head and shuffled down the hall. At a classroom door, she looked back and managed a smile. Ask, for reasons he couldn't explain, didn't return the smile but looked away.

"And that is how Ask ruins a perfectly good opportunity," Deonte said facetiously. "You have got to be kidding me. A whole summer—that's how long I listened to you talk about her. Remember how your heart broke when you saw her holding Jepp's hand?"

Ask nodded. "I do." He didn't know what else to say. It's not that he wasn't interested. He found it hard to explain, so he simply said, "She wouldn't understand." That old, worn expression summed it up about right, he felt. He recognized the gulf that now separated him from the world he knew and the one he discovered. Sheryl Ann would expect a reality in which giants lived only in fairytales and myths were buried remnants of dead poetry.

Perhaps remembering his initial reaction to Ask's first transformation, Deonte, with his eyes set on his shoes, humorlessly replied, "I get it." Deonte would also know the tradeoff now, the cost of straddling two worlds, forcibly part of one in order to protect the other. For instance, he'd never be able to wear his new shoes to football practice or in a big game. He'd always have to hide his full potential from the world of mortals. Both of them, it crossed Ask's mind, may now better understand a portion of Orla's loneliness.

And then Deonte said something that surprised Ask. "But she might. I mean, she could come to understand. With time. Like I did. Like my mother and your father did."

Was it worth the risk of exposing something people were better off not knowing about? Ask didn't have the answer to that question. He simply replied, "Yeah, I guess."

"There he is," Deonte said, poking Ask in the chest. "There's the guy who thinks hella too much and talks himself out of all kinds of things that could bring him happiness. Seriously, don't just think about what I said. Take a chance."

Ask nodded and then changed the subject before he inadvertently committed to something. "Hey, I was looking for you. Remember these?" He covertly showed Deonte the runes in his hand.

"Ah, hell. Yeah, I remember. Something to do with Grior's mission before we spoiled it, right?"

"Right. I'm not sure what they mean. The symbols are ancient and may or may not be from this world." His whisper diluted to a shallow undertone, barely louder than a breath, as he reached the end of his sentence. "We need to find Orla after school. She'll know what to do."

CHAPTER 32

THE MARK

DESPITE HIS URGENCY, ASK PAUSED when he saw Orla in the distance. The snow had finally arrived. He didn't want to disturb her because she seemed so content. She strolled the school grounds, face turned to the wind ushering in cold flurries from the north, eyes closed and smiling. He was surprised not only to discover Deonte also smiling, but that his own heart sank, just as quickly as it had lifted upon seeing her. He didn't know what that meant. They met her by the tree that had come to represent the threshold of their friendship.

The night before, Ask and Orla stayed up late talking. She confessed that Hyrrokkin's offer to forgive her for leaving the giant horde and protecting Ask had tempted her greatly, not because she wanted to betray Ask nor because she cared at all for the giants under Hyrrokkin's command, but because her people were willing to take her back. "To be wanted, even by them, after so many years of solitude... Well, it meant being part of something again," she explained.

Troubled both by Orla's consideration of betrayal and by her admittance of intense loneliness, Ask had to know, so he asked, "Why did you decide to help us in the end? When we were clearly outnumbered and should have died? Why stand with us? With me?"

Orla set a hand on his shoulder. "Because I can live with loneliness."

Ask thought about this response. So much implication, so much unspoken truth about the costs of betraying oneself, one's beliefs, one's friends. "You don't have to be alone anymore, Orla. You have my mother, Deonte, and me. I know we're not giants, but we can be your people, too."

Orla smiled softly, genuinely—a rare thing—and said, "Thanks, Ask."

The clear sky exposed so many stars that Ask couldn't name them all, nor did he want to. Perhaps Polaris did show a true north, but often, he'd learned, directions, or rather expectations, have a funny way of steering you off course. The world is full of giants, after all, set on clearing the way for their version of paradise—even if that version looks more like hell and they have to blaze a trail through everyone and everything else to get there, killing their gods and eating their own hearts. But sometimes giants did just the opposite of what you expected.

At the tree, Orla held her palm out to catch snowflakes. Unlike mortals who catch snowflakes and watch them melt against their warm skin, the snowflakes on Orla's hand remained intact and continued their journey toward the ground only when she released them. "That's a pretty cool trick," Deonte said. And then aloud he pondered, "I wonder if I could run between the flakes."

Ask shook his head to signal irrelevance, and then held his hand open to show Orla the runes. "We need to ask you about these. Grior had them with her the night we rescued my mother. She wanted us to leave her locked up when we left for our attack. Do you have any idea what she was planning to use them for?"

Orla's smile faded. She pushed the runes around with her index finger until she could see their etchings. "These are ancient and dark, Ask. They are old, even by the standards of the giants' long history. There are several sets of these runes, and most of them portend destruction, even initiate that destruction. Have you been carrying these with you for long?"

Ask felt his cheeks pinken with embarrassment. "Well, I forgot I had them. I guess they've been in the pocket of these jeans since Friday. I just noticed them again this morning."

"These stones," she said, pushing a few to one side of his hand, "spell out the phrase 'ice mark.' The symbols describe the purpose of the mark. I see the resurrection, the thief, and the blood symbols. This is curious." She picked up the round stone upon which the dark circle had been, the one that caused Ask's hand to shake, but was now missing. "A plain white stone?"

"What?" Ask flipped the stone over and over. "That's not right. There was a black circle in the middle of this." He shivered, thinking about the vast emptiness of that dark void.

"That is the mark." Orla grabbed him by the wrist. Below the runes on Ask's palm, like a cancerous mole, was the imprint of the mark, as if tattooed into his skin. Ask had never seen Orla so worried, not even the other night as they fought for their lives.

"What does this mean? What do we do?"

And then everything went dark. The last thing Ask saw was Orla looking down at him.

CHAPTER 33

THE VOID

ASK HAD ENTERED A VAST emptiness, the landscape around him like the faded images of old photographs devoid of color and damaged by age. Nothing grew in this nightscape. The ground was muted grays, treeless and desiccated, and the air still and scentless. There was no sun or moon or light or dark. Everything was stone and cold, nothing alive or dead. Nothing stirred, no wind, no water. It was as if the world had burned so thoroughly and so absolutely that it could never live again. So definitive was the destruction, in fact, that not even a corpse of animal or human could be seen. All had become and would remain dust forever.

He wandered aimlessly for some time, trying to find his bearings. After a long while, what felt to him like hours, he sat on the hard, dead ground and felt the most profound sense of hopelessness he'd ever experienced. He would die here, and his bones would crumble to dust, and no one would ever know. This nothing-scape would be his tomb.

"That's not how it ends," a voice said. At first, Ask couldn't imagine someone else stuck here with him. This was *his* hell concocted by the giants who had found a way to get rid of him for good.

"That's not true." Clearly a voice, and it could read his mind. Or was he already coming unhinged in such a place? Was the vacant world so silent that his thoughts formed words? The voice louder now said, "I'm not in your head, Ask."

There in front of him suddenly stood his father.

"How are you here?" Ask didn't trust his senses. Not in this nowhere place.

The figure of his father, not a memory this time, appeared much the same as he had the last time Ask saw him—baseball cap of the Minnesota Twins, two days' growth, and a polo. He was tall, had a sturdy build from years of hard labor in the fields, and an asymmetrical smile that always seemed to Ask cockeyed and smirky, as if the man was perpetually on the verge of delivering the punchline to a joke. The kindness in his eyes, too, the assurance the joke wasn't on you.

"The convergence. Bjornen and the energy transfer. Part of me will always be with you. I guess you could say I came along for the ride. Though, I must say," his father added, "the accommodations are lacking."

Ask smirked. "Where are we?"

"Inside the mark, of course. It transferred to your hand as you fiddled with the rune." No reproach in his voice.

"What is this place?" Ask pressed.

"Let's call it a hologram in your head of Asgard after the giants burned it to the core. Right before they made for Earth, they set it ablaze with the foundries of the underworld. Surtr bellowed the flames so hot that every root of every plant scorched to ash. Every animal cooked in its own skin and then melted until its juices dried to dust. Buildings, even those made of rock, disintegrated to their primary elements. It was a total and complete annihilation. It is what's left of your mother's home, or at least a replication of what is left."

"This is what will become of Earth if Hyrrokkin has her way," Ask said. He remembered the dream memory and Hyrrokkin's declaration that war was eternal.

"Maybe. Though the giants will need to live somewhere. I don't take them for the self-immolating types." His father winked.

How could the man be so flippant in this place? "Am I really here?" he asked.

"That's a complicated question and an even more complicated answer. Yes and no. You are not physically here, but your essence is here. So, in the sense of how energy and Bjornen's power work, you are here."

Ask shook his head. "This was their plan all along. This is what Grior was sent to do." Ask felt ashamed having so fully fallen into the trap.

"I think you overestimate their tactics, Ask. I fought those giants for a long time, and, yes, they are wily, conniving, and deceitful, but they are not known for being so elaborately and precisely strategic in their machinations. More likely, Hyrrokkin planted Grior in your custody with those runes in hopes something would develop. She probably had other plans as well. She's always preferred the shotgun approach to strategy. She aims with a broad intention and figures something will hit the target."

"And I stepped right into it." A crushing sense of failure weighed him down like many giants' thumbs pressing on him. "What do we do now? Wait here forever?" *Eventually become dust on the dead ground*, he added to himself. A lightless sun cast a mute shadow beneath them, a slightly darker gray against the lighter gray ground.

"That's not how this place works," his father said. "It is a world between. No one stays here forever. It is the nightmare world of Earth and the corpse world of Asgard. The giants use it to locate their enemies. Once they find you, you will awake."

"And lead them right back to us. So much for sending them all away." Hopelessness gripped him by the ankles, like corpse hands reaching from graves below, to pull him deep into their despair. "How do you know so much about this awful place?" Ask shivered despite lacking a corporeal presence.

"Bjornen and I are, well, much closer since we merged. I guess you could say his knowledge is my knowledge and mine is his. He's had a long and extensive history with both the gods and the giants. He carries a share of Mjölnir's memories as well. He gleaned insight into some of Hyrrokkin's mind from her failed attempts to converge with the hammer. Her mind is not too dissimilar from this place, metaphorically speaking."

Ask shuddered. How could he fight a creature whose mind functioned as a literal hell? Perhaps it would be better if he stayed and succumbed to the emptiness.

"Look, Ask. One thing I know about you is that you don't give up. This hopelessness is just not who you are. You'll be prepared when they come for you."

Something had been tugging uneasily at Ask's mind since his fight with the giants, something he hadn't confronted because doing so meant acknowledging his severe disadvantage in this war, his vulnerability, his dependency. The thought surfaced in this horrible place. "I never could have escaped that night if you hadn't told me what to do." He stared at his feet. "I'd be dead." *Like this world*, the thought occurred to him, perhaps his soul permanently affixed to its graveyard surface.

"If I hadn't suggested that one idea, Ask, you would have found another way." His father paused before continuing. "I wish I had told you about all of this, prepared you in some way, trained you, showed you how to harness the ax's power." Another pause, longer this time. "I guess I hoped you would never need to know. It's not an easy life. I didn't want it for you."

Melancholy covered this not-world like a cloak, every moment in this void an eternity. Ask imagined his feet transforming to the dust beneath him, crawling up his legs, gripping his waist, sucking the moisture from his skin, choking the air from his lungs, and finally suffocating the breath from his lips. "They'll eventually kill me, kill mom. If not today, then tomorrow or in six weeks or in ten years. I can't stop them." He felt an urge to cry, but no tears could form in the still, dry, dead air. "It's hopeless."

"It's this place," his father corrected. "It makes everything seem that way. But it will pass. You will return to the full living world. When you do, you will prepare for Hyrrokkin. You'll be ready."

From an immeasurable distance, a loud guttural cackle cracked through the silence, more maddening and frightening in its contrast against the desolation. Ask gripped his shoulders with his hands, pulling himself into an embrace. "She found us," he whispered, shaking, fear immobilizing him. "We're dead. You were right to keep it a secret from me. The ax should have gone to someone stronger, someone braver. I can't protect it. They will kill me and take it."

He pictured Hyrrokkin's immense scar-pocked face inches from his own, a massive boot crushing his sternum, her hand yanking the ax free from his dead fingers. He envisioned shrinking under that boot until his diminutive bones could no longer yield to the weight and exploded, oozing marrow and blood.

"Look at me, Ask. This fear is part of the mark. Hyrrokkin is using it to implant these thoughts to distract and dishearten you. Do you know why the ax chose you?"

That booming laugh seemed to bounce around inside his skull as if it resided there, as if it had always been there. He shook his head, afraid now even to speak. "She'll find me," he repeated silently, "she'll find me," as if it were fact, an inevitability.

"Not because you are my son, not because of some promise to me. Bjornen chose you because of you—your intelligence, your intuition, your compassion. Because he trusts you."

Ask tried to focus on what his father was saying to him, wanted wholeheartedly to believe those words, latch onto them as if they could be real too; but the vile, loud laughter felt like the last sound he would ever hear.

"Remember I love you," his father said, then. Chimes began to rattle in his ears, replacing the laughter. "Tell your mother I love her, too." He paused. "For eternity."

Ask covered his ears and his eyes. He felt dizzy, as if he'd just stepped off the Corkscrew at Valley Fair in Minneapolis, like that time when he was younger, and he'd rushed for a trash can to throw up. His father's hand was on the back of his neck that time too, grounding him.

"They found you. You're going to be waking up soon, son," his father said, positioning himself in front of Ask, pulling his hands from his eyes. "I need you to remember one more thing. I may not be able to plant this thought in your dreams, since it is not my memory, so hold on to it as you pass back into your world. Tell your mother it's time for the alliance. She'll resist, but you must convince her. Go north and seek out Freyand. She is the next protector of the spear." His father began to fade.

Before Ask woke up, he heard only "majestic," "strong," and "cruel."

His mother and Orla stood over Ask as he came to. Heim lifted his head from the base of the bed, where he lay warming Ask's feet. Head aching and threatening to split, Ask couldn't remember how he'd gotten to his bedroom. What little he remembered from his blackout also began to fade. He muttered, "Dad?"

Idun comforted him. "Son, your father is gone, remember? He, well, he's part of Bjornen now."

Ask shook his head. "He was there. In that awful place." He could no longer picture in his mind what the mark looked like, but he knew how it felt.

He lifted his hand, turned it palm up, revealing the black circle that had transferred from the stone. His gut wrenched and he threw up over the side of his bed. Covered in bile and remnants of his last meal, a new stone appeared that looked like the inverse of an eight ball. The black dot on his palm was gone, his memory of the experience in the mark nearly expelled with the stone.

He quickly blurted, "They are coming, we must go north to Freyand, and form an alliance." He then fell into a deep, dreamless sleep.

This time, when he awoke, it was as if nothing odd had transpired. In fact, he was surprised to find his mother and Orla standing nearby. "Um, a little privacy, please," he said.

"It's an aftereffect of the mark," Orla whispered to Idun. "He can't remember the danger he's in. It's rather genius, really. You mark someone, locate them, and then make them forget so you can surprise them. Koerl used that ploy often. . ." As if realizing she was talking glibly about a tactic that resulted in many deaths during the bloodiest years of the war, she added quickly, "Well, at least he won't be using it anymore."

"How are you feeling?" his mother asked.

Perplexed, Ask said, "What's going on?"

"We're just glad you're okay," she said, placing a hand on his.

Deonte suddenly appeared in his room. "Hey, man. Holy crap. You're alive!"

"Why wouldn't I be alive? We won, didn't we? We sent the giants away?"

"And," Orla added, "the mark, once expelled, also leaves in its wake a heightened sense of security and safety."

Ask didn't understand what they were all excited about. "What's the matter with all of you?"

Deonte offered a recap: "Okay, so you had these stones with writing on them. One of them had this big dot on it. It somehow transferred from the stone to your hand, and then you passed out. I ran you home, Orla and your mom did some kind of chant thing, and then you woke up a few hours later. Now, here we are. You can't remember a thing, and we're trying to sort out what you said when you woke up the first time."

"He won't remember for a while, but some of his memory will return. Those who are marked are typically disposed of quickly. . ." Again, Orla paused, as if recognizing she'd crossed a line. She added, "With time, the influence of the mark fades. He'll remember bits and pieces of what he said and, well, where he was."

Both adamant and angry, Ask replied, "You think I'd know if I'd been somewhere and said something."

He got out of bed and started getting ready for the day, despite being woozy and a little unsteady. "We're going to be late for school," he said to Deonte.

"No, we're not. It's Saturday afternoon," Deonte said. "I'm not going to school on a weekend. Forget that."

It couldn't be Saturday. How did Ask lose nearly an entire week?

CHAPTER 34

ASK REMEMBERS

IN THE DAYS FOLLOWING HIS blackout, Ask felt a bit like either an invalid back from war to convalesce in a sanitarium or a memory patient in an assisted living facility. His mother and Orla hovered incessantly. At first, this confused Ask. His mother had explicitly banned Orla from her home. Yes, she had changed her mind and allowed Orla back, but the two were still far from being friends. There was, after all, the alleged betrayal and the subsequent kidnapping. So, he wasn't sure what had changed his mother's attitude toward the giantess. He didn't mind, of course, having Orla around. She smiled more. She seemed to have found a place where she could belong. His mother had even given Orla the guest room.

Often, he would see the two women together attending to chores around the house or walking the yard, laughing, happy. It was strange, but this new friendship further isolated Ask. In the week he'd been unconscious, the world seemed to have moved on without him. When they spoke quietly across the room, he felt more and more alone. Since he couldn't remember what had happened, not even what he himself had told them upon first emerging from his blackout, he also felt useless and damaged. Somewhere deep inside him, a voice told him, "See, you are worthless. Give up. They don't need you."

When asked how he was doing, Ask would shrug and go up to his room. Nobody demanded he stay. They let him do whatever he wanted. Even Deonte, who frequently visited, deferred to Ask's wishes and checked in with his mother downstairs. He would listen to them talk before Deonte left. Ask would army crawl to the top of the stairs, where the voices below were amplified, and wait to hear them say, "He's a lost cause. Maybe someone else should try using the ax."

One morning, Ask didn't get out of bed. He figured there was no point. Plus, he didn't want to see the smiles on other people's faces. They infuriated him now. Their smiles, he was sure, were meant to mock him. If his mother or Orla came to check on him, he simply said, "Get out." He also grew obsessive about conversations too quiet for him to hear. He was convinced these were plots to oust him from the group. A group, he complained to himself, formed because of him. They planned to usurp his authority and steal his source of power, he was certain of it.

He had all but convinced himself to take up the ax and leave when it happened, as Orla predicted. He remembered.

The image of a muted landscape flashed through his mind. A fear welled within him.

Orla and his mother were seated next to him at the dinner table when the first flashes of these memories returned. He saw his father standing near him, as dull gray as pencil lead, in a world of ash and sorrow. The fear of this dead place compounded by the fear of Hyrrokkin's laughter caused him to convulse involuntarily. Yes, that laughter had signaled both the triumph of discovering a path back to him and a sinister promise to end the gods once and for all. The voice that had been poisoning his mind had been hers, somehow embedded deep in his psyche. He let go of all thoughts of leaving alone.

"Hyrrokkin's coming," he said.

"Where is she?" his mother demanded. "How soon will she return?" The fear now in her eyes, too.

Ask shook his head. "I don't know. Dad told me I would wake up when she found me. I heard her crooked, ugly, mocking laughter in my head. She was everywhere and nowhere at the same time. I know this doesn't make any sense." He placed a hand on the crown of his head, as if doing so would hold his thoughts together, press out the viscous laughter.

"It's okay, Ask," Orla said. "The giants don't appear themselves in the mark. They only use it to locate you. They use another stone, a seer stone, to peer into the void. From what I remember of the portal you created, they must be quite a distance from here. I think we have time."

"Time for what?" Idun asked. "To run? To hide? To fight?"

"To form an alliance," Ask said. He now remembered what his father told him. "With Freyand."

"You don't know what you're asking." She waved a dismissive hand. "She's as much a butcher as Hyrrokkin. You ally with her, and you might as well give away your freedom. Yes, the lion may help with the hyenas, but what happens when the hyenas are all dead? What does the lion want or need in return? More than a pound of flesh, I promise you. We defeat Hyrrokkin without Freyand."

Ask smiled, the first time in what must have been weeks. "He said you'd resist."

"You mean, your father knew I'd be reasonable," Idun insisted.

"He also said to tell you he loves you," Ask added. "For eternity."

After a brief smile, she retorted, "That doesn't make his idea any better."

"What are our options?" Orla asked. "I mean, Ask, Deonte, and I nearly died the last time we fought Hyrrokkin's horde. If Freyand isn't an option, then what else can we do? Who else can we turn to?"

"We've talked about this, Orla," Idun said. *Was this the subject of their secret conversations?* Ask wondered. "We lay low. Create misdirection. Stay close to the shield."

"Our plan is to do nothing?" Ask shouted. "For how long? Eternity? We can't hide in a bubble forever. We have to do something. If this Freyand can help, we need to make an alliance. We get rid of the giants, and then we worry about Freyand. One problem at a time."

"Think about what you are saying, Ask. Your father is right. Freyand can help us defeat the giants but consider the cost. And, with Freyand, there is always a cost, greater than anything you can imagine. Did your father happen to mention why Freyand hasn't already killed the giants?"

Ask shook his head.

"Because, son, her consciousness was imprisoned in a sort of vessel used to preserve her life when we all fled Asgard. This vessel limits her abilities. The giants knew she would be a threat, so they hunted her when their horde was much larger, tried to ensnare her before she left Asgard. They understood that once she returned to her goddess form, they would not be able to contain her. She killed more giants singlehandedly than anyone else in the war. If we release her, we unleash on this world the most dangerous being it's ever seen, and she will be angry."

Orla nodded. "Maybe we find another way."

CHAPTER 35

DENIAL'S STONE

SINCE THERE WAS NO WAY of telling when the giants would return, the days passed for Ask in a peculiar mix of apprehension and monotony. Ask and Deonte went to school, trained with Orla in the afternoons, and wrote papers and studied for tests before bed. Soon, the fear of impending doom became a prolonged period of frustrated waiting, during which time everyone was on edge. Deonte was even pulled from the starting roster of the basketball team for "starting a fight."

Adding to the frustration, December brought plummeting temperatures and snow accumulations, along with midterms prior to the holiday break. Orla spent long hours, Ask noticed, walking in the snow. One evening, after she returned from a walk down their lane, amidst fat, lazy flakes, her shirt and hair covered white in the entryway—she never wore a coat on these walks—he asked her, "Why are you, um, so happy in the snow?"

Still smiling, she said, "It's where I belong."

Ask furrowed his brow. How could anyone belong in the cold? It was uncomfortable. "But you stay outside for a long time. Don't you worry about freezing to death?"

Orla anticipated his confusion. "I'm not human, Ask, nor am I Asgardian. I'm a giant. We come from a land that is always cold. The blood coursing through our bodies, unlike humans, is cold. Because we are cold inside, we respond best to a cold environment. It feels good. My homeland is gloriously snow-covered most of the year. A frozen paradise."

What she said registered with Ask's brain, but it didn't resonate with his understanding. "But don't you worry about frostbite? Skin is a sensitive organ."

"Let me explain it this way. You know how you can train with me in your transformed state and not get cold?"

This was true. He nodded.

"It's because your internal engine is running hotter than it does when you are in your human form. When you're done exerting all that energy, you get cold, right? Well, my engine just happens to run cold all the time." Ask wondered what it would feel like to be cold inside and out all the time. It sounded terrible. He shivered.

"It's not so bad. Except," Orla paused, "summers are torture."

Deonte suddenly appeared next to them. "No lie," he said, "you're as cold as ice."

Orla rolled her eyes. "Look, Ask, your annoying friend has paid us a visit. Again."

Deonte winked at Ask. "Just got a little antsy. Any word on the lumberjack-o-meter about the giants? I'm amped."

"Is that what happened with Steve Metzler and Brian Revers at basketball practice the other day? Did you think they were giants?" Ask said, in reference to the fight Deonte had gotten into that led to his suspension from the team.

"Not my best moment, true. Since you must know, my beef with them had nothing to do with giants but with their attitudes. Steve pushed me down, and then Brian stepped on me during a scrimmage. They disrespected me, and so I applied some humility." Deonte threw a couple of punches to punctuate his point.

"Not with the shoes, I hope," Orla added. "Those are sacred weapons meant to protect. They shouldn't be used lightly."

"Whoa, Mom." Deonte held up a hand. "No, I do not wear that pair of Jordans to ball. Plus, I don't need to be superfast to dance around those fools. Yes, the punch to the face was a little much, I admit. I could have been more responsible and patient. Let's see, what else did I tell my mom? Right, I won't do it again. I will be more mature next time. Satisfied?"

Orla shook her head. "Good night." She climbed the stairs to her room.

"I've been thinking," Deonte added when Orla was out of sight. "Maybe you and I should go after this Freyand person, just the two of us."

"I don't know. We agreed to explore other options," Ask said.

"How's that going? Let's see the list of those options." Of course, Ask could produce no such list. None of them could think of anything other than preparing themselves for the inevitable return of the giants. He shrugged.

"My point exactly. Ask, even your father told us this was the way. Isn't he some kind of super brain in that ax? Maybe he can tell the future or something."

Deonte was right, of course. Freyand was Ask's father's idea. "I don't know," Ask said. "What if we give it some time? I think the giants are someplace very cold and far away recuperating."

"What makes you think that?" Deonte asked.

"Call it a hunch." He looked up the stairs in the direction of Orla's room, where the window was no doubt cracked, letting in the "comfortable" cold.

"Doesn't that mean the giants are one step ahead of us?"

"How so?"

"Think about it, man. They obviously know Freyand is a threat. Maybe they even saw or heard you talking to your father in that in-between place. Could they have overheard what he said to you? If they know what shape she's stuck in, couldn't they find her and kill her? Eliminate the one person who can help us?" Deonte explained.

Ask realized how frighteningly feasible this could be. Why else hadn't the giants attacked already? But they couldn't just rush off because something might happen to someone none of them had met and his mother considered dangerous. Ask had to think about it. A decision like this could not be made lightly. It was one thing to ignore one of his mother's requests. It was another to outright disobey her when he knew exactly how she felt about Freyand. Yes, thinking was needed right now, not action.

But, think about it, he did not. Soon days turned into weeks. Suddenly, Ask found himself at the brink of winter break. He had more or less shifted the notion of going after Freyand to the back of his mind. He'd even begun questioning whether thinking about it was necessary. Maybe, he told himself, the giants aren't coming. Perhaps he had transported them to another dimension, perhaps another time. If portals could send matter across great distances, why not to parallel universes or times buried deep in the past or futures so far ahead their existences were inconceivable in the present? He would celebrate Christmas, he decided, as he had done as a child, before the ax strapped him with the unnecessary responsibility of bearing the burden of protecting the world from giants. Who's to say they hadn't been victorious all along? Perhaps there was no longer a need even for the ax.

When Deonte revisited going after Freyand, Ask replied, "We haven't heard a sound from the giants. Maybe they've given up, licked their wounds and crawled into a cave somewhere. Maybe they're gone."

Deonte protested. "Ask, every minute we wait we give them the advantage."

Ask blew it off. He even left the ax sitting in the shed for days at a time. He'd find an excuse to skip training: "It's too cold," "I have too much homework. You want me to get into a good college, don't you?" or "I'm just not feeling up to it right now."

Orla argued at first, tried to motivate him, reminding him that the giants were coming, that he himself had confirmed it. Her admonitions and predictions, however, didn't sway him. Soon, she stopped pushing back and would go out on her own.

With the trees devoid of their leaves, Ask could see her from his bedroom window swinging her pike and practicing her footwork in the meadow where she had first instructed him. He watched her advance, pike pointed forward, pivot, oscillate, shift position, lunge, parry, and stab a pile of hay bales they had stacked for striking. He pushed down the sharp pangs of shame and guilt for not joining her deep inside himself, to the void, the place where he pretended all worries disappeared, where feelings were dead, gray ash, and everything, he would remind himself, ultimately crumbled to dust, and there was nothing anyone could do about it.

In the moments he remembered the void into which he'd descended as a consequence of the mark, he closed his eyes and forced the images even deeper, into a place where he told himself thoughts die. He attempted to console himself by reading the books of his childhood—*The Once and Future King*, *Lord of the Rings*, *The Lion, the Witch, and the Wardrobe*. He abandoned these books nearly as quickly as he opened them. Always, there was some reference to a monster, some giant or villain bounding through the pages. He wasn't safe from these images, not even when he chanced some early reads, like Dr. Seuss or Shel Silverstein, in which the world transformed in some ghastly way. Always that terrible, menacing laugh awaiting him at the flip of a page.

And, so he slept, early and late, retiring to his room as soon as he returned from school, heading down to the kitchen for a quick breakfast only moments before he needed to leave the next morning. But his sleep was restless and dark. Here the thoughts he'd worked so hard to push away grew legs and strutted across his subconscious. He dreamt constantly that he had forgotten something and found himself crouching defensively in the shadow of a massive figure. No longer did he wear his father's memories. Instead, he ran endlessly with the ax, looking for a place to bury it where it would never be found. Always, the ax would cling to his hand as if it were affixed to him like an appendage, a part of his body.

On the last day before holiday break, he further assured himself all was well by imagining Christmas mornings when he was young—the younger, the better—his mind most soothed by the abstract images it couldn't quite grasp, a vague glow of colorful lights, a generic rip of wrapping paper, a whiff of pine. Of this last memory, he stepped carefully; too much focus and he might picture himself transformed as his father pushing through snow-laden pine trees toward screams issuing from a nearby cabin. If he controlled his thoughts and made them agreeable, he would be pacified. The world would once again slip contentedly into its normal axis and spin as it should. The North Star would stay unmoved, giants would remain in books, and he could find solace in the child he was before all this happened.

He avoided Jepp at school that day. He didn't want the cast on Jepp's hand to remind him of his new strength and all it implied. He found that his strength had actually begun to wane as the days away from Bjornen passed. A few more weeks and he really would be the Ask he was before the convergence. Such a possibility appealed to him immensely. Fortunately, he found that Jepp didn't want to run into him either, so it wasn't difficult to brush the reminders of that altercation aside. He also attempted to avoid Deonte, who insisted on talking about the giants. Even when Ask told him not to worry, Deonte demanded they form a plan. He invoked the names of Hyrrokkin and Freyand, making these discussions nearly intolerable for Ask to bear, the names like banshees screaming in his ears. Deonte now had him cornered near his locker before last period.

"So, is the plan to wait it out, then?" Deonte asked.

"I guess you can look at it that way," Ask said. "There really isn't anything to wait out. I'm pretty certain it's all over."

"Did you see that in a dream? Did you visit with your father again?" Deonte pressed.

Ask swallowed hard, his throat dry. "The magic's wearing off. I think it's a sign that this is over."

"I don't understand, Ask. After you woke from, well, your coma or whatever it was, you said we had to find Freyand. Now you're saying that was all a mistake? What about the mark? Didn't you say they know where we are and are coming for us?"

"I don't remember what I said. I was unconscious and blurted the first thing that came to mind. It must have been nonsense." Ask wanted badly to get to class.

"Nonsense that specific about someone you never heard of before? I don't know, man. Something's going on with you. I don't like it."

"Look," Ask pleaded. He placed his hands on Deonte's shoulders. "We have a chance to go back to how things used to be. We can put this behind us and try to enjoy life again. Let's bury the monsters and move on."

"That would be easier to do if they were actually dead. I suggest you snap out of this funk and start training again. We need to—"

"Don't say it again. The only thing I need to be ready for is midterms." Then, he changed the subject to Deonte, reminding him there were still a few games left in the season before the semester ended. "You should check with the coach; maybe he'll let you back on the basketball team."

Deonte shook his head. "Later." He pushed past, and Ask watched his friend stomp off to class.

Ask spent the last class of the day agitated. Why had Deonte said those things? There was no need to storm off. He treated Ask as if he were the unreasonable one. His contemplations of that encounter accompanied Ask home, where they tugged irritatingly at his conscience. He found himself stewing in his bedroom, unable to concentrate on homework or escape into a comforting nostalgia. He distracted himself by staring out the window at snow amassing on his windowsill. Winds soon swirled the flakes into a blizzard. He could scarcely make out the figure standing at the end of the long driveway. He killed the lights in his room and squinted, his face close to the window. It was Orla, her hands outstretched, head tilted back, basking, it appeared, in the cold. He envied that moment of genuine joy.

But it lasted just a moment. She dropped her hands suddenly. Something wasn't right. In milliseconds, she brandished her pike. Ask's stomach wrenched. He ran down the stairs, out the front door, and down the lane. Without even being summoned, Bjornen flew into his hand. A powerful surge coursed through his body, and Ask stood beside Orla, transformed and ready to fight.

"What is it?" he inquired, his booming voice vanishing into the white void. Yes, he realized, that is exactly what it reminded him of, the blotted landscape, the interminable sameness, the blinding nothingness—it was a void, a reflection of the place where he had lost all hope.

"Over there." Orla pointed with the blade of her pike.

Ask squinted, though peering into the white nothingness took every ounce of strength and courage he had. "I don't see anything." He felt his voice quiver.

"I saw him. He was staring at me," Orla said.

"Who?" Ask didn't want to ask the question, but he spoke the word and couldn't take it back.

"Koerl."

"No," he said. "That's impossible. You killed Koerl. Put your pike through his chest."

"I know," she said.

In the darkness, amidst the swirling white vastness, Ask heard, as clear as if the voice reverberated in his head, Hyrrokkin laughing. Ask's hands shook, and he dropped the ax. He leaned forward, fell to his knees, clothes stretched, torn, and dangling irreparably around his human-sized self since he'd stopped wearing the tunic some time ago, and heaved uncontrollably for a couple of minutes. Below him, in his sickness, he saw a black stone melting the snow. The darkness had finally been purged.

Orla said, "That is the last of the runes, the locating rune. When it is expelled, it means the giants have found their mark. They've returned."

CHAPTER 36

FREYAND'S KEEPER

HAVING EXPELLED THE STONE, ASK experienced a new clarity, as if a fog had lifted from his mind, although the hopelessness he'd felt remained. An acute urgency gripped him as he sat at the kitchen table, pleading with his mother. He explained it to her this way: "They implanted fear in my mind to make me want to forget. I should have been seeking Freyand, preparing myself; instead, I put all of my energy into hiding in the past, into burying the ax."

"It was the rune with the mark, an especially nasty one. They located you and then befuddled your mind and manipulated your emotions to keep you in place. Now they're here," Orla elaborated.

"We have to end this," Ask concluded. "The power they hold over people, even when they aren't around, is reason enough. They're dangerous."

"Yes, they are, but so is Freyand. To partner with her is to exchange one danger for another, even greater danger," Idun also pleaded. "There has to be some other way."

"Time is up for finding alternatives," Ask added. He stood up. "I'm going with or without you." A line, he realized, had been drawn in the sand, a line he had finally willingly crossed. He would not be a victim of circumstances any longer. He would take up the ax and protect, like his father.

Ask called Deonte to tell him they were leaving.

He hung up after Deonte said, "It's about time. I'm on my way."

Orla told Ask to pack light. To that end, he set about gathering the equipment he needed for a long journey: a flashlight, batteries, rope, since he'd always packed it for camping trips, extra clothing, and nonperishable food—cans of beans, mandarin oranges, and peanut butter, the only items in the pantry the appropriate size for lugging long distances. He slipped the tunic on under his shirt. He had to be ready to transform at any and every moment. He also crammed a fist full of cash into his pocket—money he'd saved doing odd jobs for nearby farmers—and grabbed a sleeping bag. As he was leaving the house, he caught sight of his father's old cowboy hat balancing on the top of the bookcase his father had built. He crossed the several steps from one side of the living room to the other on impulse, grabbed the hat, and arranged it on his head—a perfect fit.

Heim barked his approval. Ask patted the dog's head, just in case he never saw him again.

Orla was waiting for Ask at the base of the stairs, dressed in her usual attire and holding her pike. She grinned, as he dropped the backpack and sleeping bag on the floor. "What?" he asked.

She shook her head. "What didn't you understand about 'pack light'?"

Outside, Deonte, who had arrived twenty minutes after the call in his mother's SUV, putting his newly acquired driver's license to use, secured the ax to Ask's backpack and stowed it in the car.

"Come on, Babe," Ask called. Babe, still a goat, wet beard and all, trotted over to the group, who now stood at the edge of the driveway. Ask wasn't sure which way to go but knew their trek would be both dangerous and lengthy. Ask looked at Deonte, and Deonte looked at Ask. They both turned to Orla, expecting, perhaps, that she had some sort of giant locater ability she could employ to guide them on their journey. She shrugged. "Don't look at me. I have no idea where she is."

"I find," a voice below them said, "when in doubt, ask the energy." Ask didn't understand Babe's counsel at first, but then he remembered his father telling him that Freyand was to become the spear's protector.

Deonte, who had volunteered to carry the spear, leaned on it as if it were a walking stick. "What the hell is that supposed to mean?" Deonte asked.

"I think," Ask said, pulling the spear out of Deonte's hands and causing him to quickly shift his weight to avoid falling, "it means we invoke the energy in the spear to guide us." He pointed the spear toward the fields consumed by the growing storm. Nothing happened. He tried speaking to it. "Lead us to Freyand." Nothing happened.

Deonte smiled. "Try this: Oh, great, magical spear, show us the way." He held up his hands as if in supplication.

In frustration, Ask slammed the base of the spear against the ground. A slight tremor preceded a ray of yellow light that emanated from the tip of the spear straight up. "Okay," Ask said. "We're in business." He pointed the spear straight ahead. The light continued to shine straight up. He shook it, thinking it might work like one of those glow sticks you wear to parties with blacklights. The light did not change its trajectory.

"Maybe you broke it," Deonte offered.

"No, it's not broken." Idun stood several feet away. "Freyand isn't as far away as you might think."

"Where is she?" Ask looked around.

"She's right here," his mother said.

Ask squinted into the snow to see if his mother was pointing toward any of the outbuildings on their property. Could this Freyand be locked up in a cellar, like the one below their barn? "I don't understand. I can't see her."

Idun stepped closer. "She's me, son."

He wanted to tell her to stop interfering. They had already decided to go after Freyand. Her stalling only prolonged the inevitable. "We don't have time for this."

"It's true. She's inside of me. To escape the giants, we merged our powers, our life force. Because we used my body—she was dying, you see—I've been able to suppress the darkness. Who knows what will happen if we release her. I keep her, well, in check."

"I don't believe you." Even though Ask's challenge was genuine, he felt ashamed for calling his mother a liar.

In response, Idun held out her hand, and the spear came to her. A golden glow surrounded her. The pupils of her eyes, as Ask now remembered seeing before, became eclipsed by an obsidian darkness.

Ask stuttered. "But Dad told me to seek her in the north. How can she be here? This doesn't make any sense."

"Because, son," Idun said, "the goddess who can separate us lives on the edge of the tundra. Only she possesses the knowledge and the ability to make Freyand reappear. Your father didn't need to know the whole story."

Ask stammered. Again, this isn't how he imagined things working out. Always these twists and hang-ups, these messy entanglements to complicate his mission. His thoughts swirled like the snow around them. Still, somehow, he stumbled upon the right question to ask her. "Why would you agree to combine your life force with someone so evil?"

A tear trailed down Idun's cheek. "She's my sister. And nobody wants her back more than I. But, Ask, we are as different as compassion and cruelty. Whereas I am the goddess of life and eternal youth, she was a goddess of death and eternal damnation." Ask remembered the apple rotting above his mother's hand and quickly turning to dust when she first revealed her power to him. "I will free her, but once we've defeated the giants, we must kill her."

The storm gained strength. The wind filled the spaces between them with its mad howling. The party hesitated at an immobilizing impasse. And then a voice issued from his mother's mouth that Ask did not recognize. Unequivocal and remorseless, the voice that was not his mother's said, "Did somebody say 'kill'? I know a thing or two about that."

Ask shivered against the cold as the storm worsened. The snow fell now as a thick white sheet. He could no longer see his mother. The blizzard swallowed everything but the porchlight, which tethered him to a safety he must leave behind, a sanctuary that would never protect him again like it once had. Soon, even that light was a ghost winking in the night. He begged for his father to tell him what to do, to guide him with a well-timed dream memory, but there was no response—only the bitter bellowing of the wind. Even the stars remained mute, slumbering somewhere above the oppressive clouds, incapable of guidance.

And then Freyand began to laugh a laugh that Ask recognized all too well, not from his mother but from a darker, more sinister place. She sounded unsettlingly like Hyrrokkin. Ask's pulse quickened. He struggled to breathe against the wind. Instinctively, he summoned the ax, which jostled free from his backpack and flew into his awaiting hand. He looked at Deonte, Orla, even Babe, hoping one of them would offer a suggestion, or take charge and relieve him of this responsibility. All were silent, waiting for him to make a decision.

Ahead, the only direction that now mattered, he could see neither where the road began nor where or how it would end. For courage, he glanced at the ax, which gave off a soft green glow. Looking back at him in the reflection on the ax's metal cheek, he saw his face transposed to that of his father's. Despite his fear of this uncertain path, he took the first step into the storm.

~

And the Tale Begins Anew

LEGEND HAS IT THAT ONE day, while Paul Bunyan was chopping down trees deep in a Minnesota forest, at the end of a long, twisting road far from civilization, a friend complained, "It's murder hauling these massive logs through all them cutbacks and turns." He held a hand to his lower back and moaned, rubbing a tired shoulder.

Always considerate, Paul said, "How can I help ease your burden?"

His friend shook his head, spat on the frozen ground, and mumbled, "Nothing doing," before hobbling over to the saw awaiting him halfway through a trunk. The situation seemed hopeless.

Not only did the crooked road create extra slow work, but winter made it that much more treacherous to travel. More than once, the company had to forgo meals because their food would take too long to arrive. Paul himself, they say, needed a lot of food, so he felt the pang of the long journey in his gut more profoundly than others.

About midday, when his stomach gargled and complained, Paul knocked down a tree with one swipe of his ax. Enough was enough. No chuckwagon could be seen climbing the windy road. Paul called for Babe. The two of them followed the road to the point where it began its twisted climb into the hills. Paul drove hooks deep into the frozen ground and attached thick chains to Babe's harness.

At Paul's signal, Babe began to pull and tug at the frozen ground. Soon, Paul, too, heaved at the chains, using his ax for leverage by driving it into the ground and dragging himself and Babe forward. Together, they pulled the crooked road straight.

Never had such a thing been done. The men in the camp cheered, for the road could now be traversed with ease, no longer an obstacle to sustenance or the painful trial awaiting them at the end of a long day.

Nearly a hundred years after this tale tall was printed, a new tale emerged in North Dakota, making its way across the plains.

As the story goes, it was the worst storm in twenty years. Dense as a fog and cold as a deep freezer full of ice cubes buried at the bottom of the Antarctic Ocean. A farmer was out driving sheep, two goats, and a handful of cows into a barn when he was distracted by a bright green light several fields away. This light illuminated a massive figure, like a giant lumberjack, swinging that light so fast and hard that he actually split the storm in half, "like Moses parting the Red Sea," the farmer would later declare.

The light also showed the large silhouettes of giant creatures advancing toward the massive lumberjack from an adjacent field. As they approached, the light moved faster, producing a strong gale, which seemed to first stop the creatures in their tracks and then to blow them backwards. The force of that gale continued to mount until the farmer himself, as far away as he was, felt the wind plow into him, knocking him on his rear end and pushing him halfway across the three acres he planned to use for corn in the spring. For now, the field was barren, and the farmer slid across the snow as if he was sledding down a steep hill.

Once again on his feet, the farmer fought to make his way back to his house, finding that all he could do was grip the ground until the wind stopped. When it did, the light was gone.

On the news, later that evening, he heard the weather forecaster describe a winter squall that toppled trees and knocked over semis on the freeway. But the farmer knew differently.

Of course, Paul Bunyan was a myth, he would admit when he told this story to his friends, shaking his head in disbelief and saying, "Don't make any sense, I know." He could never, however, doubt the powerful wind that knocked him off his feet or the light in the hands of a massive lumberjack that chopped through a blizzard.